# RUNᵢ _ ᵢ N

# CIRCLES

*Lucy Lewis Thrillers*
*Book One*

**Claire Gray**

SAPERE
BOOKS

# RUNNING IN CIRCLES

Published by Sapere Books.

11 Bank Chambers, Hornsey, London, N8 7NN,
United Kingdom

saperebooks.com

ISBN: 978-1-912546-33-6

# Chapter One

Steve texts and asks if I want to meet him somewhere for a drink. He says the air-conditioning has broken in the office again. It's late afternoon, still hot. We go to a place halfway up a hill, with thick green leaves fringing the view and insects nearly drowning out the music playing behind the bar, where a couple of young Thai men are laughing together. Steve and I take a circular table by a window, each of us with a plastic cup of white wine; sweet and sickly against our lips.

'They botched it, I think,' Steve says. He won't let me look at his teeth, which have been drilled into by a dentist on the other side of the island. 'I wanted white fillings. But they gave me gold. And the pain relief made me laugh but didn't stop the pain.'

I've been working all afternoon; a pair of Bollywood stars got married to each other on the beach. Steve would have enjoyed himself there, but I felt uncomfortable and hung back from the crowds, near to where a pile of dead crabs had been scraped out of the way, stray dogs creeping in to snatch them. I made some notes which I'll turn into an article tomorrow morning.

'I'm sure you're fine,' I say, trying to see past Steve's hand, his strategically placed drink and his big, grey moustache.

'I should have gone to the mainland for it, but, you know,' he says.

I nod, although I don't know, really. Steve Boyd, my editor, is American but hasn't left this tiny island off the coast of Thailand for years. He's from a town in the centre of the USA, just a single row of houses really, where he says the fields are like oceans. His passport lies in the back of a safe in our office; water damaged and curled at the edges. I flicked through it once and saw visas for Asian countries, long since expired. I've been working as his junior reporter for about a year, ever since I somehow impressed him during a long-distance job interview over Skype. I arrived here thinking that he must have made some kind of mistake, and I still can't believe my luck when I wake up and come to work each morning.

We haven't spoken much about the lives we led before meeting each other here, but sometimes we go out for dinner and Steve drinks too much wine, opens his mouth to speak and then shakes his head, smiles and pours another glass. I think his life, like mine, is better now that he's on the island. Although my career was just starting to take off at a local newspaper back in England, other things were happening to me which I was desperate to escape from. I try not think of them now.

We run a newspaper called the *Koh Star*, just the two of us; releasing it every Saturday, just a few pages printed with cheap ink. We write for the Western tourists who come here to play golf and go to full moon parties, and sometimes they read it but mostly the paper just sits about the island in hopeful little piles. We make just enough money to get by, filling the pages with adverts for scuba schools and bars, although sometimes Steve has to put his own money into paying the rent on our little office.

To distract him from his teeth, I talk about the Bollywood wedding for a while, trying my best to describe the clothes, even sketching the bride's dress and shoes on the back of a beer mat. I try to hum the tune that was playing as the bride first appeared, but even with Steve tapping a beat on the table I can't manage it.

'I wish I could have been there. I was sitting with my mouth open for hours. There was a lump in the chair just here.' He pats at the small of his back. 'And the dentist had a family of bald guinea pigs under her desk.'

'Really? I've read about those somewhere. They're called skinny pigs.'

'Yeah. And they cost about ten times as much as regular guinea pigs which, now that I think about it, you could just buy and shave. She made me pet them. It was like touching a load of old ladies' hands in a box. But tell me more about the wedding. What was *he* wearing?'

So, I tell him, acting reluctant although I'm not really; I like seeing how interested he is and making him smile.

'We'll put your Bollywood story on Saturday's front page,' he says, pouring more wine from the jug left on our table. 'Maybe we'll even feature a couple of your sketches. That shoe. Look at that shoe!'

'It didn't really look like that. I can't draw.'

'Nonsense. It's beautiful.'

'Are you drunk already?' I say, smiling.

'No, it's the laughing gas.'

The wine grows warm in our hands and the sun begins to set, turning the sea red for just a moment. And then night is here and it's time to go home.

I make myself something to eat in my hostel's kitchen, pumping boiling water into a mug and watching as dry noodles came to life, and specs of unknown vegetables and chemicals rise to the surface. Stirring with a plastic fork, I say hello to some backpackers who are drinking beer beside the row of refrigerators.

'Will you come for a drink tonight, Lucy?' asks Ben; Irish, blonde and perhaps five years younger than me.

I take a sip from my cracked mug. The noodles are still crunchy. I shake my head and smile at the floor. 'I can't. I have work in the morning.'

'You always say that.'

'I always have work.' I shrug and put the mug up to my face again, burning my lips. Conversations like this make my face prickle.

Ben passes a flyer to me, the kind I often see as I walk to the office early in the morning, crumpled in the gutter at the end of a party. 'There's a bonfire on the beach tomorrow. We'll go to that.'

'Maybe.' I nod.

'You sure you won't come out for one now?' he asks. 'The night's not old yet.'

'Maybe tomorrow.'

# Chapter Two

I'm walking towards my bed when there is a roar so enormous that at first I think an aeroplane must have fallen from the sky. I drop to a crouch on the tiles, hands raised above my head. Looking up, through my shaking fingers, I see that the ceiling is still there, but the light has gone out. The fan has stopped; its chord rocking wildly. And then I realise all of the glass in my window has shattered and been blown across the floor. Outside of the window, smoke moves, darker than the night sky. My throat has tightened and I can feel my lungs hanging like dead sacks. A bomb. It must have been a bomb.

I stand, dropping the toothbrush I've just finished using. As I shuffle towards the window, my feet moving between needles of glass, I'm aware that I ought to go downstairs, where other people are probably gathering. But still I keep moving in the wrong direction, reaching out as if someone might take my hands and help me.

The usual view from my bedroom is one of stray dogs lying in the shade, backpackers drinking at plastic tables, and a row of bars and brittle trees. I peer through the ragged hole that used to be a window. There's a smoking crater across the street, surrounded by debris. The buildings opposite mine are broken and burning. Fragments move in the air; sparks and torn pieces of material. People stream out of the bars, moving like fish in a current, opening their mouths to scream. The stray dogs are gone. I scream too, just once, and then press my knuckles into my mouth.

Blood everywhere. It's black in the darkness; even the fires don't properly illuminate it. Black blood on faces. On knees. A man in a football shirt lies face down on the pavement. I hear screams, the crackling of flames, and something that sounds like rain. Dogs bark. Alarms are going off. Crying and wailing like I have never heard before. I put my hands over my ears and keep them there.

My toenails are freshly painted, my hair still wet from the shower, and I'm wearing pyjamas that my sister gave me before I moved here; shorts and a vest with pigs on them. I don't think to get dressed or put on my shoes before I turn and run.

It's the way I run in nightmares; too slow, the ground feeling all wrong against my feet. The room looks almost normal as I pass through it. There's my book left open on the bed, my hairbrush on the chair, but I can feel hot air against my back and I kick a piece of glass. I nearly scream again but hold it in, biting down on my lips.

Stumbling out to the narrow corridor, I hear the building creak around me. It is too dark to see the posters on the walls, or to know if Billie the hostel dog and her puppies are in their normal place at the end of the landing. I call her name anyway, in a scratchy voice. But there's nothing, no familiar shapes in the shadows, and no animal or human noises. I reach the stairs, my body shaking so badly that it's a struggle to take the steps and grip the banister.

I run through the reception area, which has become slippery with a thick layer of dust. This room is usually bright with potted plants and a cage of parrots but it is now dominated by a mound of rubble which I have to climb to get out. It shifts beneath me, and I slice my hand on a broken piece of glass, feeling heat around the place where thick wires have been severed.

I'm shivering as I step onto the street, despite the fire that's climbing over the bar and the ice cream parlour opposite, eating up their awnings, turning plastic furniture into something terrible. A man is slumped out here on the ground, covered in the same dust as the tiles inside and with rubble in his lap, one of his shoes missing, his eyes half closed.

'You've got to move,' I say, looking at the mess of bricks and plaster which could slide down and consume him at any second. I try to clear the debris from his legs, skinning my knuckles, and then I struggle to pull him to his feet. He's heavy like metal, like someone more than half dead. In the end, all I can do is slide him across the pavement a little, where he moans and turns onto his side. Another man comes over, with blood on his hands.

'Jim?' he says, bending down and pawing at the stricken man's shoulder. 'Jim, can you get up?'

Looking around, I hope to recognise someone's face. Dozens of people are wandering each way along the road. Others are burnt and torn, laying where the blast threw them or where they've fallen after trying to escape. Some people, I think, are dead. People are shouting, searching for their friends. Men and women sob. Screams come irregularly. Each one makes me flinch.

A girl stands alone in the middle of the street, circling slowly and tottering on her bare feet. There is blood in her hair, and dirty looking wounds all around her eyes. I recognise her from the hostel; didn't we play poker together just a few nights earlier? I keep my eyes on her and move across the road which is strewn with bricks, clothing, drops of blood.

'Are you okay?' I say as I reach her side. She's not okay, clearly, but I don't know what else to ask. She stares right through me, opening and closing her mouth. I look around for help but everyone else is doing the same. And then, with a bang loud enough to make all of us scream and cling on to each other, a wave of bricks crack and tumble from the front of my damaged hostel.

'We need to move, we need to move!' someone shouts. 'The building's coming down!'

People are being ushered into the Grand Hotel, at the far end of the street. I drag the injured girl there with me. Her hand is small and hot in mine; I feel her pulse against my palm. We go into the hotel lobby, which seems too still, too clean, to be part of our world. I don't feel safe in here; I think another bomb might go off. Who did that? Whose bomb was it? Was it even a bomb? I look around for any sort of answer, but all I see are frightened people huddled on plush furniture, lying on the black carpet, drinking bottles of water from behind the bar.

'Are there medics? Is an ambulance coming?' I ask a member of staff, but he just shrugs his shoulders, blood across his uniform.

I leave the girl with him because he has a pile of first aid kits and looks vaguely official. Stumbling back outside, the heat slaps me all over again; the burning of the fires mixed with the usual sticky, night-time temperature.

And then I see Lena, my German friend who works on reception at the hostel. She is holding a bunched-up rag against her forehead, but when she sees me she runs, arms flailing; a wound clear beneath her hairline. We grab each other. I close my eyes and feel her blood trickle onto my cheek.

# Chapter Three

The Green Turtle Hostel, my home of six months, is smashed and dark. When the police arrived and saw people trying to climb in over the rubble, they told us we better find somewhere else to stay. They wouldn't even let me inside for my things. I haven't spoken with anyone I know except for Lena, who has gone to stay with her boyfriend. I half recognised some of the faces on the street last night, lit by fires and blue lights. Perhaps some of the people crying amongst the rubble were my friends. I'll look for them all, but first I need to find Steve.

I know he was planning on staying home all evening, to watch Cary Grant movies and eat a fruit pie his sister had posted to him, and I know his home is nowhere near Main Street, but I've been to the office every hour, all night long, and he's not been there. I haven't seen him amongst the shifting crowds either. It's just turned 7 am. He'd be in the office by now, on a day like today.

A maid at the Grand Hotel gave me a spare uniform to wear because when I wandered back there in the early hours I was still in my pig pyjamas and splattered with Lena's blood. The maid offered me a basket of fruit too, but I didn't accept it because my stomach was churning. I went up to a room for a while and the bed was comfy but I didn't sleep. It's hard to sleep when the hotel you're staying in has streaks of blood in its lobby.

Steve and I rent space above an internet café, not far from Main Street, where my hostel is. I keep my eyes to the ground as I walk past groups of backpackers, injured and lost, and weave between mounds of bricks and exhausted emergency workers in soiled clothing. The sun is fully up and things seem even worse than they did in the darkness. Some of the fires are still smouldering. There's a smell of chemicals in the air. My legs are numb; I misjudge kerbs and potholes. I have to grab hold of a dustbin when I trip and nearly fall.

As I pass through the town I write its obituary in my head. I think of the little green parrot who greeted me the very first time I walked into the hostel. He bowed from atop a broken House of the Dead arcade game and said hello in a Thai accent. I mourn my little square room, with its tiled floor, juddering ceiling fan and someone else's dreamcatcher hanging over the window. After I started working at the newspaper and was earning some money, I could have rented one of those cabins by the beach, but I liked the hostel. I liked the building itself; dim stairways, colourful corridors, and noisy birds both wild and caged. I also liked the people; the backpackers and the elderly owners who always looked angry but then offered sour sweets to me whenever I walked by.

*Where are they now?*

I climb the fire escape at the back of the building to reach our office, stepping around plants that Steve has put out here and forgotten to water; we never use the front door because it sticks, and spiders nest over it.

The door's ajar this time. I clatter into our small, grubby newsroom and he's here. Alive and intact. The first thing I notice is how sweaty his bald head looks as he speaks on the phone. He flaps a hand at me and smiles wildly. I smile back, but my mouth bends into something else. He's telling someone not to worry. He has a daughter, perhaps he's talking to her. Sitting down, I catch sight of my dusty reflection in the computer screen. Blonde hair hanging lank around a pinched, white face. Is it strange that I haven't cried yet?

'Lucy!' Steve throws down the phone, gets up, and sends his chair spinning across the office. He comes at me with his arms outstretched. Oh, okay, we're going to hug. I don't like people touching me anymore, but I don't want to upset him. I've seen him cry on more than one occasion, most recently at the hatching of a duck, so I know tears come easily for him. Standing up, I let him envelop me in his meaty arms, my face pressed against the floral pattern on his chest. Actually, this is the safest I've felt in hours. *I love you, Steve*, I want to say.

'I was starting to think maybe you were dead,' he says into my hair.

'Same here.' I slide my hands out of his grip and take a step back. Steve, who I see every day, has changed. He's like a man from a photograph, a walking scrap of the news, faded and damaged.

Grabbing a tub of biscuits from our lopsided table, Steve knock the blinds with his elbow and they swing loudly against the window. I twitch. When he reaches to stop them he somehow just makes the noise worse. He holds the tub in front of me until I pick out a handful of stale wafers.

'You look like you could use the sugar,' he says.

'Yeah, and I should probably sit down.'

Steve sits too, but leans forward, like he wants to be as close to me as possible. I tear the wafers apart in my lap and listen to him breathing.

'I can't believe this has happened,' he says. 'I just don't understand it.'

'Do you know what caused the explosion?' I ask quietly, afraid to hear the answer. I want it to have been an accident, not an attack.

'It was a bomb outside Bar XS,' Steve says, and although this has been my suspicion ever since I heard that awful noise outside my bedroom, it's odd to hear him say it out loud and to realise that this is all more than just a nightmare.

'Oh,' I say, resting my head in my hands for just a second.

'I'll never understand how people can do such things,' Steve says.

'People must have died,' I say, thinking in hard facts for the first time, wondering about numbers. 'I mean, I'm pretty sure I saw bodies.'

'I think so. I heard they did. I heard maybe three girls died, who were sat at a table outside the bar. That's where people think the bomb was; under one of the tables. People keep bags under there all the time, don't they?'

'Yes. They wait there and have a drink before going to the bus stop down the road. Oh, it's just so fucking horrible.'

Steve nods. 'There are no words. But somehow we're going to have to find some and write them down.'

He's in the shadows over there; the electricity is still out. Usually this office is frantic with activity; computer screens, TV, radio, flickering lights and ceiling fan. Today it's quiet; just his old laptop running off its battery, and the half closed blind still tapping against the glass. The hills are out there, familiar and beautiful, but they seem far away this morning. Too nice to be real. I go to the window, breathe against the glass and watch my breath hang there for a while, shrinking to nothing. Looking over the rooftops I can just about see the billboards that follow the line of the road to the port. Whoever's behind the bomb probably travelled here that way. And today people will leave that way; survivors fleeing an island that is no longer any sort of paradise.

'Have you been writing?' I ask, turning to look at Steve's laptop. 'Will the paper go out as usual on Saturday?'

'Yeah, but I'm discovering that it's hard to write when you're part of the story. You know, I've been down at the bombsite since around midnight. I was asking people if they'd seen you. I tried to help.' He grips his legs and holds on tight. His fingers are black. So are the knees of his jeans.

'I should have been there too. I went to a hotel and I've been walking around. I didn't really know where I was going.'

'You did the right thing staying away. What if another bomb had gone off at the bar? You can never tell when these things are really over.' He looks over his shoulder now, like he's still not quite sure it's over at all.

'Are you okay?' I ask. 'You don't really look it.'

'Sure I am. Don't worry about me.' He says this brightly but his face is yellow, and slack around the eyes. He doesn't look as bad as I know I do, but he looks bad all the same. That's what no sleep all night will do, a night spent breathing in smoke, fear and the dust from broken buildings. And watching people suffer in the middle of it all.

'Have you spoken to the police?' I ask. 'I haven't. I saw some that I recognised but I didn't feel like I'd be able to speak any sense to them. All I could do was walk and look for you. Just backwards and forwards all night. I felt like a ghost.'

Steve frowns at me. 'Lucy, you should take the day off. Go to my house and rest. I've got this. Maybe you ought to see a doctor.'

'I'm actually fine. Just this ringing in my ears. A few cuts and bruises. I have a headache but it's no worse than a hangover.'

'I'd really feel better if you went home and rested. Shit, maybe you should look into going back to England for a while. Your family —'

'No,' I say, sharp enough to make him flinch. 'I'm not going anywhere.'

'Okay, okay,' he says, not quite able to meet my eyes. 'I didn't see this coming, did you? This is a safe place. I fell asleep on the beach last week. Too many cocktails. And when I woke up my wallet was still poking out of my pocket, with money visible in it, *and* someone had stuck a parasol into the sand next to me so that I wouldn't get burned.'

'I've always felt safe too. Since I came here.' I suddenly can't remember the last time I blinked, and have to force myself to do it now. My eyelids feel hot and dry.

'Please go back to mine,' Steve says, his voice soft. 'I have a fruit pie in the fridge, and some of that lemonade you like.'

I shake my head. He sighs and tugs on his moustache. I say: 'I need to stay and help somehow. Going back to an empty house is the worst thing I could do right now. Don't you think?'

'I suppose. I'd come back with you, I mean, I *should* come back with you, but I can't. There's this sense of responsibility that I haven't felt in a long time; like maybe my job really is important, no matter how small the *Koh Star* is. I'm going back to the bombsite. You don't really want to come with me? I don't think you should. You don't even look like you ought to be walking around.'

I open my mouth to speak but then hesitate. I stand up, get a head-rush, then sit back down again so heavily that the chair bumps back against the desk.

'How do you feel? Really?' Steve asks.

'My hair still smells of smoke even though I've showered,' I say. Steve nods, urging me to go on. 'And I'm here talking to you, but all I can see is the stuff I saw last night. I saw it all, almost. I didn't tell my family that on the phone. I had to queue for half an hour in the hotel lobby to call them from behind the desk. I let them think I was far away and barely involved. But I was *right there*.'

'You could have used the phone in this office,' Steve says. 'It came back on a little while ago.'

'I left my keys in the hostel. I couldn't get in here. It's not safe to go back up to my room. Someone told me there's structural damage. Or something.'

The phone begins to ring now from its nest of tangled wires.

Steve says: 'People are starting to find our number online. Parents have been calling, worried about their children. I don't know what to tell them. And journalists from Britain and Australia, a couple from Europe, who seem to have misunderstood the nature of our newspaper and expect me to be able to give them something useful. I have nothing useful. I'm just a bemused foreigner like everyone else. I've been telling everyone they'd be better off speaking to the Thai press who I'm sure are already arriving from the mainland. I've heard helicopters flying over.'

'Let me get it,' I say, reaching past him for the phone.

The person on the other end is clearing their throat, a dry wheeze that makes me picture a snake shedding its skin.

'Shuttleworth speaking,' he says eventually, as I pull the receiver a little further from my ear because I feel like I can smell his breath.

'Bernard Shuttleworth?' I say.

'Yeah,' he says, clearing his throat again. I look at Steve and grimace. I first went to Shuttleworth's golf resort about a week after I started at the paper, to cover a story about a partially paralysed man who scored a hole in one. Shuttleworth, an elderly Australian, was dressed in crisp white shorts and a polo shirt, a hat with a tassel on top, and was fairly disinterested in the disabled man's achievement. I've been there a handful of time since and have never warmed to him. A lot of our funding comes from Shuttleworth, who likes us to print full page adverts for his resort. We deal with him reluctantly; rumours circulate about the way he treats his Thai members of staff.

'When are you coming over here to discuss the new hotel wing? You were going to write a feature on it, remember.'

'There was a bomb,' I say. 'A bomb went off last night.'

'I know. That's the other thing. I can't get through to the police on the phone. It rings and rings and then there's a recorded message. No English translation. What happened?'

'I don't know. It was on Main Street. You know Bar XS?'

'No.'

'You know, the bar where those tame mice run around on the shelves above the bottles of vodka?'

'I've not been.'

'Well, it was there. Outside of there. So that bar, the ice cream place next door to it and the hostel across the road were damaged and lots of people are hurt. People have died, apparently, but I don't know for sure.'

'Terrorists,' Shuttleworth says, and I feel like he's doing something else while he speaks to me, peering into a fridge or cutting his toenails.

'I saw people with burns all over their legs and arms,' I say, not really to him. 'People younger than me. The same age as my little sister.' I remember, for some reason, how Hannah used to love birds when she was small, and our house would be full of dirty feathers that she found in the street.

'My club?' Shuttleworth is saying. 'That's not damaged.'

'No, that's fine,' I say, thinking of the seedy club near the beach that he owns, where the walls are painted black and stray dogs eat people's vomit from the pavement in the morning.

'So, no one can come over here today? I have literature. I'm thinking of going away for a while until all of this dies down. It would be good to pass the information on to you before I go.'

'No, we can't come over today,' I say, raising my eyebrows at Steve. 'We're going back to the bombsite.'

As I say this, I get a sensation like I'm melting into the seat of my chair. The concrete on the street will still be blackened. The blood won't yet have dried or been washed down the drains along with grey bubbles of charcoal. Steve is getting up, putting his wallet into his pocket, shutting down his laptop.

'I'll come,' I spit into the phone. 'I'll head over now.'

'Where are you going?' Steve asks as I hang up.

I explain and he frowns at me as the screen of his laptop goes black and suddenly, without its insides whirring, the office seems deathly quiet.

'You sure you want to go there?' he says.

'I know, I know. I should go the bombsite with you, but Shuttleworth pays for nearly all of our advertising. If we don't go out there today and he gets pissed off, we won't have any money coming in and…' He knows, I think. He sees that I'm a coward.

'Oh, sure, I get that.' Steve nods, although his eyes say something different. 'But do you really want to be alone with that man? He's not nice. He has a way of looking at his female staff members that, since I picked up on it, I can't help noticing. There was talk, last year, of a porter being beaten with a golf club.'

'I'll be fine.'

'Yeah, you're tough,' he says, and actually sounds like he means it. 'If you want to work today, if you really won't go back to mine, then I suppose a golf resort on the other side of the island might be the best place for you.'

# Chapter Four

The trees are wild; I'm driving through a dank, green tunnel. A family of monkeys were sitting beside the road two miles back, but otherwise it's just me out here; no other vehicles since I left town.

I washed Steve's car for him a week ago, but it's already filled with cigarette ash and candy wrappers. Its paintwork is coated with a grey dust which may or may not have come from the explosions. It felt greasy when I touched it; I'd like to wash my hands.

I think about the afternoon that I spent cleaning the car, while Steve grilled fish for us and mixed horrible, salty cocktails. That was a happy day, and probably the last one we'll have for a while.

I'm whistling through my cracked lips because the radio isn't working. I'm trying not to think; but I do think, of course. Groaning, I rattle the dials again, desperate for some noise. Visiting the golf resort seemed like a good idea; a way to keep busy but stay away from the crater in the road outside my hostel. But it wasn't; I forgot that I'd be alone in the car. A burst of static jumps from the speakers; an electrical scream. I brake hard and pull over, because I can't see the road anymore, just my memories of injured people. The wheels crunch over dry earth and rocks. Slipping out of my seat, I stumble on loose boulders and throw up into the dust.

Straightening up, looking into the barbed trees at the side of the road, I realise that I've been thinking about the baby all morning. The baby who I carried inside me for nine weeks and who then abruptly, with a certain violence, was no longer there.

That whole series of events isn't the worst thing I've lived through anymore, but I wouldn't even be here if it hadn't happened. I quit my job at the newspaper in England because, after everything happened, I couldn't write a proper sentence or even think without getting confused. I wanted to shy away from anything bad or sad that made its way onto my desk. And most things were bad or sad. I'd just passed all my exams to become a senior reporter, but then it was like my mind had turned grey, like how smokers' lungs get. No one understood. I didn't try to explain, and I left without working my notice period so I couldn't get a decent reference. I hadn't even realised I was pregnant at that point.

Once I wasn't pregnant any more, and had another secret to drag around with me, another reason to hate the feel of my body, my sister found this job at the *Koh Star* through a lucky Google search. It seemed ideal; I needed to escape, I needed to avoid thinking for a while, and here was an offer of exclusively soft news in a tropical environment. So, I left behind my pokey flat, my woolly hats and neglected friends and family. And, gradually, I've been getting myself back. I've thrown myself into writing about hotdog eating contests and unusual sea creatures, so that I would never have to think about anything bad again. And my plan was going fine until now. Everything has risen to the surface; a soup topped with scum. I wipe my mouth on the back of my hand and take a deep, broken breath. The vegetation is all around me, creeping closer. I can taste the plants, their spores dense in the air.

I need to stop thinking. I need to get back into the car, otherwise I'm going to collapse out here and die, and the plants will grow over me. I half run to get behind the wheel.

It takes forty minutes to drive across the island. It's not a great distance in terms of miles; the island is the size of a small city. But the roads are bad, dipping and twisting through pockets of trees. Eventually I pull up beside the hotel buildings at Bernard Shuttleworth's golf resort; white plaster, terracotta tiles. There's nobody here. The fountain out front has been switched off. I thought, somehow, this would be a different world, untouched by the explosion, but there's shock in the air here, just as there was back in town. It's a couple of minutes before I force myself out of Steve's car and crunch across the gravel. I tie my hair back as I go, feeling dust in it, feeling heat from the sun on my scalp.

Inside the building the air is cold; it hurts my skin. Water features babble all around me. This is a huge space, with corridors leading off it like spider legs. Statues are poised and watching; naked women carved from black stone wrestle with golden snakes, but there are no real-life humans about.

Then I hear something; the soft clunk of club against golf ball. It happens again and again, so I walk over marble tiles towards the sound, coming out the other side of the foyer and into an outdoor courtyard. Trees are growing out here, their trunks covered in thick brown strands like hair. And on the other side of the courtyard, Shuttleworth is chipping golf balls over the top of a brick wall.

He is even squatter than I remember; his body the definitive pear shape. A floppy straw hat sits on his head, and his feet are trussed up in old leather sandals. There's a basket of balls to his side, and a tray on the floor filled with half eaten fruit and an empty bottle of wine. I recall a rumour I heard from a backpacker who had worked at Shuttleworth's nightclub; supposedly he's father to the gaggle of children I saw hanging around here during my last visit. But I don't always believe rumours. I look around. There are no kids today. No one at all but this old man.

'There's nobody on reception, is there?' he says, turning to face me when my feet loudly scuff the ground. 'Do you have bags?' He rests the club against the wall and comes towards me, wiping his hands on the front of his shirt. His plump face is covered with white stubble. I smile at him but have to force it.

'I'm not a guest. I'm here from the newspaper.'

He pulls a pair of glasses from the front pocket of his shirt and takes a moment to attach them to his face. 'Lucy Lewis, of course it's you. You're clearly not here to play golf. You're too young and beautiful. I'm sorry there was no one to greet you. Everyone's been leaving, you see. I think we have three rooms occupied and barely any staff left to serve them. It's a bit of an embarrassment. Come with me.'

Beckoning with a thick finger, he leads me out of the courtyard and along a concrete path which is rippled like sand on a beach. He holds open a wrought iron gate into what I assume is the backyard of his home. As I pass, he places a warm hand on my lower back and gently pushes me towards a seat.

'This is very nice,' I manage to say, looking at grapes hanging from a trellis above my head. I sit and watch as he pours lemonade from a jug filled with ice. My skin's prickling where he touched me. I don't like people to do that, especially when they're looking at me the way *he's* looking at me.

'I was about to take a break anyway. What superb timing you have. I haven't been into town yet. Is it devastation? As bad as people have been saying?'

'Yes.'

'And the police, have they been taking it seriously? I'm always inclined to think that justice is better served through people like your good self.'

'I don't know,' I say, waving away a fly. 'I can only assume they're doing things right.'

'I hope you're correct,' he says. 'But I expect you're wrong.'

'You want us to print something about your new hotel wing?' I take a sip of lemonade. It makes my tongue throb.

'Well, I did. There doesn't seem an awful lot of point now. Who's going to want to play golf on this island? I wouldn't want to holiday somewhere like this, where people can burn to death outside a bar. But I'm going to the States for a while, and I suppose you may as well get something printed in the meantime. I don't know how long I'll be. Have you visited Aspen before?'

'No.'

'Here's the literature, anyway,' Shuttleworth says. He pushes a hand deep into his pocket, and sticks his tongue out while rummaging down there. He passes me some warm, glossy prints which I cast an eye over; champagne, maid service, purple carpets.

'Okay,' I say.

'So, tell me, Lucy. What do you know? What have you heard that's not on the news?' He leans towards me and slowly puts his tongue away.

'Nothing at all.'

'Oh, come on. You're press. What are people saying?'

I shake my head slowly. 'It's still early days.'

'I can tell you something,' he says, reaching to touch my hand which I pull away. 'This is interesting.'

'What?'

'Many of my staff members have left. Either because they have family nearby who they want to be with, or because they're from abroad and want to get back where they feel safe. But one of my maids, Maliwan, she left yesterday morning, before anything had happened. And she left in a hurry. She left some of her things behind.'

'She didn't tell you why?'

'She came to see me. She said she was leaving for personal reasons and wanted to make sure she'd still be paid for the days she'd worked this month. She sends it all to her mother, I think. Some sick relative, anyway. But I can read people. She was troubled by something.'

'You think she's connected to the bomb?' I lean in but can't quite bring myself to meet his eyes.

'She's just a young girl. But I do wonder about her boyfriend. If he was involved in some way, Maliwan would be too frightened to go to the police. He might have forced her to go on the run with him. He's picked her up from here a few times and I've seen enough to know I don't like him. I don't like the way she talks about him. He has long hair, he wears a scarf in this sort of weather, and he smokes those menthol cigarettes. He's definitely a political type. American, by the way.'

'But why would he want to bomb the island? Who is he? What does he do?'

'I couldn't tell you what he does. I haven't been interested enough to find out. And I can't claim to know his motives. But I know people. I know about the things they do. Anyway, if it was him, and if he gets arrested, Maliwan will be back here with me in hours, I guarantee it.'

'What's his name?'

'Dolph. Short for Adolph. Or Rudolph? I don't remember his surname. But he's been staying at the Imperial Hotel these last couple of weeks. She was always swanning off to visit him there. She says his family have money. That's interesting to you, yes? You're a journalist.'

'It's not a whole lot to go on,' I say, trying to gauge his sanity. I go to take another sip of lemonade but see that there's a fly in it.

'It's enough to get you started.' Shuttleworth nods at me with his hands clasped together.

'Do you read our paper? You should tell all this to the police if you're worried. We're not exactly investigative journalists.' I half laugh but then stop when I see the look on his face. He stares at me and crunches on a lump of ice.

'It was really your boss I wanted to speak to. He seems like a professional sort of chap. Perhaps you can pass my information on to him. I'm sure he'll be able to follow it up. We have an arrangement, he and I, with advertisements and what not.'

'I'll follow it up,' I say. 'What about Maliwan? How can I get hold of her? Is she local?'

'Yes, a local, but she's gone. Shame. Pretty, pretty girl.'

'Gone? You don't have a phone number? An address?'

He shakes his head. 'She left her phone here. It belongs to me. And she lived here. This was her address.'

'Right,' I say, putting my hands beneath the table and digging at some dirt beneath my thumb nail; dirt from last night.

'We have to catch whoever did this. Look what he's done to us!' Bernard Shuttleworth stretches out his arm and gestures to the empty courtyard. His lips are trembling. Following the arc of his arm, I see a female child watching us from behind a screen door. Our eyes meet and she dashes back into the darkness of the building.

I say: 'I think you should talk to the police and tell them what you've told me.'

Shuttleworth snorts into his glass. As he shakes his head, a wiry little monkey jumps onto the wall behind him. It looks down at our table, and I remember something.

'Is it true what people say, Mr Shuttleworth, about you introducing monkeys to the island? Apparently there never used to be any, but then you brought some over from the mainland.'

'Not everything they say about me is true. Some of it, however, is,' he says with a wink.

Out of the corner of my eye, I see the child watching us from the door again, her little fingers around the handle so that she's practically hanging from it.

'Thank you for the drink.' I stand up, my chair scraping across the flagstones. 'I better go now.'

'Don't go, Lucy. Stay for another. I'll bring out the hard stuff.' He laughs, and lounges in the chair as if he expects me to get into his lap.

'I should probably chase up your lead, don't you think?' I say, trying to keep my voice steady.

'Good. Thank you, dear. I'll be in touch.' He smiles and splinters another piece of ice between his teeth.

# Chapter Five

As I drive away from the golf resort, following a line of dried-out trees which dwarf my car, I can still hear the ice moving around in Shuttleworth's mouth. I open the windows to gulp at the thick air. There's no wind, but leaves shaped like blades are falling from the trees and landing on my windscreen. Tap, tap, tap. It's time for me to go back to the office, back to our ruined town, and face whatever's coming for us next. I turn the wipers on; they groan, leave a grey sheen in their wake, and dislodge just a few of the leaves.

If Bernard Shuttleworth really felt that Maliwan and Dolph were involved in the bombing, he surely would have done more than mention it to a local journalist. I'll phone the police when I get back to the office anyway, just in case, and I'll tell them what Shuttleworth had to say. He was probably messing with me. I think he was. Or he's just mad. Angry, old and mad. I've thrown the pamphlet that he gave me onto the back seat and I expect it will stay there.

This headache is pressing against my skull; I feel more aware of my eyeballs than usual. The ringing in my ears is still here. A couple of cars pass in the opposite direction and mopeds flit by, but the roads are eerily quiet. I have to pull over a few times to take deep, noisy breaths while staring into my lap.

Usually I love driving. It's generally me that takes the wheel while Steve sits beside me, talking and passing across sweets. Today I hate being in the car, and all I can focus on are dead insects on the windscreen, some of which still have frail little legs and wings, flapping as I drive. I think I see a shadow in the rear-view mirror, a shape moving across the road towards me;

a creature or drone, swooping out of the sky, where smoke still lingers. I imagine the flesh ripped from my arms, and have to look down at them every so often, to make sure they're still intact. And my friends; are they safe? Is anyone looking out for Steve? I let Lena slip away with her boyfriend last night; are they taking care of each other? And what about the faces from my hostel, people I see every day but don't really know? What about the owners of the Green Turtle? They always stayed up until the early hours, cleaning and cooking strange, sweet meat. Are they okay?

I reach the edge of town, coming in through the hills which we can see from our office. This isn't the way I would usually drive; I've missed a turning somewhere. There are houses, mansions really, set back from the road. I don't know who lives up here, but people speak of movie stars and gangsters. I pull over so that a tank-like car can pass. It clips Steve's wing mirror with a thud.

'Hey!' I twist around in my seat, but the vehicle continues down the hill like a mindless crab. I get back into gear, squint out at the road, and then I'm sick into my lap.

There are napkins in the glove compartment; the kind they give out with burgers at the place beside my hostel. I attempt to mop up the mess, my eyes and nose streaming. The thin paper tears and sticks to me, but I manage to mash the stain into just a faintly dubious looking wet patch. This has happened before; sudden vomiting after a traumatic experience, so I'm not too concerned. A drink would be nice though. Why didn't I bring anything out with me? I flip open the glove compartment again, rifle under the seats, but there's just one empty can of cola.

I notice a building poking above the trees, perhaps a half mile away. That's the Imperial Hotel. I could clean up in a bathroom there. Buy myself a drink. Look for a young couple who resemble my mental image of Dolph and Maliwan. I tap my fingers against the wheel for a moment. It'll take another twenty minutes to drive to the office; the roads in town are probably still packed with emergency vehicles and with people leaving for the port. I need a drink now. I need to get out of this car for a while. I need air conditioning.

The Imperial Hotel is a mess of gothic towers, archways and decorative trees. Completely eccentric looking is how Steve described it when he sent me here to cover a story about a rare lizard found in a pagoda. It's the most expensive hotel on the island. Famous people have held their weddings here, reproduced on the pages of glossy magazines. I think about what Shuttleworth told me. I wonder if Dolph is inside right now, basking in the pool or drinking cocktails on the terrace. Is this really the sort of place a terrorist would stay? Who knows, but it's not very discreet. Neither's terrorism though. Perhaps Dolph has left already, with a fake passport and with his girlfriend dead in a hotel wardrobe. Perhaps not.

Entering reception, I can smell my own vomit, and I'm very aware of the wet patch on my shorts. Unlike the hotel at the golf resort, this place has tried to retain a traditional Thai feel; there is a lot of gold leaf on the furniture, numerous wooden archways and sharp-edged leaves. Statues and ornate lamps are placed casually about. It all feels artificial to me, and a perfume scent makes me sneeze as I push through the doors. A middle-aged white woman is at the desk, surrounded by plants with heavy, vibrant flowers. She watches my approach with pursed lips. No one else is about, although there were a few cars parked outside. I can hear a television playing nearby; a news report.

'…victims from Sweden and Germany,' the report says in muffled tones. 'And many more still missing.'

'Hello,' I say to the receptionist, as personably as I can manage. 'I was wondering if I could please use your bathroom?'

'Over there,' the woman points, her face softening. Something about my appearance has marked me out, I think, as harmless and perhaps not quite right. I can't place her accent. Swedish perhaps. I can feel her watching me as I walk, unsteadily, to the bathroom, where I work on my clothes with towels and expensive soap. I try to avoid looking at myself in the mirror; I only catch a glimpse of my hands, tense and pale as bone.

I get a glass of mineral water from the bar, where a couple of old ladies are talking quietly together in French. I've decided to down the drink and get out of here, back to Steve, but the bubbles catch in my throat so that I can barely breathe. I pick up a black napkin and press it against my lips, avoiding the eyes of the French women who I'm pretty sure would like to engage me in conversation. Turning to face the reception area, which is attached to the bar via a wooden archway of carved flowers, I hear the receptionist talking from behind the desk.

'See you again, Dolph,' she's saying, with a smile in her voice.

I don't hear a reply as I put my glass down on the bar and clatter across the room. The receptionist is alone and has picked up a feather duster. She's picking bits of cobweb out of it. She hides it behind her back when she sees me.

'Dolph?' I say, breathless. 'I was looking for him.'

She sees something in me to make her wary this time, and doesn't answer. Her narrowed eyes move, however, towards a small window overlooking the car park. I go to press my face against the glass, and see a skinny man with messed up, shoulder length hair. He's throwing bags onto the backseat of a battered old car.

'He's leaving?' I say. She still doesn't answer. I hesitate for a moment but then run outside and down the steps, calling his name as I go.

# Chapter Six

Dolph stands frozen beside his car. I stop moving at the bottom of the steps and we hang there for a moment, separated by wavering air, joined by our eyes. Then he slams the door and scrambles around into the driver's seat. For a second, I can't think what to do, but as Dolph speeds out of the car park and heads down the hill, I sprint to Steve's car, ignoring some pain in my feet as they slap against the concrete. But the keys aren't in the pocket of my shorts like they ought to be.

'Shit,' I say, and slap myself on the forehead like a character from a cartoon.

I go back inside to the bathroom, which still smells slightly of my vomit. The keys are sitting there on the marble, in a little pool of soapy water.

I try talking to the receptionist again, but she says no to everything that I ask. I suppose they're paid to be discreet at an exclusive place like this, and I probably don't look like someone who ought to be given information, with my hair all over the place and stains on my clothes. I leave her my card anyway, but it sounds as if she drops it into a bin as I walk away.

I leave the hotel and roll down the hill in Steve's little car, realising that for a moment or two I've not been thinking about last night, or about what happened to me back in England. It feels better to be thinking like this. Constructive. I picture Dolph's face as I drive; the look in his eyes as he heard me yell his name. I know I caught him in the middle of something bad.

Steve is in the office when I arrive back. I tell him about my time with Shuttleworth and about what happened at the Imperial Hotel. Steve doesn't think much about any of it, but I still feel a little flicker of hope, like maybe there is a way to reach the other side of this pain if I just throw myself into work.

'He doesn't sound like a terrorist,' Steve says. 'Rich American enjoying luxury hotel. Thai girlfriend. Menthol cigarettes. I don't know.'

'But he was scared of something.'

'Isn't everyone scared right now?'

'I think maybe he was scared of *me*.'

'Who knows.' Steve shrugs. Then he adds: 'I'm sorry you had to waste your time with Shuttleworth. He's a nasty old man.'

'It might not have been though. A waste of time, I mean.'

I call the police to pass on my information, dialling the direct line for Officer Kadesadayurat, who is a friend of Steve's. I still have to wait a long time for an answer, listening to scratchy noises and the occasional beep. And I don't get to speak with Kadesadayurat. A woman answers in halting English. She takes down what I have to say, but I don't think she really understands. I can hear other conversations going on in the background, in various languages. So much despair, all over the world, radiating from one small spot of disaster on a boozy street.

The office is as hot as ever, despite the fans that revolve above our desks, making sheets of paper dance. The air conditioning rarely works. Steve tells me that the phones have been constantly ringing since he returned from the bombsite. Relatives of missing people are calling. Despite there being official help-lines available, people are contacting us for any sort of news. They seem to have great faith in an English language newspaper's ability to help and advise. It's all hopeless, I think, but as I take a turn at answering calls, I try not to let people hear that in my voice. I write down names and descriptions of people who are unaccounted for. I must have seen some of them last night, destroyed on the seared ground. Between calls, Steve puts his head in his hands. Sometimes he looks at me as if he's going to say something, but then he doesn't. We go on like this for hours.

'Go get something to eat,' Steve says to me eventually. He's sweating in his chair, empty drink cans crumpled around him.

'It's okay. I'm eating the biscuits.'

I'm not hungry but Steve keeps offering snacks to me and eventually I had to take something. Crumbs are scattered over my keyboard, under my fingers as I slowly type. I'm not even sure what I'm writing; some sort of first-hand account of what happened last night. I can't bring myself to read back through it; it might all be nonsense.

'Biscuits aren't enough. When did you last eat a meal? Or sleep? Take a break.'

'Oh, I'm okay.' My eyes drift towards our little television. The power's been back on for a while and we're tuned to the news with the volume low.

'...not officially confirmed, but sources suggest the bomb was hidden in a suitcase in front of Bar XS, a popular venue amongst backpackers and tourists. Officials are appealing for witnesses...'

There's no exact death toll, and no one can say who did this to us or why. But there's my street, again and again, destroyed for the world to see. It makes my eyes itch.

The phone on my desk begins to ring. Steve slides across on his wheelie chair and snatches up the handset. One of the wires from beneath his computer gets dragged over with him, caught around his foot. Shaking it away, he switches off my monitor.

'Go,' he hisses, and nods towards the door, which is propped open with a dirty pair of walking boots.

'Okay, okay. I'll be back in ten.'

The other phone starts ringing but Steve waves me away as I try to answer it.

'Okay,' I say again.

Actually, it's a relief to get outside. I'm glad to be away from the phones and the news reports, even though this road is empty and strange. The internet café beneath our office is closed. The signs advertising scuba schools and nightclubs, usually out all along the pavement, have not been displayed. There are no backpackers sitting in the cafés or on the balconies of the hostels. There's no music; just the sound of drills.

Thinking of all this, vaguely aware that I'm shaking my head, I reach a food stand. There are normally stands like this all along the street, but this is the only one today. The birds have gone too. I've got some money from Steve to tide me over until I somehow get a replacement bank card. My purse, and everything else, is lost inside the hostel. I use Steve's crumpled up notes to buy a box of noodles. The elderly woman selling them pats my hand and mutters something reassuring.

I eat as I walk. People ride past on mopeds, their belongings piled up behind them. I wouldn't want to leave the island now, even if I felt I had a place to go. How can people desert it just as it needs them the most? I flick a dark little mushroom after them as their bikes whine and bounce. But then I feel bad and self-righteous and become, abruptly, aware of the scent of my own sweat.

I decide to go to Steve's place, to shower and change, but then I remember I don't have any more clothes. Everything's back at the hostel. I've lost absolutely everything; all my material belongings and my sense of home too, because this is no longer the island I know. At least I'm not hurt; just some cuts on my feet which are making me walk funny, and this noise in my ears that won't quite go away. It's disgusting to feel sorry for myself when people are dead and maimed. But I do feel sorry for myself. I can't help it, and I want my stuff back. I decide to go get it.

If I continue down this street I'll get to the roped off crater where the bomb exploded, and where international news crews are now gathered. Steve's spent much of the morning there, talking to the police, paramedics, victims. But I'm not ready to go back just yet. It would be like poking a stick into a friend's open wound.

I dart along a side street and come out behind my hostel, where the back door is hanging open same as always. There is just a strip of police tape blocking the entrance at waist height. I purposely keep my eyes away from the small swimming pool that's back here, sunk in a box of concrete between the hostel and the place where the greasy kitchen next door keep their dustbins; Steve's told me that a plastic sheet has been pulled over the pool to hide what's been left there by burnt people who fell in last night, looking for relief.

Around the back door, which residents tend to use more than the front entrance, some posters have been put up. There are photographs with notes scribbled next to them. Messages have been scrawled on the backs of receipts, and across pages ripped from notebooks. People trying to reach their loved ones. I gently run my fingers across the bricks, around these pictures and notes. Look at their smiles. None of us saw this coming.

I put my noodles down on the steps, duck under the police tape and go inside. Usually I would walk in to the sound of music, laughter, the clunk of cans falling to the bottom of a vending machine. Today I hear work going on out front, my own quick breath, and the creaking of the building. The whole place is dark, but I'm still acutely aware of my surroundings. I didn't come this way last night because the corridors twist and turn; I thought I'd get trapped. But the way seems clear. I can smell plaster and soot, a tang up my nose which might be blood. Are there bodies under that rubble in reception? I pass the rooms of people I know, but just watch my own feet. No one else is in here; I can feel the building's emptiness in the air. I keep walking, aware of my stupidity with each step I take.

In my bedroom, I dart like an insect, grabbing only what I really need and staying away from the edge of the room; in fact, I don't even look at it, although I can feel the heat of the sun against my skin. I recall walking into the living room of my home one night when I was very young, and my parents were watching a horror film. I remember my mum saying, 'No, sweetie, don't look.' I think of that as I pack my things.

# Chapter Seven

We stay in the office until after dark. I'm melting into my chair. The light fades and noises from the street grow louder; shouts and passing vehicles. It's not the usual sort of noise; there's panic out there, and it reminds me of last night. I begin to tap my feet. Steve has his nose right up by the screen as he reads news reports online. I'm finding it hard to focus on anything other than the shadow of my limbs on the carpet. It looks like the shadow of a dead tree; boughs ready to snap.

Steve types loudly for a few minutes and then swivels to face me. He says: 'I feel like a war correspondent. You know, that's what I always intended to be.'

I look up at the clock. 'I keep thinking of how things were this time yesterday when we had no idea. The person, or people, who left the suitcase in front of XS; do you think they were hanging around all evening, watching people get drunker? People who were about to become victims. We might have walked past them, Steve.'

'Yeah. I don't know. But I expect they've left the island by now.'

'I feel like they're still here watching us,' I say, trying to hide a shiver.

'We should go to the port,' Steve says. 'Talk to the people who run the boats. They may have noticed any suspicious arrivals or departures, right?'

'Yeah, we should. Maybe tomorrow?'

'I think it's a good place to start.' Steve nods.

Eventually we stop answering the phones, and let them ring through to a recorded message; Steve's voice, wavering and

41

sincere. We can hear requests being left in the background as we type up what we can, and upload information onto our website. I'm steadying my hand to pour coffee when we notice a voice on the phone which sounds different to the others.

'That's Kadesadayurat.' Steve grabs for the handset while mopping at his forehead with a stained cloth. We've been hoping to speak with Kadesadayurat all day, but he's been impossible to get on the phone, unsurprisingly of course. He's been a friend to the newspaper since Steve interviewed his wife five years ago, way before my time; she makes jewellery, and we all get together sometimes to drink whiskey. He gives us stories when we're running low on them.

I put a mug beside Steve's keyboard and watch while he speaks on the phone. I hold my own coffee but don't drink it, just let the steam pass my face. What could be worse than the night we've just lived through? But still I feel icy as I watch his face change. He nods and says that we'll come to the police station right away.

'What's going on?' I ask.

'Someone at the golf resort has reported Bernard Shuttleworth missing. It looks like he's been attacked and taken. The police want to speak to you about your conversation this morning.'

# Chapter Eight

Steve walks with me to the police station. The night's hot and there's a hum of nervous energy in the air. A helicopter circles over another part of town. Somewhere nearby a dog is whining.

'I don't think I'll be able to help them,' I say, breathing in a sweet smell, seeing empty beer bottles in the gutter.

'You'll be fine. Just remember to think before you speak.'

'It's not like I'm a suspect or anything though.'

'No, no.'

'Except, I could be, I guess. This must be my fault somehow. I should have paid more attention to the things he said. I should have been more focussed.'

'You did just fine. But the thing is, you might have been the last person to see him before it happened. Whatever *it* might be.'

'I didn't kill him, honestly,' I say, trying to be funny. Steve doesn't laugh.

Actually, I feel guilty, like I *did* kill him. There were moments during our meeting this morning when Shuttleworth looked at me in his leering sort of way and I hated everything about him. What if the police see that hatred in me now, and what if it makes them think I murdered him? I keep walking, but perhaps it would be more sensible to turn around and run.

Vans are parked outside the small police station, and groups of people stand around them, looking professional. Other people sit alone with bags, staring at nothing. There is a noise like a generator, and a murmuring of voices which comes from all around us and occasionally peaks like the screeching of a bird. I notice a woman sitting on the steps with bandages up her arms and some of her hair missing. She looks like a backpacker and vaguely familiar, so I smile at her as we pass. She doesn't smile back, although her eyes track my movements.

Revolving doors take us into the reception. Harsh lights beat down on lines of crumpled people in plastic chairs. Phones are ringing. Doors open and close. I feel my lungs tighten, and take a step closer to Steve. The air conditioning works in here; it's cold. Too cold.

We introduce ourselves to the female officer at the front desk. She remembers Steve from a past meeting, and they talk for a moment about how awful everything is. I barely know any Thai, so can't follow. I've been meaning to take lessons. Steve learnt by forcing himself into conversations with the locals. He's close to fluent now. He's making an effort to be friendly with this lady, but I can see him picking at a scrap of sticky-tape attached to the front of the desk; I know he's as nervous as I am. A sickness rises inside me again. Oh, please don't let me be sick here. It'll make me look like I'm guilty of something.

Eventually we're led along a corridor filled with dark glass. Offices on either side are crowded and people have spilled out so that we have to step around them. Everyone's shouting, arguing, waving pieces of paper around.

'Wait here.' The police officer leaves us at an unmanned desk.

We sit in silence. Steve's leg twitches and touches mine. A man at the next desk is poking pencils into an electric sharpener while he talks on the phone. Someone nearby is humming an operatic tune that I recognise but would not be able to name. Other people are talking in groups. The noise is a big, solid thing. It reminds me of the noise in a school canteen, only with a different, nasty edge. It's at this moment that our mobile phones regain their signal for the first time since the bomb went off, and begin to chirp like frantic animals.

'Seems like people care about us,' I say, looking at texts coming in from friends I've not spoken to in years. There are messages from people I know from the hostel too, alive after all, and most of them are already far from the island.

Steve switches his phone onto silent and says: 'I can't face them. I've been online to prove I'm not dead; that'll have to do for now.' This isn't like him, and my nausea goes up a notch.

A man shuffles past the desk as I try to text with shaking fingers. I see blood on his trousers. Behind him is a policeman I don't recognise. I know most of them; it's only a small department. Steve has mentioned how extra police officers are being shipped in from the mainland to help deal with things. This policeman stops beside my chair, puts a hand on the back of it and leans in.

'Thank you for getting here so quickly.' He's young, perhaps the same age as me, which isn't that young really; I'm nearly thirty. He seems young compared to the other officers moving around behind him, their faces clenched.

'I thought we were going to see Kadesadayurat?' Steve says.

'Busy.' The policeman introduces himself but I don't catch his name. He turns to me. 'Lucy? We need to talk about statement you made on the phone. Perhaps you can help find Mr Shuttleworth.'

'Sure, of course I'll help,' I say, a little too quickly. I immediately rattle off an account of our conversation at the golf resort. I start to talk about the monkey I saw there, and ask what my companions think; did Bernard Shuttleworth bring all the monkeys here with him? But Steve shakes his head at me and the policeman clears his throat.

'He okay when you left?'

I nod. 'I left him drinking lemonade.'

'Okay.' He looks down at the notes which he has written in both Thai and English. 'You said you ran into one of his staff's boyfriends at a hotel? Tell me, please, what happened when you spoke to him?'

'I didn't actually speak to him. He left before I got a chance. I can't really tell you anything except that he was in a rush.' I stop to think for a moment. 'I can describe his car for you. And him. I can describe him.'

'His hotel already did that. They were very helpful.'

'Oh.' I look around and wonder why no one's offered a coffee to Steve and me. Everyone else seems to be drinking one, from crinkly plastic cups or chipped mugs. Perhaps it's because they think I'm a murderer and they don't offer drinks to those.

'Did you see anyone else at the golf resort?' Steve asks me, and the policeman nods like this is a very good question.

'No. He said that they only had three rooms occupied. I didn't see any of those people.' I remember the child watching us from the doorway but don't say anything about her. Then something else comes back to me. 'Actually, as I was leaving I did see a car coming along the road towards me. I don't know if they stopped at the resort but there's not much else around there.'

'What kind of car?' the policeman asks, pointing his pen like a dart.

'A blue one?' I shrug.

'Same one you saw Dolph driving?'

'I'm not sure,' I say. 'It could have been. But then he was already at the Imperial Hotel as I arrived there, so I don't suppose the timing works out.'

'Is there anything else?' the policeman asks, ignoring my questions.

'I don't think so.' I stare at my battered feet, trying to think of something useful. 'What do you think happened to him, honestly? You think Dolph attacked him?'

'Like we said on the phone; Mr Shuttleworth has gone missing.'

'But you think he's been attacked? Someone hurt him?'

'We don't exactly know,' the policeman says, looking around, distracted. Steve, beside me, seems to have relaxed. His leg is no longer twitching.

'And what happens next?' I ask, trying to catch the policeman's attention as he watches his colleagues, who are trying to catch a bomber.

'We find him. It's a small island.'

I say: 'Do you think Dolph's involved in the bombing?'

The policeman doesn't say anything but he gives his head the smallest of shakes.

We show ourselves out of the building. On the steps, beneath a fluorescent light and a cloud of humming insects, we turn to each other.

'What do you think happened?' I ask, desperate. I need to know if whatever happened is my fault somehow, but mostly I just need to know what the story is, because stories are how I see the world. Without them, it's all just chaos.

Steve, lighting up a cigarette, says: 'My guess is that one of his workers came back and did something to him. They would have known the place was near enough deserted.'

We start along the street, beneath palm trees and the lights of an aeroplane blinking high in the sky, oblivious to all that's happening down here. Neither of us knows quite where we're headed.

'Don't you think that's a bit dismissive of the evidence though?' I say. 'He talks to me and then he's attacked or kidnapped, apparently. It just seems like the two must be connected.'

'I think it's a coincidence,' Steve says.

'You really believe his staff members hate him that much?' I have heard some of the rumours about Bernard Shuttleworth, but I know Steve will be aware of every horrible detail.

'He's rich enough to live above the law. He doesn't treat his female workers well. What do you think of him?'

'I don't like him.' I pause and lean against the glass front of a café.

'Are you all right?' Steve goes to put a hand on my shoulder but stops just short. He's noticed that I don't like to be touched. He's my friend. Friends notice that kind of thing.

'We should have looked into the rumours about him,' I say. 'We're as bad as the police, letting him get away with whatever he wants.'

'But we're not that sort of newspaper,' Steve says, with an uncomfortable smile.

'We should have tried.'

'I did try once. Before you got here. But it's like you said; he practically keeps us afloat. He didn't cooperate when I tried to question him, and he made it clear that he'd no longer be advertising in the *Koh Star* if I, you know, persisted. So…'

'Oh,' I say, trying not to show how disappointed I am.

'And anyway, it looks like he might have got his comeuppance,' Steve says. He's seen how disappointed I am.

'Maybe. I guess that means we're screwed then. Financially.' I continue walking. My skin stays cold for a while, where it was pressed against the glass. A moped passes us; the only vehicle on this long street. I think about Shuttleworth and where he might be now. He didn't seem, this morning, like a man anything bad could happen to. But no one's safe anymore. I've seen what we look like inside our skins and it's awful. I think I've got to the truth of something. This must be how it is to live in nature, to be something's prey and always vulnerable.

'Come stay at mine tonight. Don't go back to that faceless hotel. You can sleep on my futon. We'll have a bit of wine and some pizza. Girls night in.' Steve laughs.

'Yes,' I say, desperate suddenly to be sitting on that futon. 'That would be good.'

# Chapter Nine

I wake up on Steve's dusty sofa, my fingers brushing an empty wine bottle on the floor. My mouth is dry, my lips cracked and tongue fat. I don't remember falling asleep. When we arrived here last night, Steve and I ate pizzas topped with meat we couldn't identify, and although I hadn't asked to see them, he got out his laptop and showed me photographs of his daughter from when she came to visit last year, before I'd arrived on the island. I let him talk about her, and about the things they did together, and we tried to forget that the world has changed.

He's left some freshly printed newspapers on the coffee table. It's Saturday; the day the *Koh Star* comes out. Sitting up, I take one from the top of the pile. It feels twice as thick as usual and there's an image of the bomb site on the front page. I can see my hostel, ruined in the background like it was never a real place at all; a place where people slept and ate and smiled at each other. I fold the paper and put it back down.

'Good morning,' Steve says from somewhere across the room. I raise my head with an effort and see him perched on a stool by the window, eating a donut and reading the back page of the *Koh Star*.

'Morning,' I mumble.

'I've counted three spelling mistakes,' he says. 'You'll probably spot more. But still, I think this might be the best work we've done in a long time.'

'Do you think there will be any tourists left to read it?' I ask, sitting up as he pours us each a coffee from a grimy looking cafetière.

'I don't know. But there's important stuff in here. If even one person reads it I think it'll help them. So, I'd count that as us doing our job well.'

'Yeah, you're right.' I don't think Steve feels as positive as he's trying to sound. His hands shake as he passes over my coffee, and his eyes have sunk even further into his skull since yesterday.

'Speaking of work,' he says, 'are you still coming with me to the port? It can't hurt to ask around, see if anyone remembers anything suspicious. Anyone odd arriving or leaving the island around the time of the bomb. And, I don't know about you, but I feel like I want to keep busy today.'

I agree with him, and after a quick shower and a change of clothes, I drive us out of town and towards the port where the majority of visitors come in and out of the island. The road is winding and potholed, busy with mopeds and cars crammed with people. Steve has brought along a big bottle of sparkling water and we drain it within twenty minutes of being sat in the slow-moving traffic. The interior of the car is so hot that we can taste metal, like the vehicle's frame is melting.

When we get to the port a worker is checking backpackers' tickets as they queue beside a huge banana plant. We line up to speak to him; the offices seem to either be closed or bursting with people anxious to find a way out of here. Small, brightly-coloured fishing boats are resting in the turquoise water, and beyond them are other boats of varying size and modernity waiting to take people back to the mainland. There are usually one or two boats coming in and out of here every few hours. I count six here right now.

When we reach the front of the queue the worker holds out his hand for our tickets. He doesn't look at us; he's frowning towards the ticket offices where the crowd is swelling like the sea. As Steve begins speaking in Thai, two young girls with henna tattoos on their arms and bandages on their legs, slip past the man and try approaching the first boat.

'No, no,' he shouts, rushing to block their way. 'I tell you before. No ticket, no boat.'

'There aren't any left for today but we need to *go*,' one of them wails in an Australian accent.

The man ushers them back past the banana plant and I watch as they wrap their arms around each other and disappear into the crowd.

'Ticket, ticket,' he says to us impatiently.

'We're from the *Koh Star*,' Steve explains. 'We wanted to ask a few questions.'

'We didn't realise how busy you'd be,' I say. 'We should have known.'

One of the ships blows its horn, making people duck and cry out. I have to swallow a whimper myself, and take deep breaths to slow the fluttering of my heart.

'No time for this,' the man says, pushing us aside. 'Go to office.'

I crumple up my empty can and toss it into a bin that is already close to overflowing. Insects rise from it and then settle again.

'I suppose we ought to try their office, then,' Steve says, eying the crammed buildings warily.

'Excuse me,' someone says beside us. 'Did you say you're from the *Koh Star*?'

A sunburned English man is drinking a bottle of lager with the label peeled off, and is just throwing a cigarette away towards the dustbin when we turn to nod at him. He has a baseball cap pulled low over his eyes, which have the same sleepless look as Steve's. He's maybe in his mid-twenties but his shoulders are hunched like an old man's and his voice sounds raw, as if he's been shouting or crying.

'I've read your newspaper,' he said. 'It was useful for finding out boat times.'

'Oh good, good,' Steve says, distracted, trying to steer me in the direction of the office.

'Wait,' the man says. 'I want to tell you guys something.'

'Okay?' I say, stopping.

'Everyone's saying that the bomb was in a bag out the front of XS. But it wasn't. It was in front of the café next door. In one of the big plant pots, probably.'

'You mean the ice cream parlour? How do you know?' I ask. I can picture the plant pots. I was able to see them from my bedroom window. They reminded me of giant pineapples, and the yellow leaved plants always looked half dead.

'My mate Gaz,' he says, pointing to a man perched on top of a pile of backpacks, smoking a rollie and leafing furiously through a Thai phrase book. 'He used to be in the army. Been to Iraq and Afghanistan. So, he's seen lots of explosions. Came here for a break. Funny eh? Anyway, he was able to tell just by looking at it. He knew where the explosion started.'

Steve steps towards Gaz as if he wants to talk to him, but the other man shakes his head. 'He's already spoken to the police. He's not going to talk to you. Look at him. He's done talking for a while. I just wanted to mention it because I don't know if the police were listening to us. It didn't even seem like they were writing much down. They definitely didn't care that he'd been a soldier for ten years. I know there's going to be experts coming in and telling folk exactly what happened. What type of bomb it was and all that, but the other thing is, I tried to go in that café the afternoon *before* the bomb went off, to get a bottle of water, but it was all locked up. Deserted. I'd been going in there every day all week until then. I don't know. I just felt like I ought to tell someone.'

# Chapter Ten

We have lunch back at Steve's place; cold slices of the pizza from the night before. They leave a film of grease on the roof of my mouth. We switch on the television and watch a news report with English subtitles scrolling at the bottom of the screen in bright yellow. Not all of it makes sense, but we learn that the death toll has risen to twelve, and still more people are unaccounted for. A middle-aged white lady is interviewed at the port we've just come from. The subtitles give up as the lady speaks in what sounds like Polish, but we understand the catch in her voice, the lines around her eyes and the way that she turns away at the end, mid-sentence, a hand against her face.

'Thank goodness for the ice cream parlour theory,' Steve says, poking his crust into ketchup. 'Or this morning would have been an utter waste of time.'

We never managed to get anything from the people working at the port. We hung around outside their offices for a while, drinking more of that strange juice and watching people surge onto the waiting boats. Eventually the office workers came out to lock the doors and put up signs saying they'd be back in the morning; tickets were sold out for today. They shook their heads at our questions, said that the police had already been around and they didn't know anything about anything anyway.

'I actually noticed it was closed that day too,' I say, thinking about what the man at the port had told us. 'I was going to get a drink on my way to the Bollywood wedding.'

'Is that unusual, for it to be closed?'

'Yeah.' I nod. 'I think so.'

'So, that's what we look into next. We find the owner. First, though, I'm going to have to lie down for a while, Lucy. I don't think I can sleep but I need to rest. My head is pounding. I'll see you in an hour or two.'

'Yeah, sure, I understand.'

After he's gone I put my hands over my face and press down until my eyes hurt and I see stars. What am I supposed to do today? Now that the initial horror is over and I've been left alive, it's hard to settle on a new path to follow. I decide to phone the police, to see if they've found Shuttleworth. Pulling my mobile out from the sofa cushions, I see that my German friend, Lena, has texted me. I reply to say that I'll meet her at a café in town.

I can't get through to anyone when I call the police. There are beeps, crackles and then a Thai voice that is abruptly cut off. I give up for now and pour a glass of juice from the fridge. As I sip it I try to decide whether Bernard Shuttleworth is alive or dead. There is so much death around us right now. It's difficult to sense his amongst it all. I think maybe he's alive. Maybe the police will call me later with an update, and they'll tell me that it's all been a mistake.

Lena texts back to say that she'll be half an hour, so I take a moment to look around Steve's home. I've been here before, but never alone. It's a one storey, open plan sort of space, with cobwebs and occasional lizards on the ceiling, dusty light coming through slats in the blinds, books everywhere, magazines too, and speakers arranged about the place, many with their wires trailing to nowhere. He has two electric guitars and a stereo system about four feet tall. The whole place is dim and warm, and smells of rolling tobacco and unhealthy food.

I linger beside a set of shelves, reading the spines of books. On the top shelf, hidden behind a stack of science fiction magazines, I discover a pair of photographs. Their frames are delicate and ornate, which suggests to me that Steve wasn't the one who framed them. One is of a baby in a Moses basket, and I assume this must be his daughter, Jenna. The other photograph is of Steve when he was about twenty years younger, with his hand on Jenna's shoulder. Jenna's holding a plump rabbit, squeezing it against her chest. A woman stands beside them, a slight smile on her face. This lady, like Jenna, is very pretty, but there's something about her eyes and the distance she's keeping from the others, like maybe she'll say something unpleasant when the camera turns away. I've never stopped to think about Jenna's mother. Steve doesn't mention her.

Time to go. The road outside Steve's house is a brown strip of dust. The buildings are packed close together, built with wood and breezeblocks. I'm the only person out here, but I can hear people speaking in Thai, also an American drama on TV, and metal scraping against metal. There's this sense that people are all around me, but hidden. I walk slowly, feeling their eyes on me.

Lena will probably want to speak about the people who have died. Their names haven't been released yet but there has been talk of Swedish women, Australian teenagers and a British TV talent show star from years ago. All just rumours. Steve and I keep searching for confirmation and we're told there will be a press release soon. If I hadn't seen what happened the night before last, I'm not sure I'd be able to accept that people who were enjoying the island just days ago no longer exist. As it is, their fates are clear to me, and I feel it with a dull ache all through my body.

I'm thinking this, when I notice two Thai women on the other side of the street. I'm closer to the centre of town now, and there are people about, a semblance of normality. These particular women are drinking milkshakes on the curb, huddled together like children, luggage piled up around them. But what I really notice is the way that they're dressed. They're wearing Bernard Shuttleworth's golf resort uniform, which consists of black and gold blouses, pleated skirts and long white socks. It's pretty hideous, which is why I remember it so clearly from my visits to the resort in the past.

I cross towards them, pausing halfway to let a moped pass. The women glance up and I see that they are just girls really. One looks like she has recently been crying and the other has on a lot of gold jewellery.

'Do you speak English?' I ask as I step onto the pavement, smiling hopefully.

After a pause, they nod.

'You work for Mr Shuttleworth?'

The girls look at each other and then nod again. 'Actually, we leave today.'

'I heard about your boss going missing. I've met him before. Does anyone know what happened?'

The girls discuss this in Thai for a moment and then shake their heads. 'We don't know anything,' they say.

'Okay. That's okay. Can I ask why you're leaving?'

'His wife closing,' the girl with the tear-stained face says.

'I didn't know he was married.' I'm truly surprised, and probably stare at them for just a beat too long, so that I start to seem strange.

'Why you asking us?' the same girl says. She has one hand on her bag, like she's afraid I might steal it.

'I'm just curious. Sorry.' I'm about to leave but then hesitate. 'Do you know Maliwan?'

The girls nod, and smile a little. They like Maliwan, I see.

I ask: 'Do you know where she is?'

'No. You her friend?'

'Sort of, yeah. You have no idea where she might be?' I smile and hope that I look young and normal, like someone who might be friends with Maliwan.

They shake their heads.

'Do you know her boyfriend? Dolph?'

They look at each other and then tell me: 'No, we not see.'

I remember something that Shuttleworth said and decide to try it. 'Could she be with her mum? Her mother. She's sick, right?'

The girls stare at me but don't shake their heads. Maybe.

'Where does her mum live? You have an address?'

'You are police?' the sad-looking girl asks.

'No, I'm a journalist. For the *Koh Star*. I need to talk to her. It's really important.'

'We can tell you address. But will you help us? We need to get bus and we haven't been paid.'

I get some money from my purse and the girls hold out their hands. I decide to see this through, even though I can feel their mistrust of me and I doubt they're going to give me anything real for my cash. All the same, I let the notes go, and one of the girls writes an address in English across a page of my notepad, her gold bracelets jangling.

'I don't remember exactly,' she says as she writes. 'But you find it. There's a...' she speaks with her friend in Thai for a moment, searching for the right word.

'Pond,' the other girl says.

'Okay, thank you.' I hug the notepad to my chest as I walk away. They were messing with me, probably; when people say they need money to take a bus they are nearly always lying.

I don't look at the address until I get back to the other side of the street. Maliwan's mum lives up in the hills, apparently, where not everyone has electricity and where the clouds hang low. Perhaps she does live there. Perhaps she knows something important and I'm doing the right thing.

My phone begins to ring. I scrabble for it in my bag and see that Steve's calling.

'They've announced a press conference,' he says before I can speak.

I stop walking. Lena, the address, and everything else can wait.

# Chapter Eleven

We've gathered outside the town hall; a spiky building that I've always disliked. It casts shadows like giant insects. A statue of an ancient Thai King stands in its courtyard. Strips of gold on the statue and building are twinkling as foreign journalists point their cameras at the police chief. He's speaking from the top of the concrete steps. His face, and the triangle of chest visible at the top of his shirt, are wet with sweat. Watching him makes me want to mop my own forehead.

I arrived late and had to squeeze through the gathered crowd to reach Steve's side. All around us, people are writing, recording, gently jostling for a better view. TV cameras glide and dip like birds. There is a smell of sweat and electricity. Behind this ball of journalists, normal people are watching, standing where there would usually be plastic chairs, fried chicken stands and ice cream stalls. Some of these people, I think, are here because their children are dead. I'm looking at them as the police chief talks. They are white, middle-aged, dressed too warmly for the weather, and they stare like beaten animals. Steve nudges me and whispers something, making a scribbling motion with his finger. I get out my notebook and start writing; I'm better at shorthand than he is.

'Sixteen people,' the police chief is saying, using his hands to hush shouted questions. His English is good but I see people straining to understand his accent. Armed police stand behind him in the doorway.

'They are Europeans. Young people. Their families are coming here. The death toll will rise.' He stutters slightly as a man in a suit reaches out to him from the shadows of the doorway, as if to keep him from telling more. No names are given.

And then there are questions. An Australian journalist asks how many people were injured. The police chief screws up his face and says maybe thirty. Most have been flown to the mainland and some to Singapore. Some of these people might still die? Yes, they could. Steve and I don't ask anything although we had both planned to. I have a folded piece of paper in my pocket with several questions written on it. They're good questions but my mouth is dry. If I try to speak I might scream instead. The scene goes on around us and maybe Steve feels the same way I do; that the world is ending and we have to get away from these people and the snap, snap, snap of cameras.

'We will find those responsible,' the police chief says, but his voice is weak.

'No one has claimed responsibility?' a woman close to me asks, pushing forwards and shouting across the crowd.

'Not yet.'

'But who do you *think* it was?' she presses.

'Cannot say. Not at this time.'

'Was it a suicide bomber?' asks a man with an Irish accent.

'We believe the bomb was hidden. Not a suicide bomber.'

'Hidden where?' someone demands.

'We are still working that out,' the police chief says, and Steve and I glance at each other.

Afterwards, I sit beneath the statue of the King, chew a stick of gum and watch the vehicles slowly disperse. Some reporters are yelling and grinning at each other, like they're on an adventure holiday. Steve joins me. He leans against the statue and stares at the sky. I watch his shoulders move as he breathes. Neither of us says anything for a while.

'I somehow thought things would feel less horrible once someone official had stepped in and taken charge,' Steve says.

'Me too. But it still feels the same. Worse even. Because now we know that the official people are as lost as we are.'

'Oh, that reminds me. I bumped into Kadesadayurat when I arrived here,' Steve says. 'They haven't found Shuttleworth. And this Dolph character *is* missing. He's a Marine Biologist and shares a house with a few other scientists. They're concerned about him. They thought he must have been injured or killed by the bomb but of course several people, you included, have seen him at the Imperial Hotel since then. He probably just got scared and left the island like everyone else. Maliwan's not been seen either. Her mother thinks she's dead, and she's quite possibly right.'

'Maybe she is,' I say, looking down at my feet. 'That could be why Dolph looked upset. But why was he staying at a hotel if he has a house here?'

'Well, I don't know. That is sort of odd.'

I look towards the town hall, where the doors have been sealed and shapes move on the other side of the glass. I imagine that the people inside are staring at the ground much like Steve and I, asking question after question but getting no answers.

'It's strange that no one's claimed this attack,' I say.

'I guess. But it's still been less than forty-eight hours.'

'Did Kadesadayurat say anything else about Shuttleworth?' I ask. 'Don't they have any idea what happened to him?'

'Well, they don't think you killed him.'

'That's a relief. Although, it's not very thorough policing, is it? How do they really know I'm not involved?'

'Honestly, I don't think they care too much at the moment. They know how he treated people and they have terrorists to hunt.'

'You know he's married?' I say, shielding my eyes as the sunlight pulses around the roof of the town hall.

'They're separated. She lives in the States, I think. Don't waste too much energy worrying about the Shuttleworths. His disappearance isn't your responsibility and I don't think they're connected to the bomb in any way. I know he gave you what he thought was a lead but he's a strange guy; I doubt he knew what he was talking about. Are you coming back to the office?'

'I need to meet Lena but I won't be long. I haven't seen her since the other night. I'll swing by the office afterwards.'

'I'll be there,' Steve says with the faintest of smiles.

# Chapter Twelve

Lena's sitting outside the coffee shop. She notices me just as she's finishing a cigarette; she crumples it into a clay pot in the centre of the table, which is covered with laminated menus and emptied coffee cups. She stands up to greet me with the gentlest of hugs and kisses me with lips that smell like blackcurrant and leave a stickiness on my cheek. It's impossible not to look at the cut on her forehead. It's healing, but the dried blood is as black as her hair.

'Good to see you,' she says without smiling. She stops a passing waitress and asks for two more coffees.

I've known Lena since I arrived at the hostel. She was working on reception when I paid for my first week's stay. She's been travelling for two years and doesn't see an end to it. She spends most of her time resting in chairs, curled like a cat and smoking, or reading, or drinking from glass bottles which she taps her coloured nails against. But when something excites her she becomes a spark of energy, igniting everyone around her to party or protest. I was wary of her at first, and still am a little. But she seems fond of me and tells me about her life whether I ask her to or not. I don't tell her much at all. She doesn't seem to notice.

Today, Lena is changed. Her face looks plumper than usual and she keeps her hands still in her lap. She's been staying with her boyfriend since the night of the bomb. He's a Thai fisherman. Five or six of them live there together, laughing, eating and smoking. I visited the house with her about a month ago. We drank vodka on a mat made from reeds. There was very little in there besides a smell of fish; some crates, boxes, piles of clothes. I don't think she should be staying there right now. I can't imagine what she does in there for all those hours, hanging around people she can't communicate with verbally, as her Thai is as basic as mine. I want to tell her that she should be with her family or with her friends, but I don't say anything because I know I would hate it if she said something like that to me.

'Look who I have here.' Lena reaches into a mound of blankets beneath her chair and pulls out a puppy; a furry slug with a pink nose and rheumy eyes.

'Cute,' I say, although it isn't; it looks sick.

'It's one of Billie's puppies. Don't you recognise him? The others all died in the explosion, but not this one. They were downstairs. I found him under his mother's body when I tried to get back inside for my stuff.'

'Shit,' I say. The hostel dog. 'They even got Billie.'

We drink, she smokes and cradles the puppy, and we try to capture something of how we used to be. It's hard to know what to say, other than to list the names of people we knew, and to state their various fates. And then we agree that what happened to them, and to us, is terrible. Our real thoughts, the ones we have when we're alone, won't translate into words. We both know this and stare at each other, trying out telepathy. It doesn't work. We give up and talk of other things, chasing normality. I feel like I've failed; this is not the conversation we ought to be having. I think of Steve alone in the office and I want to leave this place, but can't. She keeps reaching over to touch my knee. I expect Steve's worrying about how long I'll be; chewing on the end of a pencil, writing his thoughts on post-it notes so that he'll remember to bring them up with me later.

I tell Lena about the press conference and, interested, she asks what I learnt.

'Not very much, I'm afraid,' I say, taking out my notebook and looking at the single page of shorthand.

'Very weird. Like hieroglyphics,' Lena says, tracing her finger over my biro marks. 'And what is this?'

'Oh, an address I got today. I don't think it's anything important.'

'Address for who?' Lena, who I think is pleased to have someone she can properly converse with, keeps pressing me until I tell her about Mr Shuttleworth and Dolph and Maliwan and my conversation earlier with the girls in the street.

'You absolutely must go to this place,' Lena says.

'I will, I will,' I say, eating the crisp little biscuit that came with my coffee.

'No, I mean right now. What if the old man is being held there? You should really check.'

'I don't know,' I say. 'Maybe.'

We hug again as we say goodbye. I notice red marks above my elbows as I walk away, from where her fingers dug in.

'I'll see you again soon!' I shout back to her, but she's already rounding the corner, lighting a cigarette and frowning at the ground.

# Chapter Thirteen

Steve isn't at work when I arrive there. He's scribbled a message on a love-heart-shaped post-it note; he's gone to meet someone from the mayor's office. I stand by my computer for a moment and tap at the keyboard just to make a noise. I wipe dust from the screen with the palm of my hand. Going to the shelves beside the window, I gently flick through the sheets of paper that Steve has piled here; notes from his conversations with people at the bombsite on Thursday night. He took so many eye-witness accounts that we couldn't use them all in this week's newspaper. We're going to type them all up anyway, but I can't bring myself to read them right now.

I look outside and see Steve's little car parked crookedly on the pavement. I could get to Maliwan's mother's house and back in less than an hour, if I needed to. I pick up the phone from the nearest desk, and read Kadesadayurat's number from a list taped to the wall. It rings for a long time, but then someone answers in Thai, speaking quickly and talking over me as I try to explain myself.

'It's to do with the missing man,' I say. 'Bernard Shuttleworth. I've got this address, see. What? I'm sorry, do you speak English at all? I'm really sorry.'

They hang up on me and I try calling the main police phone number, but I'm on hold for so long that I'm able to watch an old man limp nearly the whole length of the street, leaning on a battered pair of crutches.

'Oh, fuck it,' I say out loud, slamming down the phone.

I grab a post-it note from my desk; these ones are shaped like rainbows. *I'll be back soon.* I leave this by Steve's love-heart, lock up and go to the car, which has not cooled down at all since we drove back from the port.

The address in my notepad leads me out of town and uphill. It's a steep climb, and as the car struggles I pass homes built on high verges. The jungle is threatening to reclaim them, growing around their walls in thick tangles. Everything is wet. The trees look rotten.

I try not to look at the empty passenger seat beside me. It would be better not to do this alone. If Maliwan's mother really does think that her daughter was killed the night of the bomb, then this is going to be hard. I haven't done a difficult interview since moving here, but I have done this kind of thing before. I'd only been working as a journalist for a month when my boss sent me to visit a woman whose son had been knocked down by a drunk-driver. I hate this, but I know how to do it. If the address is genuine and Maliwan's mother is out here, I'll be able to talk to her, and I'll find out something useful. I know I will. I have to. I always used to be good at dealing with horror, until I had a personal horror of my own. I wind down the window to let some air blow across my face. I fill my lungs, choking on the heat. I press a hand against my stomach and tell myself not to think about the pregnancy now. Not ever.

Eventually the track narrows. I slow right down, peering out at dogs resting in the shade. They all look related; white fur and crooked bat ears. There is a smell of wood smoke. Plants begin to scrape the sides of the car. And then a three-legged cat steps into my path, staring.

'Screw it,' I say when the cat refuses to move.

Stopping the car, I get out. The air is thick with moisture. I hear a waterfall not far away. In a different life, this is the sort of place I would visit with a camera and a packed lunch. I climb a muddy slope away from the road, come out of the trees and here, right in front of me, is a little pond filled with weeds. There are burnt-out incense sticks on the ground beside it. Further up the slope is a tiny wooden home with a closed screen door. A couple of chickens scratch at the ground beneath it. Finding this place has been easy, but there's an air of abandonment to it that makes me think either those girls were lying, or Maliwan's mother has moved on. I think about what Lena said; that maybe Mr Shuttleworth is being held here. I can see other buildings dotted around between the trees, some with washing hanging outside them, others with push bikes propped against their walls. If there are bad people here, I can scream and surely someone will come out to help me. I look back towards the car and curl my hand around the phone inside my pocket.

Still, I edge closer. The building is decaying in the sun. There's an odour. It smells like sickness. Like a bad hospital. The door is hanging open just a little. Reaching out, I knock on the metal rim. It makes a tinny noise, hardly louder than the buzzing insects.

'Hello?' I push the door open a bit further. It's dark inside. The smell gets stronger; medicines and antiseptic, sweat and urine. Suddenly I don't like it. I want to run outside, breathe some clean air, but I force myself onwards.

As my eyes adjust, I realise that someone is sitting at the other side of the small room. They are slightly reclined, as if asleep. Sunlight creeps in with me, showing a mat on the floor, an old woman's gnarled feet. I feel my stomach shift, but if this woman is dead — and she certainly looks it — it's surely a better death than the others this island has seen lately.

Crossing the room with my fists clenched by my sides, I see that her eyes are closed inside a leathery face. Her hair, jet black, is pulled back. I don't know what to do, but then she's awake and clawing at me, squawking like a bird.

'No, stop!' I stumble backwards. 'I just want to help. Are you ill?'

'Yes, I'm ill,' she says in a bone dry voice, 'but not too ill to fight you.'

'I saw you through the door. I wanted to make sure you were okay.'

She sinks back into her chair, seemingly unable to leave it. When she begins to cough, I pick a bottle of water up from the floor, but she ignores it.

'I'm really sorry.' I glance at the door and the sliver of light around it but stay where I am. 'Look, I'm from the newspaper. My name's Lucy Lewis.'

'You're here about Maliwan.'

'Yeah.' I nod earnestly, trying to look like I know something; *anything*.

'My daughter. And she's always been the good one. It makes me sad that people like you are after her now. If it had been one of the other girls, I'd understand.'

'I'm not *after* her,' I say. 'Who else has been here?'

'The police. This morning. That's why I'm so tired now.'

'Here, have some water.' I hold out the bottle as she coughs and shakes.

'I don't want that. There's some Pepsi by the window.'

I get her a can, and smile, trying to look friendly, even though I'm imagining her grabbing at me with those long fingernails. I'd have to beat her off, knock her out of that chair. 'Your English is really good,' I say.

'Why are you surprised? I'm educated. I used to be a nurse in Bangkok.'

'Oh?'

'I saw some bad things in that city, but nothing like what's happened here.'

'I'm sorry to hear about Maliwan,' I say, unnerved by the sudden tremor in my voice. 'You think she was there when the bomb went off?'

'I haven't heard from her. She wouldn't let me worry.'

'What about her boyfriend? Dolph. Do you know him?'

'Yes, he's an American. Very good for her. She's a good girl. They come to visit me in his car. That's it. Are you going back to the town? Can you help me find her? I've heard the bodies are piled up in the streets, all without names. Look for her, won't you?'

'It's not that bad. There aren't any piles. It is bad though. I can take you into town, if you want?'

'When I feel well enough, I will go,' she says, and I worry that she will never be well enough. She coughs again and it sounds like there are ball bearings bouncing between her ribs.

'You haven't heard from Dolph?' I ask, speaking quickly so that I can finish this.

'No. The police tell me he's alive. They say other things about him which I don't believe. He didn't protect my daughter. I suppose he's afraid to see me.'

'You don't think he had anything to do with what happened to her boss?' I say. 'Or anything else?'

'My daughter wouldn't be with someone who does bad things.'

'Okay. I'm sure you're right. But do you know where I might find him? Where's his house?'

'I never went to his house,' she says, grimacing so that I see her pale gums.

'Okay.' I flap my arms and look around the dark room. It's tidy, barely anything in it, but feels dirty, like a layer of dust and grease is lying over everything. 'Do you have anyone to look after you?'

'I have friends. I have family. What do you think? No one cares about me?'

'No, no,' I say, shaking my head so hard that it hurts my eyes. I begin to back towards the door. I can no longer remember what I hoped to find here.

'They were here on Wednesday. The night before the bomb. They brought me some fish and all these cans of Pepsi. They know I like it. She's very good, Maliwan; she's a very good girl to me.'

'She sounds it.'

'She works very hard.'

'At the golf resort? Was she happy there? She wasn't going to leave?'

'Why would she leave? The money is very good.' She begins to say more but then covers her face with her hands, wheezing loudly enough to fill the whole building with the sound. I think that I can feel her hot breath all over me.

'I'll leave you alone,' I say, going for the door. 'I'm sorry to have troubled you. And for your loss. Really sorry.'

I hurry outside, slamming the door back into its frame. As the sunlight fills my eyes, I slip on the wet ground, landing on my knees. The noise of the hidden waterfall, very close, is enough to drown out the memory of that woman's dry breath, but I feel tainted by the smell of the place, and by this feeling that I just took a step in the wrong direction. My face is burning. I don't belong here. If Steve had been with me, things would have gone differently. He would have had her smiling by the end of it, and would have probably made some move to hug her, make her more comfortable in her chair. I expect he would have rustled her up something to eat, or helped her out into the daylight. And the thing is, he would have *enjoyed* all that. Perhaps I was that way too once. I can't remember.

# Chapter Fourteen

I get a text from Steve just as I'm parking outside the office, and I go to meet him for a milkshake at our favourite beach café. He says he needs the sugar but I think he just wants to do something normal. I don't tell him where I've been. All I did up there in the hills was upset Maliwan's mother. I wrap my hands around the icy cold glass and try to think of something to say. There's nothing, so I suck noisily on my straw.

We sit cross-legged on cushions and watch the sea. I went snorkelling out there last month and made eye contact with a turtle. It's as if that happened to someone else now, or like I saw it in a film. Steve's eyes are fixed on the horizon while he tightly folds a paper napkin until it tears.

It's practically empty in here. I recognise an elderly black lady; she's an artist and lives in one of the huts over there on the sand. I went to cover one of her shows a few weeks ago, and drank strange, spicy tea out on her decking. I try to catch her eye now but she won't look my way. A couple of backpackers are sitting together, silently eating pancakes. To the side of the bar, a young Thai woman is gutting a fish. There's a copy of the *Koh Star* left open on the table beside ours.

'I spoke to someone in the mayor's office,' Steve tells me.

'Yeah?' I kick off my shoes and rub the soles of my feet, which hurt like little bits of glass are embedded in them.

'They're holding a meeting tomorrow for people whose businesses have been affected by the bomb. It's an open meeting; we can go.'

'The ice cream people might be there,' I say.

Steve nods. 'It's been a long day today, hasn't it?'

'And it's still not over.'

'It is for me,' Steve says, pressing on the bridge of his nose.

'Are you okay?' I ask. Steve's never ill and never anything less than enthusiastic. He works all the time; he never stops writing or thinking.

'Yeah. Don't look at me like that. I'm just exhausted. This has been a lot.'

'Sorry,' I say. 'It's just that I care. Do you need me to do anything?'

'You should come home too. We could both use a rest.'

'I kind of don't want to stop working,' I say. 'When I slow down my brain speeds up, if you know what I mean.'

'Yeah, I know what you mean. I was feeling that way too, but now I've hit a wall. There are things you can do, but only if you're sure you really want to.' He gives me a few options and the one I pick is to go to a scrapyard on the outskirts of town. The owner pulled people out of the wreckage the other night, risking his own life.

'It might be good to have something positive to say in next week's paper,' I say.

'Make sure you get a photo of him. I've spoken to his son on the phone and he said just to turn up; they'll be happy to talk with you. The son's English is very good. He speaks it with a sort of Australian accent.'

'Okay,' I say. 'I can do that. Are you going to be all right? You're sure?'

Steve nods. 'Just tired.'

I wait for him to smile but he doesn't. I've finished my milkshake. His has lowered by perhaps a centimetre. He does look tired, I suppose. I don't like seeing him so flat. I push the straw around in my glass and realise that we were here a week ago. We arrived to eat in the early evening and a rain storm came down around us. The candles on the bar flickered in the breeze, and lizards ran in across the ceiling. It was one of those moments when you feel a sort of romance with the world, spoiled only when an Australian man in a wetsuit made eye contact with me, came over and started talking. Steve looked at us with a little smile on his face, like he was trying to encourage me into something. But thinking about it today, I would gladly go back in time. The look on Steve's face right now is much worse. And I felt uncomfortable with the Australian man because, I suppose, of that other unresolved trauma in my life — the one that brought me to the island — but that trauma, although awful, was at least less outrageous than these new ones. I know too much now to ever lose sleep over something like the way that guy in the wetsuit touched my knee.

'Shall we go, Steve?' I say now.

He nods. He leaves his milkshake.

Later, I drive to the edge of town, leaving Steve at home with a black and white movie.

I don't know what they do at the scrapyard or how they make money on an island this small. It's not something I've ever considered before, despite driving past it many times. It seems abandoned when I pull up beside it now. I peer out at a wooden building, surrounded by vehicles in various states of disrepair. Everything is cluttered and dirty, dull even beneath the sun. I sit in the car for a moment, absorbed with a desire to sleep, to let myself fall away into nothing. But I force myself out and walk towards the building, passing towers of tyres, fridges with their doors hanging open, farming machinery, metal benches, a couple of religious sculptures.

'What do you want?' a voice says in English, with an accent half Thai, half Australian. I hear him before I see him, and freeze. I don't spot him until he moves out of a doorway. He can't be much older than fifteen and is wearing a baggy pair of shorts, metallic blue. As he comes closer I see that his skin is covered by a fine white dust, like he's been spray painting.

'I'm from the *Koh Star*. The newspaper.'

'You want my dad? He's out.'

'Oh. Do you know how long he'll be?'

The boy shrugs, and then turns to play with the dials on the front of an old cooker.

'I heard that he rescued people on Thursday night. It'd be great to talk to him.'

'He's with his girlfriend,' the boy says.

'I can come back.'

He nods, and pulls one of the dials off. As I start to leave he flicks the dial away and I hear it land somewhere to my left. Glancing over that way, I notice a car parked crookedly in the dust, one of its rear doors hanging open.

'How long have you had that car?' I call to the boy, who is about to step back inside the building.

'What?'

'That one,' I point. I go over, stepping around engine parts which are piled on the ground. The car's blue paintwork is gleaming, freshly washed. An air freshener shaped like ballet shoes hangs from its rear-view mirror, and there is a Free Palestine bumper sticker pasted crookedly beside where I'm standing. I recognise this vehicle.

'I don't know,' the boy says. 'Yesterday?'

'Where did you get it?'

'Someone sold it.'

I try opening up the boot. Nothing happens. My toes slip in the dust.

'What you doing? That's my car. Don't touch.' He's on his way over here now, moving fast.

'Who sold it to you?'

'It's not stolen.'

'I can pay you to tell me,' I say, opening my bag and rummaging inside for my purse. I drop my keys, a pen, a ball of chewed gum wrapped up in a receipt.

'You don't need to pay me,' he says, picking up the pen and handing it to me. 'I just don't want to get him in trouble.'

'You won't. Who?'

He hesitates for a moment longer, then says: 'His name's Mike. We like him. He plays guitar on the beach and always wears a big hat. He's English, like you. You probably know him.'

I do know who he means. I've never actually spoken to Mike but I've heard him play. He strums folk songs, mumbling the words beneath the shade of his panama hat. He doesn't play for money. I've seen him throw coins back at people after they've dropped them at his feet.

'Thank you,' I say. 'Thank you so much.'

'Is this going to be in the newspaper? We were supposed to talk about the people my dad saved.'

'We'll still do that. I'll come back later.'

'Okay,' he says, but I don't think he believes me.

# Chapter Fifteen

I find Steve sitting on the living room floor with a cat, stroking its wiry fur. Strands of hair are loose all over the rug. Steve takes a while to look up as I close the front door with my elbow and rush over to him. When he does look up, he only half smiles.

'I think it's a stray,' Steve says. 'It just wandered in.'

I tell him what happened and he nods for a while, staring down at the animal, which is paralysed with either fear or ecstasy.

Steve says: 'It's a shame you weren't able to speak with the owner of the scrapyard.'

'I still can. But don't you get it? They have Dolph's car. Let's go to the beach and talk to this Mike guy.'

'I don't think I do get it.' Steve looks at me with an empty face, like he doesn't even care. This is a man who gets so excited by the crime dramas we watch together on DVD, that he has to pause them in order to tell me his theories. He skips to the ends of novels and reads them backwards. He even gets excited writing news stories about stolen snorkelling gear, and that time a chicken was killed on Main Street in what he called a hit and run. Steve gets excited about things, and now here he is, in the middle of something real and terrible, and he's just staring at me.

'It could mean that something's happened to Dolph, or perhaps he dumped the car. There are lots of things it could mean,' I say.

'Like, for instance, he's gone back to the States for completely innocent, understandable reasons, left his car behind, and the crazy man from the beach stole it.'

'Maybe. But, I think we should go and talk to the crazy man, regardless.'

'I don't think so. I'm so tired, Lucy. Look, it's nearly night.'

'Well, then I'll just call the police and tell them,' I say, gritting my teeth and hoping he can see how I feel about him right now.

'They're only interested in finding the bomber at the moment. They don't think Dolph is the bomber, so...'

'Then let's go to the beach ourselves,' I say, flapping my arms. 'Why not? Why would we not do that?'

'Oh, I don't know,' Steve says, and then the cat bites down on his fingers. I think I hear it pierce the skin.

'Are you okay?'

'Yes,' he winces, watching as the cat skitters away towards the bathroom. 'Fine. Come on, then. Let's do it. It'll be a waste of time though.'

We go to the beach. There are better, more beautiful beaches elsewhere on the island. This one, walking distance from the centre of town, is a narrow strip of sand lined with frail trees. A stream runs into the sea, where sharp black rocks poke from the water. Crabs and pale fish wash up with the tide. There are usually stalls selling food and drink, and vendors with jewellery and clothes. Not so much today. It's only two days since the bomb went off; the dust has barely settled and normality is a long way off.

Generally, Mike is somewhere to be found, playing his guitar and rolling his big, yellow eyes. Today we can't see him. Steve buys us each a coconut with a straw poking out the top, and we walk across the sand, dodging modest waves. The sun is dropping low in the sky and the air has a faint chill to it.

'He might have been blown up for all we know,' Steve says.

'No, he brought the car in to the scrapyard after the bomb went off.'

'Oh, yeah, of course. Sorry, Lucy. I'm starting to get mixed up. I need to have a proper sleep.'

And then we hear it; someone plucking at a guitar, feverishly fast. But we can't see him anywhere.

'It's just a recording, is it?' Steve says, but it sounds as real as the waves and the warbling birds. Thinking of the birds, I look up, and there Mike is in the branches of a tree. The tree pokes out from a mess of rocks, dry plants and scraps of litter, all faded from the sun. The branches appear to be dead, like maybe they were struck by lightning years ago. Mike is wearing his usual hat, along with a denim waistcoat and football shorts. Painfully thin, his legs dangle like they don't work.

'Hi there,' Steve calls. Mike doesn't reply. I feel like he might spit on us; he has that sort of look on his face. We walk closer and I let Steve do the talking.

'We're from the *Koh Star*. Would you mind coming down from the tree? Or we can come up?'

'You don't want to talk to me. I've got nothing to say that's quotable.'

He is English, like that boy said. And he doesn't sound as crazy as I expected him to. He's quite well spoken, in fact.

I say: 'We know you took a car to the scrapyard yesterday. We just want to find out where it came from. I think it might be important.'

He's still playing but his fingers slow a little.

'It didn't seem like an important car. Couple of idiots abandoned it.'

'What did they look like?' I put a hand against the warm tree, and look up at the soles of his feet.

'How come the police haven't been here asking questions, if it's so important?'

'They still might,' Steve says. He looks around, as if the police could be here any second. I'm pleased to have him here with me.

'Maybe if I talk to you, you could stop that happening?' Mike says.

Steve shrugs, like perhaps he could. 'What can you tell us?'

'Young couple. That's a man and a woman. She was Thai, he wasn't. Arguing, or just emotional about something. They walked off and left it. Heading out of town. Anyway, I went over there. Keys still in the ignition. They obviously didn't want it, did they? I need money all the time so I took it. Not a lot else to tell.'

'When was this?' I ask.

'Couldn't say exactly. It was definitely yesterday, though. I don't think I was hungry at the time, so it would have been after I had my chicken. Early evening.'

'Was there anything inside the car?'

'There were some socks in the boot. I took those. Nice long white ones. That's all.'

'Nothing else you can tell us?' My neck begins to ache from staring up at him.

'Actually, yes. The car was muddy. Lots of orange mud all up the sides and where their feet had been on the mats.'

'Okay, thanks.'

'I like to be helpful when I can,' he says, and looks down at his fingers, picking up the pace again. He's really good, but the way he plays makes my skin tighten, like there's a message in the music, some sort of warning. I shake my head and it's gone.

The sun will be setting soon. We walk away from the beach, past an abandoned building site. This was going to become a shopping mall, but I don't know if it will now that the bomb has exploded and the population has shrunk. The island could be deserted in a year, reclaimed by the animals.

'So,' I say, 'what do you think?'

'He's living life the way he wants to. We shouldn't pity him or call him mad.'

'No, I mean about what he said.'

'Oh,' Steve says, and rubs his moustache. 'I think that if he really did see Maliwan, we ought to tell her mother about it. Tell her that she's alive. Imagine thinking your child is dead. And then imagine finding out that she isn't.'

'I think it was her too,' I say, skipping and nearly grabbing his arm. 'It was them, wasn't it? They dumped the car here. That's what I think.'

'We have to be sure.'

'It was them, and they're running away from something.'

'It does seem that way.' He won't look at me. I try to peer at his face, tripping over my own feet as I do so.

'We should phone the police,' I say.

'I'll speak to Kadesadayurat.'

We stop to watch as a huge sea bird takes off from the scaffolding of the unfinished mall. I shiver as its shadow passes over us.

'Maybe we'll find them ourselves,' I say, and look to Steve for a response but he's watching the bird, and even after it's out of sight his eyes remain distant. I have to pull lightly on his sleeve for him to follow me home.

# Chapter Sixteen

The meeting the next day, for businesses affected by the bomb, turns out not to be a meeting at all.

'Something must have been lost in translation,' Steve mutters. It happens to us a lot.

We've been waiting for twenty minutes behind the town hall, where the mayor's office is sandwiched between a tourist information centre and a chemist. There's no one else here; just some birds singing and fighting on the roof of the building. Everything is locked up.

'Let's just go,' I say and then add, to cheer him up: 'Isn't it a nice day? We should go out for a second breakfast somewhere by the sea.'

'I don't know if I can eat. And this light is hurting my eyes. It'll be worse by the water. It'll reflect right into our faces. Have you seen my sunglasses anywhere? I feel like I've not had them for days.'

'No,' I say, briefly floored because I've never known him to be so negative or to turn down food.

We're just beginning to walk away when the owners of the Green Turtle Hostel appear from the direction of the car park. I first recognise them by their silhouettes, because that's how they used to appear to me when I crossed the dark reception area of the hostel and they would be working in the harsh lights of the laundry room or kitchen.

'Oh!' I cry, waving a hand. 'Hello!'

They grunt at me as they pass by, unsmiling, the way they always used to when we met in the hostel corridors.

'They're the owners of the Green Turtle,' I say to Steve. 'I've been wondering about them.'

'That's fantastic,' Steve says. He smiles at the couple, who are probably aged in their seventies and are plump and bespectacled. He says something to them in Thai but they ignore him and continue to the doorway of the mayor's office.

'It's closed,' I call to them. But they stoop to pick a piece of paper up from a pile weighted down by a rock, half hidden behind a shelf of maps and scuba leaflets on the doorstep. They read through it, shake their heads and grumble, and then walk back the way they came, giving me the smallest of nods as they go by.

'What is that?' I ask, but they keep walking.

Steve goes to pick one up but he can't read the Thai. 'I need to learn,' he says. 'I don't know why I haven't.'

'No, look on the back,' I say. A bad translation has been made into English. 'I think it's just explaining how to claim money from the government for help with rebuilding and, you know, other costs. There are some phone numbers and things, look.'

'Yes.' Steve nods, staring at the paper in his hands as it buckles slightly in the warm breeze. 'Sorry, Lucy. When I spoke to the mayor's secretary yesterday, I definitely got the impression that this was more of a formal meeting.'

'Don't worry about it. I mean, the owners of the ice cream place could still turn up. I'm sure I'd recognise them.'

We decide to wait a while longer, and sit beside the pile of paper on the doorstep, looking through leaflets from the shelves but not really absorbing any of the information. No one else arrives.

'Let's just go,' Steve sighs. But then a moped rounds the corner and stops on the patchy grass.

'Who's this?' I say.

The rider removes his helmet and we immediately recognise him as the owner of Bar XS, a middle-aged Australian who people had been saying had left the island already. We'd also heard a rumour that he'd been blinded by the explosion, but as he walks towards us he smiles and waves. We regularly print coupons and adverts for Bar XS, and Steve has spent the odd evening over there, taking photos of tourists to stick in the newspaper when we don't have very much to say.

'Hi, Aaron,' Steve says. 'How are you doing?'

'Have I missed the meeting?' Aaron asks, looking along the empty street.

'Doesn't seem like there is one,' Steve tells him. 'They've left some paperwork.'

Aaron picks a page up, glances at it and folds it into his pocket.

'How is the bar?' Steve asks. 'Have you been able to get back in there?'

'No offence, guys, but I really don't want to talk to the press about any of this. Some people would be selling their story all over the place but not me. I'm not like that.'

'Oh, we wouldn't pay you,' Steve jokes, but Aaron doesn't seem to hear him. He's looking at the windows of the building, which are reflecting the sunlight, scattering white rays across our faces.

Aaron shrugs. 'It's all locked up, huh? Well, this is goodbye for me. I think I can get some sort of insurance pay-out but then I'm out of here. The dream is over. I was thinking about moving on anyway. It was getting too touristy here. Do you know what I mean? There were no real travellers coming through anymore.'

'Would you mind if I just ask you a couple of things?' I say, trying to meet his eyes. 'Not for the newspaper. Just because I want to understand what happened.'

'You can never understand a thing like this,' Aaron says. 'There's no sort of reason to it.'

'But were you there that night?'

'I was at home. I'd taken the night off. I came down to see what was going on though. Got to the bar about two in the morning. Honestly, just the worst thing I've ever seen in my life. You see it too?'

We nod.

'Yeah. There wasn't much I could do. The police wouldn't let me inside. I snuck in yesterday. There was smashed glass everywhere and the smell is awful. I couldn't even describe it to you. Part chemical, part blood. Awful.'

'Some people are saying that the bomb went off right outside the bar. Do you know anything about that?' I ask.

'That's what they're saying. I don't know. I've heard people say it was maybe next door. The ice cream parlour.'

'We heard that too,' I say. 'Do you know the owners?'

'Bob and Mary.' Aaron nods. 'Those aren't their real names. They don't expect western people to be able to pronounce their Thai names so they picked out English ones for themselves. Bob and Mary. They're nice people.'

'Have you seen them since that night?' I ask.

'They've been away, visiting someone on the mainland. They weren't here when it happened. I think they were planning to be back by now but I haven't seen them around.'

'Who's been watching the place while they were away?' asks Steve.

'I dunno. Someone was.'

'Do you know where Bob and Mary live?' I say.

'They won't want to speak to you guys. They're very private, very sensible people.'

'We can be sensible too,' Steve says with half a smile. 'We're not that bad. Don't you have an address?'

'I couldn't tell you exactly.' Aaron checks his watch and then looks towards where some chickens have appeared beneath the trees.

'Vaguely?' Steve says.

'Near the hairdressers. One of the flats behind there.'

We thank him. He grunts and goes back to his moped, straightening its wing mirrors which are attached with tape, and then leaving, scaring the chickens as he passes them.

# Chapter Seventeen

We've been trying to phone Kadesadayurat but can never get though; there's just a clicking on the other end of the line that reminds me of insects. Steve has sent a series of text messages instead, relaying our conversation on the beach last night with Mike. Kadesadayurat texts back to say thank you. He doesn't comment on the information.

'Do you think he's dead?' I say.

'Who? Bernard Shuttleworth? Maybe. Try not to think too much about it. You don't need that weight on your shoulders.'

Steve's managed to source a small bag of weed from somewhere and he tells me he's going to spend the rest of the morning smoking it in the little courtyard behind his house, where barbed plants grow through the cracks and the sun heats the flagstones to the point where they can burn you through your clothes. He drags a wooden chair out there and, fumbling, puts some headphones into his ears and starts scrolling through the music on his chunky old iPod.

'You want to join me?' he asks, seeing me watching him from the open kitchen window while I wash up our breakfast things.

'No, I don't like to smoke,' I say. I hate the feeling of having my brain fold in on itself, crossing thoughts and memories that ought not to be crossed.

'Don't judge me,' he says, although I'm not. 'I need this. I need to drift away from all these awful things for just a few hours.'

'That's cool,' I say. 'I'll go and see Lena for a little while.'

The streets are busier today, but the usual population seems to have been replaced with people who ought not to be here; dazed looking foreigners, policemen from the mainland and soldiers too. Beyond the familiar buzz of mopeds and the sizzle of food cooking on street stands, I can hear the clunk of heavy machinery, and I think this is coming from the bombsite. I walk away from this noise. The heat presses close. I sweat against my clothes and feel my hair damp upon my forehead. I'd like to go for a swim, but I won't. I think it would be obscene to do something like that, something with the sole purpose of making *me* happy. I need to keep pushing ahead; thinking about the victims, the missing and the potential culprits. I feel like I have a deadline to meet and I need to tie everything up neatly. As I'm thinking this, I walk into the back of someone who has stopped suddenly in my path; a white man dwarfed beneath his beat-up backpack. He says something to me in a foreign language, his eyes narrowed. I can tell it's a swear word.

'Watch it,' I say quietly. But as I walk away, I look back and realise that he is close to tears. I walk on, faster.

I walk to the other side of town where Lena is staying with her boyfriend, the fisherman, and his friends. I'm out of breath when I get there. She's alone. I suppose they're all out on the water.

She's pleased to see me. We sit on the floor and take turns holding the puppy.

'How are you doing?' I ask her, when the conversation falters and we're both left listening to the puppy's shallow breathing.

She takes a while to answer. All of the muscles in her face are tense. 'You're lucky you have your job, you know?' she says eventually. 'I wanted to volunteer and pull people out of the rubble. But everyone's out now, or dead. I missed my chance to help. Now I feel like I'm waiting, but I don't know what for. At least you have a purpose.'

'I'm trying,' I say.

'Do you remember Ralph?'

I nod. I remember his foot touching mine beneath a table when he was aiming for Lena's. I remember the pink gemstone he wore around his neck, and I remember him picking up my phone for me, when I dropped it in the laundry room and thought the screen had smashed; it hadn't.

'Half of his face is all burned up. He's in hospital but I'm scared he's going to die.'

'I hope he doesn't,' I say. We both nod. Lena touches my hand with her fingertips. Her hand looks like a spider. I say: 'What about Ben? Remember him? One of the Irish guys. I haven't seen him. We were talking that evening, before it happened.'

'Oh, Ben, yeah. He likes you,' Lena says, smiling.

'Have you seen him?'

'I haven't seen any of those Irish guys.'

'Oh.'

We're silent for a few beats, thinking about what this could mean.

On the wall behind Lena is a collage of postcards showing scenes from the island. I think Lena must have put these up. I remember there being a similar display in her room at the hostel. One shows images of the temples here on the island; ancient ruins deep in the jungle. Lena and I went out there a few months ago. When we got back into town we were covered in orange dust. I remember that now. It was orange, like the clay we used to use at school. Mike, the guitarist, mentioned Dolph's car being covered in orange mud when he found it.

'Do you want to get out of here?' I say, suddenly noticing how dim the light is in this room, so that I can barely see her eyes at all. Only the cut on her forehead stands out clear in the gloom.

'I should. I have done nothing these last few days. See how pale my skin has gotten? But where can we go? I want to lay flowers by the hostel but I'm not ready to go back there. Besides, I hear there are camera crews all around, and I don't want to see them.'

'I was thinking out of town,' I say. 'Steve's having some time off and trying to relax. Maybe that's a good idea. Don't you think?'

'Might be nice to see a beautiful part of this island. Instead of this broken town.'

'Like, maybe the temples?' I stretch my arms towards the ceiling and look again at the postcards on the wall.

'We could do that.' Lena thinks for a minute, picking at a loose thread on her shorts. 'We could hire bikes to go out there. The track to the temples won an award for the best cycle route in Asia. Something like that. Maybe not the best, but definitely up there.'

'Sure.' I nod, although I haven't ridden a bike in years.

'I definitely need some exercise. Look at my arms.'

'They're fine,' I say.

'I'm losing muscle definition.'

'Well, I think we should do it,' I say. Aside from this sudden desperation to see something beautiful and untainted by the current tragedies, I also want to see if there are tyre tracks out there — maybe Dolph went through that way before abandoning his car. I don't know why he would have done, unless he decided to go sight-seeing. There's nothing out there except for the ruins, the trees, the monkeys and stinging insects. No one will be going there at the moment; no tourists, no locals trying to sell things. But maybe Shuttleworth's out there, tied up or buried beneath the dust? My throat closes and I don't say any of this to Lena. I merely smile, and manage to say: 'We can forget about everything for a while.'

'The temples are beautiful,' she says. 'I'll bring my camera. Just let me fix my hair and wash my face.'

I watch her go, and then, just faintly, hear water running. I should probably tell her about Dolph's car. She needs purpose right now, just like I do. She can help me look for signs of visitors in the mud. But what if she tells me I'm being an idiot about it all, and the orange mud means nothing, perhaps even the car itself means nothing? If she said any of that, I'd be left empty; with just this sickness in my stomach, the bruises on my skin.

# Chapter Eighteen

Lena and I hire bicycles from a man in a rickety shed. He's pleased to have customers and lets us pick out the nicest ones. He asks us where we're going and we tell him the temples. There's just a split second when we see something negative in his face; perhaps he's wondering how we can engage in tourism so soon after tourists were killed. Lena swears in German and pushes her bike out onto the street. I stand there for a moment, on the brink of explaining about Dolph's car and the mud. But it's my secret, and perhaps it would make me sound like even worse of a person, or crazy. I thank him in clumsy Thai and follow Lena outside, the frame of my bike rattling.

We estimate that we can hit the first temple in an hour; the more distant ones are perhaps twice that far. Lena has a map, folded and worn, which we put into her bike's basket, along with a bunch of bananas to eat on the journey. She doesn't know that we're searching for something, but she seems to share my anxiety to visit every temple. She plans our route, and there's something comforting about her familiar bossiness.

Mopeds share the road with us for the first mile, flitting in every direction. Some carry more than one person; little kids watch us with giant eyes, balancing effortlessly as their parents weave the bikes about. One man rides past with a dead pig strapped up behind him. Its eyes are open. Lena and I exchange a glance.

Buildings fall away, and then patchy fields turn to trees. Plants are packed densely together, pressing in on this track as it becomes narrow and uneven. I clench my teeth and my head starts to ache, but I keep on pedalling.

As we approach the first temple, the sky begins to darken, clouds hanging low over the trees.

'I think there might be a storm coming,' I say. But we're not afraid of the weather. And then, reaching the top of a hill, we see the ruins ahead of us, grey stones fighting off the trees.

Our legs are covered with orange dust; just like they were the last time we came out here. I've got blisters on my hands from gripping the handlebars too tightly. Lena passes me a banana, which I struggle to peel. We leave the bikes lying side by side at the edge of the track.

This temple is easy to reach from town, and so people have been stealing stones from its walls for centuries. Islanders have used them to build with, and to pave their courtyards. The ruins have an aura that we can feel even now, when there's so much going on to distract us from beautiful things. I finish my banana and bury the skin beneath some loose leaves and dust, feeling like the building itself is watching me.

We walk through its chambers; rooms without ceilings frame the deep, grey sky. In one corner a bees' nest is humming, insects darting in and out of the windows. There are no people. No sign of anyone having been here for a while, although as we're leaving we see some burned incense sticks on the ground. I don't know what I'm looking for, but it's not here. Lena doesn't say much, although her face is straight just like mine, and her eyes flick from corner to corner.

We cycle on, towards the heart of the island, where vines and ferns creep. The track thins even further and dust climbs up our bodies, mixing with sweat and turning to mud. Insects are busy all around us, and the forest shivers and sighs. We stop at more of these small, skeleton temples but only discover resting reptiles and a family of monkeys. Lena takes photos with her old Pentax, a proper one with film inside it. She doesn't ask me to be in any of the pictures, but she does get me to take one of her with a baby monkey in the background. I don't talk to her about Dolph and Maliwan. I'm not even close to mentioning it. There are moments when I think she is drunk; she stumbles and mutters things in German, while kicking at stones, patting her hands against sun-dappled walls. I don't feel like I can talk to her, or like she wants me to. There's something about being the only two humans out here that has started a weird sort of energy fizzing between us; it's like all of our fear and pain is finally getting communicated, and we can see how damaged we are but are powerless to help each other.

I'm aching and hungry, but we keep cycling and reach the island's most famous temple. It's a pyramid of sorts, and barely damaged. Jagged steps lead to its summit above the tree line, and faces are carved into the walls. They're screaming, a lot of them. Dark doorways are fringed with cobwebs. The air around the building seems cooler than elsewhere. I can feel my body temperature drop as I breathe.

'Magnificent,' Lena says, and that's when an explosion rips through the sky. My spine splinters into a thousand terrified needles, but then I open my eyes and realise that it's not a bomb; it's just thunder and lightning, right over our heads. The rain comes down; hard little pebbles of it, splashing the orange dust up in arcs. We run to the nearest doorway and stand there together, the noise and smell of the rain all around us. Lena's arm is pressed against mine; cold and damp. I resist moving for a while, but then put my hand up to smooth my hair, stepping away from her.

'I don't think this is the kind of rain that stops,' I say, glancing sideways at my friend. I hope she's not mad at me for bringing us out here for no good reason, and dragging her into the centre of a tropical storm.

She's not mad. She says: 'Then we should keep going,' and steps out of the doorway. Rain engulfs her. She laughs and stares straight up through it, past the temple and into the purple clouds.

I just hope we don't get struck by lightning. It feels like exactly the kind of thing that could happen.

'Come on!' Lena shouts through the rain.

I step out after her. Instantly I'm soaked, and colder than I've felt in a long time, although the trembling is familiar. The treetops are bending beneath the weight of the rainfall, and water runs down the sides of the temple. All of a sudden, I don't think we're going to find anything out here. I'd like to go back to Steve's house now. I feel embarrassed for suggesting we come out here, embarrassed for bothering the police with my theories and thoughts. I should be in town doing something real; interviewing victims, speaking to their relatives on the phone. I expect that's what Steve will be doing, after his afternoon off. I should listen to him when he tells me things; he's been a journalist for years. He knows people and he knows what he's doing.

Thinking these thoughts, staring at the ground, I follow Lena along a winding path. The trees keep some of the water from us, but sharp, wet shrubs grab at our legs. This path was too narrow and bumpy for the bikes, so we've left them lying on the main track. We're halfway back to them when we hear a shout.

Lena freezes and I bump into her; hurting my nose and getting some of her wet hair caught in my mouth. We stand with our heads cocked to the side like animals. The voice comes again. It sounds like a man; his words damp and thick like the rain. There's a garbled sentence but I can't make it out. It ends on a high note, practically a scream.

'Hello?' we shout back. But nothing. We only hear the rain now.

'Who was that? What did he say?' Lena touches my arm with cold fingertips.

'I don't know,' I say. 'But we should help him.'

# Chapter Nineteen

We run. I'm not frightened, although I'm conscious that I ought to be. Mostly I feel good, knowing that I'm running towards something real, something more than just an idea. We tumble from the bushes and onto the winding dirt track, our feet kicking up mud.

There's no one here.

I bite down on my lip as I stop running. Taste blood. Lena points through the rain. One of our bikes is missing.

Tracks are visible on the ground where someone has left the forest, gone in circles around the bikes and then taken one, continuing along the path in the direction we were headed. It's all written in the wet, orange mud.

'He can't have gone far,' I say, looking at Lena and at the rain running down her cheeks. I scramble to pick up my bike, which is the one left behind. I catch my ankle on the pedals and see beads of blood appear in a line on my skin. Over my shoulder, I say: 'I'll come back for you, I promise.'

As I bounce over rocks, Lena shouting something after me that I don't catch, the rain smacks against my face and runs into my eyes. I try to taste it because I'm thirsty, but all I get is mud, and my own salty sweat. I'm probably not going very fast but it feels like I am; I'm flying. And this is the happiest I've been since the bomb exploded. I'm going to catch this bicycle thief, and when I have him, I know that things will start making sense again. I knew that someone or something would be out here. I can't wait to tell Steve.

But I don't catch anyone. I don't see a thing. After a while I lose sight of the other bike's tracks. Perhaps he left the path and ran into the forest, or perhaps the rain has washed all trace of him away. I stop and listen. Just the rain hitting the trees. The sun glows white and frail through the clouds. I haven't cried much these last few days, but I could cry now.

I cycle back to where I left Lena. She's sitting beneath a tree, her forehead on her knees. Hearing me, she gets to her feet and we meet in the centre of the path. When I stick on my brakes, a little shower of mud hits her ankles.

'Lost him,' I say, unable to meet her eyes. We look around at the forest, like he could be out there watching us. And he could be.

'Who do you think it was?' Lena looks over my shoulder at the empty path.

'I don't know,' I say, although I think it was Dolph. I feel it with a groundless certainty. 'He's disappeared now.'

'He sounded like he wanted to be found, the way he was screaming.'

'That's true. But there were stretches of path that went totally straight, and I could see a long way ahead. No sign of him.'

'I think he was running from someone,' Lena says. 'He was looking for help. When we didn't reach him quickly enough he continued running. Or cycling.'

'And they've found him now, whoever he was running from. They snatched him off the path. You think?'

Lena shrugs. We don't know. We stand there in the rain, and realise that we're not as brave as we always hoped we were. The noise that the man made, sketchy as it was through the distance and the rain, has left me weak; he sounded the way people did the other night, after the bomb exploded.

'Should we go home?' I ask, ashamed to give in like this but at a loss for anything else to do.

Lena nods, but first she takes a photograph of me on the empty path, the place where our bike was stolen. I don't smile, and I shiver as the flash goes off.

# Chapter Twenty

Our remaining bike begins to squeak as we take turns riding it. Progress is slow and after a while it feels like we're not moving at all.

The rain stops but our clothes don't dry. We can no longer feel our feet as they slap through puddles. Things seem even worse when night begins to fall. Mournful birds call from the trees. Bats flit overhead. There are all kinds of animals out here, talking to each other in their own languages and rustling through the undergrowth. At one point a troop of monkeys cross the path. Another time a wild dog limps out from the trees. It eyes us for a moment with its jaw hanging open and its eyes glowing a pale shade of blue. I just have time to fear it might attack us before it continues on its way.

Lena has suggested a couple of times that we sleep out here. If she says it again I might agree and curl up beneath one of these heavy trees, let the insects crawl over me. This is all my fault. I decide to apologise and tell her how stupid I've been.

But then we hear an engine.

'Terrorists?' Lena says.

We scurry into the trees. The engine sounds big and meaty, a monster of a vehicle. It's our first instinct to hide; surely anything out here with us, in the dim light and far from town, must be bad.

'But, then again, it might be someone who can give us a lift home,' I say, as we crouch in the damp darkness. I can't walk much further. I never exercise, other than to run after Steve when he forgets something, or to swim slowly in the shallow sea; my body can't carry me much further. And I don't want to sleep out here; I really, really don't.

'Perhaps you're right,' Lena says, looking at her feet as they sink into the dirt.

'You stay here,' I say. 'If they seem dangerous, keep hidden. Okay?'

I step into the road, wet leaves slapping at my face as I move. Lena follows me, of course, and we stand there with our arms outstretched, asking for help. There's a car in sight now. It is big. A Bentley or a Rolls Royce; something like that. Headlights bright enough to hurt the backs of my eyes. The noise of it rips the night apart. It knocks against plants at the edge of the road, snapping branches and scattering leaves.

It's nearly upon us. And now I'm sure that either it will run us down, or someone will stick a gun out of the window and shoot. Or worse, they will take us and do things to us. I don't want to be tortured. I don't want Lena to be hurt, out here following my stupid hunch. The car stops, braking sharply so that little stones and water from the road spray everywhere.

It's dark inside the car. The window rolls down and a female voice, American in that clipped, old fashioned way that you hear in black and white movies, says: 'Girls, I nearly flattened you. This thing can practically drive itself. I was dozing.'

'We were hoping for a ride into town?' Lena says, bending towards the open window.

'What accent do I hear? Are you German?'

'Yes,' my friend says, a little tentatively. I can't see the driver. All I can make out are some lights on the dashboard and the dark dome of a woman's head.

'I love *Deutschland*. My father was from Berlin. Just for that, you can join me. Try not to damage the upholstery.'

I climb into the back. The seats are leather and bigger than Steve's couch. I can't find my seatbelt, fumble for a moment but then give up. Mud is flaking from my body but I'm too tired to care. The driver turns to glance at me as Lena introduces us.

'Hi.' I smile and raise a hand. It's an effort to do even this.

The woman is fairly old; I'd put her somewhere in her seventies. She has short grey hair, kind of wiry like a dog's. Her lips are made up big and red, but she has very small eyes, with wrinkles at their edges. These make her look like she laughs a lot, but who knows. Perhaps she scowls. She doesn't tell us her name. A silence hangs where it ought to be.

'And what are you two doing out here on your own? You must be up to no good,' she says, and pulls off very quickly. I wish that I had a seatbelt on. I notice, then, a smell of alcohol.

'We just came out to see the temples,' I say quickly, and this is when I realise that we left our remaining bike behind, abandoned at the side of the road back there. We'll never get it back. I feel bad. I feel bad for the abandoned bike and I feel bad for the man who hired it to us this morning.

'Strange day for it,' the woman says.

Lena looks back at me over her shoulder, and then she turns to the woman and says: 'Someone stole my bike. A man. We heard him shouting.'

'A person can hear all sorts of things in the jungle. Did you see this man?'

'No, but we heard him. And the bike was gone. I don't think it was monkeys,' Lena says. She looks at me again over her shoulder, frowning.

She's going to say more and I don't think she ought to, so I lean into the gap between their seats and say: 'Perhaps it was nothing. We were in the middle of the storm.'

'Yes, I expect it was the wind you heard. Or ghosts in those ancient temples,' the woman says with a smile in her voice. She's up to no good herself, I think. As if to prove me right, she picks up a bottle from somewhere between her legs and takes a swig of what smells like whiskey.

'Are you sharing that?' Lena asks, relaxing and sinking lower into her seat.

'It's two hundred dollars a bottle. So, no.'

'What about you?' I ask our driver as Lena sits up straight again, folding her arms. 'Where are you off to? Or where have you been?' I ask so many questions, all of the time. But it is my job.

'I'm going to see my lawyer, ugly chump. I'm late, obviously. I suppose I'll have to take a hotel room and see him in the morning.'

'You live on the island?' Lena asks.

'Sometimes.' She brakes then, hard, and I hit my face off the back of Lena's seat. I hear Lena crash against the dashboard, and the bottle of whiskey hit the floor.

'I thought I saw a snake in the road,' the woman says. She stalls the car, stops for a drink, and then we continue on our way.

Lena and the woman talk about Germany for a while. Their voices rise and fall. When the woman laughs it sounds like a cough. I've never been to Germany, so I sit quietly and watch as the trees thin and we get closer to home. What was this lady doing out in the jungle? The road doesn't go anywhere except to the temples, so far as I know. I have questions but I decide not to ask any more and neither does Lena. Something keeps us quiet. Lena seems to be enjoying herself, taking gulps from the bottle which is being shared after all, although not with me. I see her face reflected in the windscreen like a light. When she smiles I smile too. I'm glad to see her happy, but I can't join in. I grip my knees and try to think in straight lines.

We reach the town. It's quiet everywhere. The bars seem mostly to be closed. The woman laughs hard and rides up onto the pavement for a bit. I realise that I haven't been breathing for a while, and as I gulp on the warm, dry air, I'm struck with a feeling that we might never get out of this car. I want to reach out to Lena, grab her arm, but she seems a million miles away and I can't push myself far enough out of the leather.

'Where the hell is it?' the woman says then, tapping the steering wheel with her nails. I hear things thudding about inside the boot as we turn a corner too sharply and drift into the wrong lane.

'What?' Lena asks.

'The Grand Hotel. It's where I always stay.'

I give directions, struggling to make my voice heard over the engine and their half drunken laughter. I get an urge to smack Lena across the back of her head and remind her of the noise we heard in the jungle. Don't laugh. Don't feel happy. Something terrible was happening to that man and we left him out there.

We go through a series of red lights. The woman pulls over about a block before the hotel and tells us to get out.

'We don't actually live near here,' Lena says. 'Won't you drive us all the way?'

'I don't care where you live. This is as far as you're getting with me. I can't arrive at the hotel with a couple of grimy backpackers in tow. I have a reputation to keep.'

'Lucy's not a backpacker; she's a well-respected journalist. And I'm a traveller. There's a difference,' Lena says, her voice slurred from the expensive whiskey.

As we get out, the woman is lighting a cigarette with a trembling hand. Lena offers to help but is waved away. We say thank you for the lift but she waves our thanks away too, and then she drives with a stuttering roar towards the hotel.

# Chapter Twenty-One

I'm woken by the sound of something heavy hitting the floor. As I push away my blanket and sit up, Steve exits through the front door, sending hot air rippling through the room. I notice what I was too tired to see when I got in last night; empty wine and vodka bottles, cigarettes stubbed out on plates, a smell of vomit, and rice spilled over the floor. There's a bottle still gently rolling on the rug. Steve must have knocked it over as he rushed out of here. When did we last speak? I expect he's headed for the office. I'll meet him there.

In the shower, I scrub hard to get all the mud from my legs. The sick smell is stronger through here, and I notice a pink residue left on the inside of the toilet. Drying myself quickly, I get out of the room.

I leave the house with a glass of orange juice still in my hand. When I get to the office I realise that I've put the glass down somewhere. Across the street is a cat much like the stray one that Steve was petting the other day. It's chewing on a dead lizard. I watch for a second, and then clatter up the steps. A smile is forming on my face as I open the door. I'm excited to tell him about yesterday's developments, horrible as they were.

Steve is hunched at his desk. He peers over his shoulder but then turns back to the screen. He's on a news website, scrolling down the page too quickly to actually be reading anything.

'Sorry I'm late,' I say, breathless all of a sudden.

'It's fine,' he grunts, and still doesn't turn around.

'Oh, well, I'm sorry anyway. I should have set an alarm.'

I move to my own desk, unsure of what to say next. I stack some notepads on top of each other, taking care to keep the tower neat. Steve has left the TV and radio off, so all I can hear is the whirring of the fans, and noises from his computer, which is old and tends to struggle. I clear my throat.

'I suppose I'll go back to the scrapyard today. And we could go look around the flats near the hairdressers, see if there's any sign of Bob and Mary. Were those their names? I should have written them down. And I need to tell you some stuff. Listen to this.'

'Where were you yesterday?' His voice is muffled by his hands.

'I told you, I went to see Lena while you were having a smoke. Did you come in to the office to do some work afterwards? Did you need me? Sorry, I meant to come in, but then...'

'No.' He spins around in his chair. 'Where *were* you? You were gone all day and I was worried. You didn't call.'

'You didn't call either.' I try to sound haughty but actually sound like I might cry, which is how I feel. I don't like the way he's looking at me; I've never seen Steve angry before, and now he's angry at *me*, which I didn't think possible. Perhaps I'll just get up and leave.

He says: 'I tried to call. I tried for hours but couldn't get through.'

'Oh. That'll be because I didn't have any signal.'

'Like I said, where *were* you?'

'At the temples,' I say, making it sound like a question.

'At the *temples*?' He half rises from his chair. 'Why?'

'Lena wanted to get out of town.' I shrug, hugging myself, trying to squeeze the lie out because I suddenly don't want to tell him that the trip was my idea; I should have gone out there with him, not Lena.

I don't tell him anything else, although I had been planning to. I'd thought he might come with me to see Officer Kadesadayurat, to help me explain about Dolph's car, about the voice in the jungle, and all the rest of it. But I don't say a thing. I grab a pencil and pick at the stained eraser on the end of it. I'm afraid that Steve won't do the right thing with my information, if I give it to him.

He rubs at the bridge of his nose and says: 'I needed you.'

'Why?'

'I just, you know, started thinking about things a bit too much yesterday. And there was no one to talk to. Not even that stupid cat; it scratched me up real bad.'

'I'm sorry,' I say.

'It doesn't matter.'

'It does. I'm here now.' My voice breaks on the last word. It's getting hotter in here, and hard to breathe. I wait for him to say something but he doesn't. So I say: 'Is there any news? About anything?'

'Well, one more person died in hospital.' He waves his hands like he's swatting a fly, although I can't see one. 'Fuck, they were all just like you. *Just like you.*'

'Like me?' I whisper.

'Young. Like you and like my daughter. And here I still am, old and useless.'

'You're not useless,' I say, in a voice that reminds me of my mother. 'Or particularly old.' I get out of my chair but don't know what to do next, so just stand there on the balding mat.

'How did you think I'd feel when you disappeared all day?' he says, his voice hard. 'It got dark and you were still gone.'

'I'm sorry. I wasn't thinking of myself as being disappeared.'

'I thought you might be dead. I think that all the time now, about everyone, because it could be so. And there's nothing I can do about it. And there's something else. I've been speaking a bit with Jenna. I'm thinking about going to visit her for a while.'

'What? In America?'

'She's living in Ireland at the moment. She's teaching out there. But, yeah, all this has made me want to see her. I think it's a parental instinct sort of thing; even though she wasn't the one in danger the other day, I feel like I need to be near her. I need to see her. I'm going to go next week, I think.'

'I guess I wouldn't understand that.'

He shakes his head for a moment, and then says: 'I expect your parents are desperate to see you.'

'How long will you go for?' I ask, ignoring what he just said because, although I would love to see my parents' faces again, I can't go back to where they are. I'm not ready yet and don't think I will be for a long time.

'I'm not sure,' Steve says. 'Probably not for very long.'

I can tell, from the way he's looking at me, that he knows he's betraying me. We were supposed to get through this together. We were supposed to do something good with the newspaper.

'What am *I* meant to do?' I say, in a little whine that I hate. 'I'm trying to help somehow, but I can't without you.'

'No, we can't help anyone. We'll only make things worse. I don't know about you, but I make the wrong decision every time. Let's leave it to the professionals.'

'But, I really think Dolph and Maliwan...'

'No,' Steve says, holding his palm out like he's telling a car to stop. 'You're wasting your energy with that.'

'But at least I'm doing something. I'm not running away like you're about to. This is just so ... disappointing.'

'And it's a waste of police time too. I know Kadesadayurat thinks so. He won't say it to you, but he does.'

Then no one speaks for a while. I sway in the middle of the room, while a standing fan I've never seen before rotates beside me, gently shifting my hair. Steve picks up a glass of water, holds it in his lap and stares into its depths.

'Can you leave me alone?' he says finally, without even looking up. 'I've got such a hangover and I just need to think, okay? I can't do it with you staring at me.'

'Sure. I've got important stuff to do anyway. I doubt you'd want to help with that.'

I pluck the car keys up from beside his keyboard, and he watches as I walk to the door. I expect him to stop me, to say something that'll fix all this and make us both smile, but he doesn't. He lets me leave.

# Chapter Twenty-Two

I immediately realise that I don't feel like going to the scrapyard, the flats behind the hairdressers or anywhere else right now, but I'd rather drive in circles than sit in the office with Steve. Journalists, in my opinion, ought to have certain instincts, and all of mine are telling me to go after Dolph and Maliwan and to track down the owners of the ice cream parlour. I don't know what else to do. Steve — he's just crying to himself, drinking alone and puking all over his house. I meant what I said to him just now; it is disappointing. I never realised how much I look up to Steve until now; now that he's letting me down.

I drive at speed, but then get stuck on a narrow road behind a pickup truck, a group of backpackers huddled together in the back of it. One girl has her arm in a sling. All of them look at me in alarm, drawing closer to each other. I touch the brake and turn down a side street. Litter is strewn on the ground; a plastic bottle pops beneath my wheels and spins away against a wall. I just keep on going, making turns, switching lanes, weaving around pedestrians and mopeds. As I drive, I think. I run through everything that's happened since the night of the bomb. I try to fit the pieces together. And I can't help but think about my other, original horrible thing. The thing that led me to this island in the first place. It's always tagging along, niggling at me to remember it. The baby could have been a real person by now.

I blink and notice where I am for the first time in a while. The bike hire place is just near here. I pull over, thinking that I should pay for the bikes Lena and I lost yesterday. It would help to do something good.

It's just a short walk over a grass verge. Big black birds watch me, and only flap away at the last minute as I limp through the dust and dry grass.

A row of bikes stand outside the shop, all shiny and unwanted. As I approach the open door, jingling some loose change in my pocket, I realise that I'm breathing very fast. I make an effort to slow myself down, feeling around my throat for a pulse but not able to find one. I entertain an idea that I died Thursday night, and now I'm stuck in a version of the island that is a sort of hell, like in a Twilight Zone episode or something.

The man from yesterday sits inside the building. He has on a John Deere hat and is eating watermelon from a polystyrene box. Bits of bike are on the floor around him. He doesn't look happy to begin with, but when he sees me his lips tighten even further.

'Tell me why someone tried selling me my own bike this morning?' he says, putting the food down on the floor and wiping his hands on his trousers.

'Um ... they did?'

'That crazy man from the beach. You give it to him or what? You seemed like nice girls. And now you're back. You going to rob me?'

'No! I came to apologise. We ran into trouble yesterday, with the storm and everything. In the end, we lost the bikes. I want to pay for them. We're both sorry.'

'How you lose them?'

'All the rain and everything.'

'Give me two hundred dollars and we'll forget it.' He knows that I'm lying.

I pay him although it seems far too much. I just don't like the way he's looking at me; like I'm a criminal.

'Which bike was it?' I ask, although my face feels warm and wet and I just want to get out of here.

'What?'

'Which bike did he try to sell you?'

Silently, he points to a bike at the side of the shed. It's Lena's; the one that was stolen in the jungle. Stolen by a screaming man. I say: 'Did he say where he got it?'

He shakes his head and kicks at a bike chain on the floor, sending it slithering away.

I go straight from there to the beach, parking crookedly on the kerb and scaring away a flock of birds. As I run onto the sand one of my shoes comes loose, and I nearly fall stooping to pick it up. Mike's nowhere to be seen. A few people sit in groups, drinking and talking. There are figures out in the water too, just standing there like statues. I head towards where the beach is most rocky. I've seen him around there before, sitting in the jagged patches of shade, surrounded by dismembered crabs and empty bottles.

He's here. I catch the sound of his guitar first, and then I see him against a fallen log, which has been worn white and smooth like ivory. He is wearing the same clothes as last time and I can smell him as I approach. Sweat and old alcohol. I step up beside him and see ginger in his beard, which is longer than it was a couple of days ago. His eyes are closed as he plays but he knows that I'm here and says hello.

'Hello,' I say, trying to keep my voice steady. 'How are you today?'

'Not too terrible.'

With my sandy hands in my pockets, I ask him about the bike and he nods. 'It washed in with the river this morning.'

He points down the beach, towards where the river, usually modest, flows into the sea. It's swollen from yesterday's heavy rain.

I forget to thank him or say goodbye; I just walk away towards the river, my eyes on the haze above it. As I get closer I realise that I've been able to hear it for a while, and I see that it has *really* swollen. It's rushing towards the sea with frantic speed, spilling over its banks and across the sand. Leaves and snapped branches are travelling with it.

So the bike came this way. It left the area around the temples, joined the river and found its way to Mike. For a while, I just stare at my toes as they sink into the wet sand. I can smell the sand. I can taste salt on my lips as I chew on them. I have an idea.

Spinning around, I run back to the car with Mike's music twinkling in my wake. I can feel my idea spreading; its flowers are blooming, cutting off the light supply to the other thoughts I have; thoughts which are dark already, and deserve to wither and die.

# Chapter Twenty-Three

I've been driving for ten minutes and the trees are closing in. As my heart rate slows and my grip on the steering wheel gradually loosens, I realise that I don't want to do this by myself. It's hard to think things through when you're alone. The words go around and around, turning into shapes and faces and making me want to give up on everything. So, I make a U-turn and head back into town, thinking: Steve or Lena, Steve or Lena? My clenched jaw begins to ache.

Outside the fishermen's place, children are playing in the shade beneath some sheets of corrugated metal, and chickens scratch at the ground, shaking their heads as if very angry. With the engine switched off, the car fills with a hot, steamy silence. I almost drive away again, to pick up Steve instead. But I pull the key from the ignition, look for a second or two at the keyring, a Mickey Mouse one from Disney World, and then get out of the car. It rolls along the street for a bit after I slam the door, despite the handbrake being on. The children point and laugh.

'Stop, stop!' I shout, shuffling after it, and eventually it does, like a weary animal. Even Steve's car is turning against me. The three of us used to be a team, driving and talking all over this island. Again, I consider going back for him, but don't. I'm not going to give him anything until he makes a gesture, tries to make things right.

One of the fishermen is sitting outside the building, doing something with a knife and a net. He smiles at me around his cigarette. As I make for the door he shakes his head and says something along the lines of: 'No, don't go in.'

'What?' I go ahead anyway, unhooking a piece of metal that's keeping the door closed.

The noise is what gets me first; flesh smacking against flesh, panting, groaning, and Lena's head grinding against the floor. Lena cranes her neck up over the fisherman's shoulder. She screams but the corners of her mouth twitch upwards. I freeze for a second, my eyes full of tensed limbs, sweat and shadows, and then I run outside, slamming the door so hard that it bounces in its crooked frame.

'I tell you,' the fisherman outside says. He has his left foot balanced on his right knee, and he jiggles these about, causing his sandal to slip off and hang from his toes. He's laughing.

'It's not funny,' I whisper.

Back in the car, I pull my hair from my hot face and straighten the rear-view mirror for no reason. It takes a couple of goes to get the engine started, but then I drive away quickly, causing the children to jump to the side of the road. Looking back at them, I see a boy throw a can after me. It bounces, skimming over potholes and catching the sun. I pull on my seatbelt and pick up speed. The town spins past; a kaleidoscope of doorways, trees, skinny animals and bicycles. I'm better off alone. I can get things done properly this way, just like I used to at my old newspaper. I've been relying on Steve for too long and Lena was always a shitty friend, now that I think about it.

I come up against a road block not too far from the bomb site. I don't know if its connected to the bomb, but men in hard hats are standing waist deep in a hole in the ground, where pipes and dirty water are exposed. I stop in the road for a moment but one of them, a cigarette hanging from his mouth, shakes his head at me and points back the way I came. I turn around and have to head back along the coast road.

I just breathe, think in circles, and keep one fist curled in my lap. Logically I know that Lena's done nothing wrong, and yet I can't think of her now without feeling a warm sort of pain. Steve too. Why isn't he here with me? Why can't he see that doing this, following a hunch and a feeling, is all that we can do right now? It's like the two of them have purposely engineered things so that I have to go on alone.

My thoughts are moving the way they did back in England, when I'd quit work and was spending a lot of time sitting in bed doing nothing. I remember flicking through one of those crappy women's magazines my sister had brought round, and thinking: How do we know that the before and after photos were taken in the order they're telling us? Perhaps we're not looking at a miraculous transformation but an unremarkable decline? The way I felt back then is how I feel now; like everything's a dirty lie and I'm the only one to realise.

'Oh, just shut up,' I say to myself out loud, and that's when I notice a small crowd on the beach, near to where I was speaking with Mike just a little while ago. I slow down and spot Steve, standing apart from the other people. They're all staring in the same direction.

I pull over and stop the car, then run onto the beach, my feet sinking into the sand and slowing me down. Some of the people have their phones or cameras out, but Steve has his arms hanging by his side, holding one shoe in each hand, his canvas trousers rolled up towards his knees. Same as everyone else, he's looking towards the swollen river which cuts through the sand and into the turquoise sea.

'They're bringing him out,' someone shouts.

I come up beside Steve and he looks at me, meeting my eyes. He doesn't say anything. We both look back towards the river, and see men dragging a body out from where it had become caught on a washed-up branch. For just a moment I can see everything. The white shirt pasted to the body. The wide-open jaw. Eyes open too.

'That's Mr Shuttleworth all right,' Steve says under his breath. I watch him write the name down in his notepad; I think he does this just for an excuse to look away. When I look back up from Steve's green biro, the body has gone, zipped inside a bag.

'That's that, then,' I say.

'That's that,' Steve says, still staring at the river.

All this time, I'd been hoping that Mr Shuttleworth's disappearance would turn out to be a misunderstanding; he'd hurried off to Aspen or wherever it was he was headed, and had left his house in a mess. Perhaps a bat had got in, and he'd smashed things up with a broom trying to get rid of it. The bats on this island are huge, and fly low over your head with menacing squeaks.

'Did I ever tell you about the first time I saw a dead body?' Steve says.

'I don't think so.'

'I was eight years old. It was a car accident outside the house, and I still dream about that one. Twenty years later I watched my mother die slowly in a hospital bed, and throughout my career I've seen all manner of corpses. But now, I think, I've seen too many. I reached my limit the other night. This one is one too many. I'm done with it.'

I don't know what to say, but he doesn't seem to want a response anyway. He shakes his head and kicks at the sand. He doesn't watch as the bag is loaded clumsily into the back of a van that is parked at the edge of the beach, where sand has blown onto the tarmac and a puddle has swamped a storm drain.

'This river flows from where the temples are,' I say.

'I think so.'

'I know so. I already checked. Can we go somewhere to talk?'

'Oh, Lucy, I'm sorry,' he says, grabbing one of my hands as the crowd begins to move around us, heading off the beach and towards the road back into town. 'Our conversation earlier didn't go the way I wanted it to at all. Usually, when I talk to you it makes my own thoughts jump into order, but today they just got even more scrambled.'

'It's okay. I don't think I've been acting the way I ought to either.'

'We have been through a lot these last few days,' Steve says. 'We tend to forget that.'

'Are you really going to stay with your daughter?' I ask. 'It's fine if you are. I'm sorry for reacting the way I did. It just surprised me. I'm not sure what I'm going to do here without you.'

'I'm still going to go, yeah. But not yet. We're mixed up in all of this whether I like it or not. Bernard fucking Shuttleworth has just washed up dead on the beach. I can't leave without knowing how that happened.'

'Okay,' I say, and smile. But then I remember how Shuttleworth's shirt looked just now, like the greasy plastic they wrap around fish at the market, and my smile melts.

# Chapter Twenty-Four

'I had a text message from Kadesadayurat telling me I should get to the beach because someone had found something. That's all,' Steve says. We're back at the office, sitting by the window at our cluttered little table. The sun tumbles in over us, casting shadows for even the little biscuit crumbs that we've dropped as we talk. I have a piece of paper in front of me, but I haven't made any notes yet.

'He didn't tell you anything else?'

'No, and he wasn't there when I arrived. The people who first spotted the body were still there; some French tourists. And a group of foreign journalists had arrived before me. They were so excited. First the bomb and now this.'

'Really?' I say. 'They were excited?'

'They were trying to hide it but I could tell they were thrilled. They kept shuffling closer to the river but the police arrived and sent them back, again and again. I recognised one of the policemen but he wouldn't talk to me. None of them would talk to me. Kadesadayurat isn't getting back to me.' Steve picks up his phone to check the screen, and then shoves it back into his pocket, shaking his head.

'Did you speak to the French tourists?' I ask.

'Yes. They're leaving tomorrow. They were trying their best to have a nice last day.'

'What did they tell you?' I ask, positioning my pen above the paper; I hate a blank page.

'The daughter saw him first. She thought it was a big plastic bag caught on the branch and was going to get it and bin it. She has a thing about plastic getting into the sea and then the turtles eat it. But it was a man. She screamed and her parents came running. That's it. That's all I got.'

I pull the laptop across the table to where I'm sitting, accidentally crumpling my notes. I wait for a map to load and then swivel the screen around to show Steve. The blue line of the river runs from behind the temples that Lena and I visited, then meanders back around the edge of town and into the sea.

'I think his body came from here,' I say, pointing to the temples.

'Why? It seems more likely that he came from somewhere in town. There are lots of industrial buildings where he could have been held. It wouldn't be far to the river from these ones here.' Steve waves his hand vaguely, scattering dust from the screen.

'Yeah, but listen; when we went to the temples yesterday, Lena's bike got stolen. And, around that same time, we heard a man shouting. Scared sort of shouting. We couldn't find the bike or the man. But then this morning, the bike washed up along that exact same river. Mike found it, you know, the guitarist.'

Steve tilts the screen so he can get a better look at the map. He's frowning; I have his attention with this. 'You think it was Bernard Shuttleworth doing the shouting? And he took the bike?'

'Maybe.' I nod eagerly, before I lose him.

'Were you out there looking for him?' Steve asks, with one eyebrow raised. Part of me wants to say yes, because although I wasn't specifically expecting to run into Shuttleworth in the jungle, I do think I've been very clever. But I know that he'll be hurt when he realises that I didn't bring him in on it all right from the start. I should have done, even if he was busy getting stoned and feeling depressed.

'I had a feeling that *something* was out there,' I say, drawing a flower on my piece of paper so that I don't have to look at him. 'Do you remember Mike saying there was a lot of orange mud on Dolph's car? The mud out in the jungle around the temples is orange. There's some sort of mineral out there that does it. I read about it once. I just thought it might be worth checking out. I definitely would have brought you if I really and truly thought something important was going to happen out there, you know?'

'Okay,' Steve says, and then pauses. He gazes out of the window, chewing on his thumb. 'So, you think that someone killed Shuttleworth in the temple region? That's your theory?'

'Yes, and I think maybe Dolph did it. He looked so shifty when I saw him at the hotel, and he wouldn't have just dumped his car for no reason.'

'But why would he do any of that? What do you know about him to make that seem feasible?'

'Nothing really,' I admit. 'Just that the very morning before he disappeared, Shuttleworth told me that he thought Dolph might be involved in the bombing. He didn't have much of a reason. But still, he said it. And now no one knows where Dolph is. Or his girlfriend. There's something, isn't there? It all adds up to something.'

'Something.' Steve nods.

'But there's more,' I say. I tell him about the woman who Lena and I met on the road back from the temples and who gave us a lift in her big, expensive car. I say: 'We need to find out why she was out there last night. She has to be involved somehow.'

'She's staying at the Grand Hotel?'

'That's what she said.'

'Then it seems to me that we ought to go there and find her. One other thing though; how does the ice cream parlour fit into it all?'

'Maybe it doesn't.' I shrug. 'Even if the bomb was in one of their plant pots anyone could have put it there. It doesn't necessarily implicate the owners.'

'No, but I think we should try to speak to the owners anyway. We need to know why they were closed that afternoon. We should be thorough, right?'

'I agree,' I say, feeling just the smallest thrill of excitement, like we're on a rollercoaster and it's started to slowly climb up, up, up. 'And, most of all, we should go out to the temples and see what we can find. We should probably follow the course of the river.'

'I don't know,' Steve says, the expression on his face faltering. 'That seems like it might put us in unnecessary danger. But maybe we can catch up with Kadesadayurat soon and find out what he knows. I'd imagine they must be thinking along the same lines we are.'

'I expect so,' I say, nodding and folding up my sheet of notes. I'm going to visit the temples, and I'm pretty sure I'll be able to persuade Steve to come with me. I've missed a lot of opportunities lately; I missed something, I know I did, when I was talking to Shuttleworth at his resort. I missed my chance to speak with Dolph at the Imperial Hotel and I missed the shouting man in the forest. If there is something waiting to be discovered out there, I'm not going to miss my chance to find it.

'Don't look at me like that,' Steve says. 'I'm with you on this, okay? I just don't want anyone else to get hurt. Let's start by checking out the building where the ice cream owners are supposed to live. It's not so far away. And then we'll swing by the Grand Hotel.'

'Okay.' I notice him sucking on his thumb, like he's trying to get poison out of it. 'Are you all right?'

'Yeah, sorry. It kind of stings where that cat bit me. I expect it had some sort of disease. Mouth parasites.'

'You shouldn't really take in stray animals around here,' I say. 'They can have rabies.'

'I mean it, you know, Lucy,' he says. 'I really want to help. I love this island. I've asked Jenna to bury me here when I die, out in the jungle. It might be illegal but I don't care. She'll find a way. She's resourceful.'

I laugh. 'It's a good island.'

'It saved me, I think. I was at a low point in my life when I came here. We don't have to go into it but things were bad.'

'Oh yeah?' I say, looking at my fingernails and hoping that he isn't about to ask me to share anything.

'I ran away, you see? It wasn't strictly necessary to run all the way to a new continent, but it helped; travelling in cramped buses all through the night, counting out foreign banknotes, drinking alcohol in bars with sticky floors in places where no one spoke my language. I got lost in it all, for as long as I could. I wandered through Vietnam and Cambodia, and then eventually settled here. I don't know what would have happened to me if I hadn't started up this newspaper. But I did, and it worked. I was on my own for years until things got too busy, and then, well, you came along.'

'Yep.' I nod, remembering the advert that had seemed too good to be true when my sister showed it to me, the Skype interview that I thought I'd bungled, and my first real glimpse of Steve as he stood in a Hawaiian shirt, waving and sweating as I stepped unsteadily onto the dock.

'I was hoping that life could stay this way forever; drinking with friends like you, petting stray animals like that stupid cat, writing meaningless, beautiful words and taking meaningless, beautiful photographs for our stupid, but not all together meaningless, newspaper. But now things are uglier than they've ever been, and I'm starting to realise that I didn't escape from anything when I fled my home. The sadness followed me here and now it's arrived and tainted everything.'

'You're talking like it's your fault,' I say, staring through the window at the roof tops and the distant green hills. Steve's looking out there too, at the island we love.

'I sort of feel like it is,' he says. 'Is that dumb?'

'It's definitely not your fault,' I say. 'How could it be?'

'I realise it's not like I armed the bomb or anything. I'm just having to admit for the first time in what, fifteen years, that I've been very selfish hiding here in my little haven while my old, damaged life goes on without me. And now this life is terribly damaged too.'

'We can help with this though,' I tell him. 'We don't need to run away anymore. We can stay here and help fix things.'

I don't tell him that I ran to this island just like he did, or that I've been hiding here. The words nearly leave my mouth but then merely fall out in a sad little sigh.

'I would really like to fix something.' Steve nods.

# Chapter Twenty-Five

The hairdressers is closed, but two small children sit in its doorway eating noodles from a polystyrene box balanced across their knees. A woman is sweeping the pavement beside them; gravel, hair and bits of plastic which twinkle in the sun. The building that looms behind the hairdressers is a pale grey cube, around five stories high, with cracks in its plaster and lines of washing hung across the balconies.

We've parked in front of the hairdressers and we're both gazing up at the apartment block, shielding our eyes from the sun while we finish our iced coffees.

'I can't picture them at all,' Steve says, unwinding his window to let a fly out. 'You really think you'd recognise them?'

I screw up my eyes and try to think back to the last time I visited the ice cream parlour. It was probably a few weeks ago, when I bought milkshakes to bring into the office. I can picture the woman's smile. Wrinkles around her mouth. She had a roll of Pokémon stickers beside the till, and had given some out to the children who were queueing with their parents in front of me. I tried to recall the names of the Pokémon while she counted out my change.

'Yeah, I'd recognise her. She was always there. Him, I didn't see so much. He's older, I think. I used to see him smoking sometimes; when I looked out of my bedroom window he'd be across the street, having a cigarette outside the café.'

'Bob and Mary,' Steve says, sucking up the last of his drink, crumpling the cup and tossing it down beside his feet.

'There's a bin right there,' I say, pointing out of my window. As I look, a man and woman appear around the side of the hairdressers, following a path leading from the apartment building. They're walking close together. Their fingers are touching but they are not quite holding hands. The woman is hunched, looking at the ground. The man is smoking, keeping his hand up close to his face.

'Oh!' I say, waving a hand at Steve and reaching to open my door. This could be them.

Steve is looking the other way, out of his window. I glance over. A police car has just driven slowly by.

The couple have disappeared. I look up and down the street. They can only have doubled back on themselves, or gone into the hairdressers. But the children are still sitting there with their noodles and the door is still closed behind them.

'Kadesadayurat was driving that car,' Steve tells me. 'There were two other policemen in there with him. Bastard's not answering my calls. You know what we should do?'

'Follow him?' I venture.

'Follow him,' Steve says, grabbing hold of the dashboard like he's willing the car to move.

I look one final time at where the couple were walking just seconds ago. Was it really them or was I just desperate to believe that it could be? If I get out of the car now and run along that path, I might be too late to catch them, or perhaps I'll reach them and find that they're strangers. Either way, it'll be too late to follow Kadesadayurat.

I pass my drink to Steve because the cup holders are already full of empties, and then I accelerate hard after the police car, which is just turning right at the end of the street. When I make the turn we can see them continuing straight; they're just overtaking a man leading a donkey along the road.

'He's sure to recognise my car,' Steve says.

I shrug. 'Let's see how far we can get. Maybe he won't mind us tagging along.'

It quickly becomes clear that Kadesadayurat is heading out of town. As the buildings fall behind us and the traffic thins, I drop back further, keeping a group of mopeds between us.

'He's going to the temples,' Steve says, when even the mopeds have dropped away and it is just our two vehicles sending trails of dust into the hot air.

'I think so.'

'You were right, Lucy. You are so clever.'

I smile thinly because I still might turn out to be wrong and, anyway, what a thing to be right about.

We continue along behind them, keeping far enough back that we often lose sight of them as the road curves and the trees rise. The journey seems shorter today than it did last night in that drunk woman's car, almost like I should still be able to see the town in my rear-view mirror. We're approaching the point where the track narrows and dips towards the first temples, but then Kadesadayurat surprises us by pulling over to the side of the road.

'What are they doing?' Steve says. 'There's nothing around here, is there?'

'I'm not sure.' I slow down but don't quite stop.

'No, keep going. You're making us look suspicious,' Steve says, waving a hand.

'But I'll pass them.'

'They might not look.' Steve sticks his head out of the window, squinting ahead at the parked car. 'I can see them. They're facing away from the road. They've gone down into the bushes. What are they doing? Oh, they've all stopped for a piss.'

'Oh,' I say, suddenly very aware of my own bladder and the distance between it and the nearest toilet.

Steve's laughing. 'Just pass them,' he tells me.

I slow slightly as we go by, and Steve winds his window the whole way down, trying to listen to what they're saying over the sound of our engine.

'A waste of time,' he says. 'Something like that. They don't want to be here. Something else is happening elsewhere. That's all I got.'

'Should we wait for them?' I say, touching the brake, not sure how to proceed.

'We know where they're headed, don't we? Let's go ahead and wait for them. He can't accuse us of following him if we get there first.'

'Okay,' I say, but as soon as we continue on alone, I feel like the sky has darkened a shade and dropped lower, so that it's pressing down on our little vehicle, as it bounces and rattles across the potholes.

# Chapter Twenty-Six

'Let's stop here,' Steve says.

The track has narrowed and the car is beginning to struggle against the mud and thick plants. I switch the engine off. Silence, almost. A mosquito moves about inside with us, humming. Many more insects have perished on the windscreen. Something in the engine is ticking.

'Maybe I should pull over a bit,' I say. 'In case someone wants to get past.'

'You think anyone else will be coming out here?'

'Well, Kadesadayurat,' I say.

'Their car looked nearly as beat-up as ours,' Steve says. 'I doubt they'd get it much further than this.'

'Still, I'd feel better if we weren't in the way.'

'Down there,' Steve says, pointing to a little dip at the side of the road, partially hidden by vines hanging from the trees. 'It'll be out of the way and it's sort of subtle. The police might not even notice it. Not that it matters. We're doing nothing wrong being out here.'

'I know.' I nod, but somehow I feel like we are.

With a lot of groaning from the engine, and with mud spitting up all around us, I manage to manoeuvre the car off the road. We climb out and sink ankle deep in sludge.

'Oh, we're not prepared for this,' Steve says as flies descend around us.

'We'll be fine. This is a few miles further on from where I cycled to with Lena. From here it should be possible to walk to the three temples I have in mind. They're the temples nearest to the river.'

'We should wait here though,' Steve says, planting a hand firmly on the roof of the car. 'Don't you think we should wait for the police to arrive and then follow them?'

'It doesn't hurt to look,' I say. I'd thought, now that he was out here, Steve would want to keep on going.

'But it might hurt. That's exactly my concern.'

So, we get back inside the car and sit silently together, arms folded, staring out at water oozing down the trunks of the trees and dripping onto rocks below. Drops are hitting the roof of our car too, an irregular beat. We wait and wait. The police car does not appear.

Steve puts the radio on and dials through the different stations until he finally manages to catch something, although it is muffled and cuts in and out. A female voice is speaking in Thai. I can tell it's the news by her sombre tone.

'Is she talking about us? The island?' I ask.

'Yeah,' Steve says, frowning as he concentrates. 'She just mentioned the police in Melbourne, Australia. Something to do with members of a group. Closing in on someone. It's so hard to hear.'

He twists the dial, attempting to make it clearer, but then we lose the voice completely and there is nothing but the hiss of empty airwaves.

'I think maybe things are starting to happen,' I say. 'We're all making progress, right?'

'Let's just go home,' Steve says. 'We've obviously got this wrong.'

'You serious?' I say.

'We shouldn't explore alone, Lucy. It's stupid and it's dangerous.'

'We came all the way out here. We can't just give up. You wait in the car. I'm going to have a look around.' I'm not sure, at this point, if I really am brave enough to get out and walk off into the trees alone, but luckily Steve doesn't call my bluff.

'Okay,' he says. 'We'll have a quick look. Ten minutes. Just to get a feel for the area. And then we're going back to the police station and we won't leave until Kadesadayurat sees us and fills us in on all of his news. Okay?'

'Okay,' I nod. 'Thank you. And don't worry. I'm sure no one will be here, dangerous or otherwise. Why would they wait around after doing whatever it was they did to Mr Shuttleworth?'

Insects follow us as we struggle uphill from the road. In places the plants grow so thickly that we have to change course. I hear the river and the air feels wet. Birds move in the trees, making ugly noises like they're afraid. The slope is steep and we have to grab at branches to keep from sliding backwards.

The ground levels out and I think I must have made a mistake; there's no temple here. Everything is thick, green, damp and suffocating. But then I wipe the sweat from my face and really look around. There's a carved archway beneath a curtain of vines, and further chambers and grey walls, trees growing amongst them, on the verge of flattening the building and reclaiming the land. I stop beneath the archway to catch my breath. The touch of the cool stone is a relief, although when I look closely I see horned creatures nesting in its pores.

'Goodness,' Steve says, puffing beside me. 'It feels like no one's been here for centuries.'

'I know, right? It looks like there's a clearing beyond that wall over there. Shall we head that way?'

'We can do. My God, this is another world, isn't it?'

I brush dust and plant matter from my arms, and then push further into what's left of the temple. The place feels alive, as if the creeping plants and ancient stones can sense us, like they're turning to watch as we walk by, the gravel crunching, mud bubbling around our feet. I know there are creatures in here with us; I can hear leaves moving, insects working, and I can taste their presence in the steamy air. But there's nothing human here. I think that perhaps Steve is right and no one has visited this place for years.

'Anyone here?' I call, just to see how it sounds.

A scrabbling noise kicks up while my lips are still parted; someone running over loose rock. The sound bounces between trees and crumbling stone, but I think it's coming from the other side of the wall, where the forest is thinner. My first instinct is to flee, and I turn so sharply that I slip and have to grab at a carved pillar. It's covered with slime, which I can feel beneath my fingernails. Wiping this on my shorts, steady again, I realise that the person isn't running to attack us; they're running away. The noise is growing distant, but the air is disturbed here, even the clouds seem to have shifted from above the tops of the trees. Something has changed.

'Someone's actually here,' Steve hisses.

Making as little noise as possible, bracing my hands against the trees, I head towards the clearing on the other side of the wall. I tell myself not to think, because if I do the fear will get in. I can feel it trickling through my veins, making my fingers tingle and my throat tighten. But it hasn't reached any organs yet, so I keep moving. Steve is behind me. He grabs at the back of my shirt and pulls me towards him. I think he's going to insist that we go back to the car but he doesn't, he whispers at me to be careful, and we continue on together, holding our breath.

All I can hear now are the jungle noises, which are frightening in their own way. It's as we reach the clearing, where sharp plants twist towards the red-hot sky, that I shield my eyes and see a man slipping away into the trees; a skinny guy in dark clothing. He's absorbed by the plants almost immediately, but they continue to move in his wake. We could leave now, go back to the office and pretend nothing ever happened. But instead we quickly share a look, nod at each other, and run after him.

My feet clap against the ground and every stone pokes sharp through my canvas shoes as we dive into the jungle.

'Ergh,' I say as my face rips through a spider's web. Steve stops beside me, trying to catch his breath as I spit at the ground, pulling the web from my eyes with hands that suddenly won't stop shaking. When I can see again, I realise that the man is right there in front of us, crouched beside a mutated tree root. He's like a demon, twisted there; his body has become part of the jungle. Steve has seen him too; I feel his hand reach for my arm and hold on tight, just below the elbow.

The flesh has thinned on his face since I saw him last, and his hair is wet and matted, but this is Dolph. I recognise him as soon as my eyes meet his.

I was right about someone being out here. Out of nowhere, and out of place in this dank twist of trees, I get an explosion of joy. It's as if a drug has just started working inside of me, but I try to stifle it because it's not appropriate to feel like this, and it's making my legs shake, making me smile. With a new strength, I force my way through the damp plants to reach him. My legs start to bleed in a couple of places where thorns catch my skin, and another spider's web wraps itself around my arm.

'Lucy, careful,' Steve hisses. He's right behind me, but has lost his grip on my wrist.

'What do you want?' Dolph asks, not moving except to dig his fingers deep into the side of the tree that he's crouching beside. Water falls from the leaves and drips down his dirty face. I recall Steve mentioning Marine Biology. He does look like a scientist. Or an artist. Sometimes there's some cross-over between the two.

'To talk to you,' I say, pleased at how calm my voice sounds. 'You're Dolph, right? My name's Lucy, I'm from the *Koh Star*. This is Steve, my editor.'

'Okay,' Dolph says, with a nervous grin now. He looks around, as if there might be a news crew following behind us. 'It's just you?'

'Yeah,' I say, instantly regretting it; it would be better for him to think we have back up.

'I've seen you before, haven't I? That was you at the hotel?'

'You ran away.'

'No, I was just in a rush. I'm always in a rush. Don't take it personally.' He pauses, runs a hand through his hair, and then says: 'Why would you want to talk to me?'

'Is your girlfriend here too?' I would feel better if I could see Maliwan.

'Um...' Dolph says, still with a little smile on his face. 'Can I ask why you're interested?'

'I'd really like to talk to her as well.' I glance around for something I could use as a weapon, just in case. There are a few small stones which I could fling in his face, and a soggy looking stick which might be useful if I could get it into his eye. He's not a big man, and perhaps we'd be able to fight him off if it came to it. But he's rubbing at his chest now as if his skin itches, and chewing on his lips which are bleeding already. He might be crazy, and crazy people tend to be strong no matter what their size. I think that he could be a murderer. But

138

the awkward jutting of his elbows, his pierced ear and long hair, make him seem liberal and academic and like he should be inside a library or at a music festival. I don't see terrorism here anymore. But murder? Yes, perhaps.

'What do you guys want?' he asks, not smiling any more. He puts his hands around the tree and hangs on as if he might otherwise float away.

'Okay,' I say slowly, glancing at Steve and changing my mind again; perhaps this man did make the bomb. Maybe a liberal academic *can* pick up dangerous ideas. Steve is silent behind me, but I can feel a cloud of tension spreading around him. I can smell it; the fear that comes before panic. The sort of smell that can make animals stampede. I lick my lips and start talking, my voice unsteady now, and a tremor running through my whole body. 'I spoke to Bernard Shuttleworth the day after the bomb went off. He thought Maliwan's boyfriend might be involved. That's you, right? And now Shuttleworth's dead, so...'

'No, I'm not involved in any of that.' Dolph's lips start to tremble, and he hits the tree with one balled up fist. Damp pieces of bark fall to the ground.

'Then what are you doing out here?' I look at the ground and think of pencil shavings.

'The police don't think I'm the bomber, do they?' Dolph almost laughs as he says this, like he thinks the idea ridiculous. His eyes, though, are screwed up tight.

'I think they've maybe considered it.' It comes out in a whisper, but is very loud all the same, hanging over the sounds of the birds and the drip, drip, drip of water, the rushing river and the insects, calling and fighting between the leaves.

'So, they haven't caught the bomber yet? The real one? I've been wondering.'

'Well, no,' I say.

'Then you should be back in town, helping them, not out here harassing me,' Dolph says, straightening up and taking a step towards us, crushing plants as he moves. He doesn't seem so small now that he's standing. He has unfurled like an insect.

'We're not harassing you,' Steve says, in a more assertive voice than I'd expected. 'We just want to politely ask some questions. Were you aware that Bernard Shuttleworth is dead?'

I realise that I've raised my arms, and I take a couple steps back, catching my clothes on the trees. Steve does the same; this is how the two of us look when we find a spider in the print room at work.

'No. I had no idea. How did you even find us?' Dolph asks.

'Orange mud on your car,' I say, looking over my shoulder to check that no one is creeping up from behind. All I can see are plants, and no clear route back to where we left the car. 'And then the bike washed up on the beach so I figured whatever happened must have happened near to the river. And then...'

'What bike?' Dolph interrupts, spitting slightly.

'It belonged to my friend. It got stolen out here. I thought...'

'We never saw your bike.'

'Oh.' We all stare at each other, equally baffled. 'I was here yesterday. Well, not far from here. And we heard shouting. It was a man and he took our bike.'

'I haven't been shouting and I definitely haven't seen any bikes. Could it have been the police? Do you think they're out here too? We haven't seen anyone at all. Are the police coming? Honestly, this is so ridiculous.'

I shrug and look at Steve, suddenly unsure of how to proceed. 'I thought it could have been Bernard Shuttleworth,' I say.

'I don't think so. You said he's dead.' Dolph looks at me like I'm very stupid. Then he shakes his head and laughs awkwardly. 'I mean, I've no idea. About any of this. No idea.'

He did it, I think. He killed Bernard Shuttleworth. My ankles are trapped in a coil of stalks and spikes. Everything around us is dark and dirty, the ruins of an ancient civilisation decaying beyond the trees, and I hate myself for coming here and putting Steve and myself at risk, because many miles away my parents are waiting for me and watching news reports which I know will be making them cry, and Steve has a daughter who he wants so badly to visit. I crouch and manage to snap a plant from around my leg. Orange mud and something black and flaky coat my hands afterwards. Spying a rock, I pick it up. It fits snugly in my palm.

'Do you have any connection to Australia?' Steve asks. 'Melbourne, specifically?'

'You've got it wrong, okay?' Dolph says, jabbing a finger towards us so that I stagger back, snapping twigs and thumping against Steve. 'I had nothing to do with the bomb and neither did Maliwan. That's ridiculous. We don't know anything about her boss. We're just out here camping, okay? There's nothing wrong with that.'

I stare at Dolph, trying to read him but failing. All I can pick up on is his pain.

'Come on, now. What have you done? What exactly?' Steve says, in a flat sort of voice.

'Nothing, I swear.'

'We know he died out here,' Steve says, and he sounds so sure of the fact that I forget to feel frightened for a moment.

'I don't know anything about that.'

'Why would Bernard Shuttleworth think you were involved in the bombing?' I ask.

'I don't know. I had an argument with him one time about Palestine. He couldn't believe I sided with the Arabs. Maybe, in his mind, that makes me a terrorist. I don't know. Why would you even listen to him? He says all sorts of things.'

'We try to listen to everyone,' Steve says. 'It's part of our job.'

'Then listen to me. I know nothing about any of this. I'm not lying. Do I look like I'm lying?'

'I guess not,' I say, looking at a throbbing vein on his forehead.

'Then, please, just go away. Will you?'

'Okay.' I've had enough, and want to feel safe again. This could be our last chance at safety, although it might not be a chance at all; there's something about the way he's looking at us. He wants something, I can tell. We begin walking unsteadily back the way we came, gripping branches and pushing leaves from our eyes. He's going to grab me. I can practically feel his fingers on my skin; it's hard not to scream.

And then he shouts: 'Wait!'

I look back over my shoulder. Dolph is following, bent forwards as if in pain.

'What do you want?' Steve says.

'I'm sorry to ask, okay, but do you have any food or drink? Someone was supposed to bring us some. I've been waiting here but she hasn't showed.'

'No, we didn't bring anything with us,' Steve says. We move on, away from him.

'Wait, wait. Could I get a ride into town with you, please? You came by car?'

'I don't think I want anything to do with you.' This is a harsher sentence than I meant it to be, and I see in his face that I've hurt him. He's used to pleasing people, I think; being amiable. Did Steve say something about a wealthy family? Living out here, torn to pieces, dirty and wet, must be making Dolph crazy if he wasn't already. Steve looks at me, and I realise that he would have responded differently to Dolph if I hadn't jumped in.

'I just need a ride. I don't want to cause you any trouble. I'm really not a terrorist or whatever it is you think. Please?'

'What about your girlfriend? Isn't she out here too? Are you just going to leave her?' I ask.

'No. I need to talk to her. Can you wait a while? Please, you could be our only hope.' He paws at his face and stares at me through his fingers.

'I don't know if we should help you. I'm still not sure what you've done.'

'Please, just wait here, okay? She's not far away. I'll be back in ten, fifteen minutes.'

Steve and I look at each other. I see that he wants to help, so I nod. Steve's a nicer person than I am.

'We'll come with you. We'll come and see her,' Steve says.

Dolph hesitates for what feels like a full minute, and then he nods. 'Okay.'

# Chapter Twenty-Seven

'I don't trust him for a second,' Steve hisses at me. We're walking a couple of metres behind Dolph, who is ducking and weaving through the forest, struggling to keep his hair out of his eyes and to hear what we're saying.

'Me neither. I know this was all my idea but I really think we should go home.'

'I do too. But, listen, what if Maliwan is out here and she doesn't want to be? Imagine if we left right now, and then in a few days' time she turns up dead on the beach too.'

'But that could happen to us,' I whisper, my voice scratching my throat. 'We could be dead on the beach.'

'Do you want to wait here? Or go back to the car? Maybe you should. I think that would be sensible. But I just won't be able to take it if I leave and then something happens to her. I can't do it. No more dead bodies, you know?'

'Yeah, I know.' I sigh, remembering Maliwan's mother alone and slowly dying in her dark house. 'I'm coming with you. But are we really going to let them into the car with us?'

'I don't know. I'm winging it here.'

'We're nearly there,' Dolph says loudly, looking back at us with his dark eyes and with a fly crawling up his chin towards his mouth. He waves it away and then continues on through the leaves which stick to him like slugs.

'We'll see if she's okay, take in the situation as much as we can, and then get the hell out of here,' Steve says to me, his whisper turning into a cough that he buries in his fist.

'I really think he might be the bomber, Steve. At the very least he murdered Mr Shuttleworth. Please, we have to be careful.'

'This is it,' Dolph says.

We emerge from a curtain of leaves, blinking as the sunlight hits us. The temple in the centre of this clearing is small and dark. It is more intact but less beautiful than the others; like it's purely functional, reminding me of a bomb shelter or a bunker. It feels deserted in a different way to the other temples; I can picture its dusty chambers filled with insect carcasses, bat droppings and small bones. It casts a bleak shadow over the Thai girl who is sitting beneath a dead tree, using a stick to draw shapes into the ground and then scratch them out again. I have a long second to take in the scene before she sees us.

'Who are they?' she snaps, throwing the stick down and jumping to her feet in one smooth movement.

'Maliwan?' I say.

'Who are you?' She glares at us, the muscles in her face twitching.

I wonder how we look to her; I have mud up my legs and my hair is falling out of my ponytail. Steve is red-faced and dripping sweat onto his striped shirt. She's squinting at me now like maybe she recognises me; like maybe she thinks she's cleaned my bathroom before, or made my bed. I rattle off my spiel about being from the *Koh Star* and I try to smile, because whether she's a victim or an accomplice we really want her to like us at this point.

But the girl darts to a bag which I hadn't noticed before in the shadows of the tree, beside its lumpy roots which are rippling with insects. The bag is a big, khaki-coloured backpack, stuffed so full that one of its seams is beginning to split. She flips open the lid, undoes a zip and pulls out a knife.

It's a few inches long and silver. She waves it around, making light dance over our faces. I brush the glare away like it's another insect; another crawling, biting, stabbing thing.

'I don't think we need that, Mal,' Dolph says, running his fingers through his hair and pulling his scalp tight.

'You're scared of it,' she says. 'That's why you say that. But we do need it.'

'I'm not scared of it,' he tries to argue, but we can all see him flinching as she moves it about.

'You're scared of it like you're scared of the beetles running over your feet in the night. So, I have to do this and I have to crush the beetles, don't I?'

'Okay,' I interrupt. 'Honestly though, he's right, you don't need a knife.'

'We're not taking sides or anything like that,' Steve adds. 'We're just out here to talk. We're just journalists.'

'Pamela didn't show up. I think maybe they can help us,' Dolph says. He kicks his feet in the dirt and fallen leaves. The four of us are standing in a circle now, like we've just met at a party.

'But why do they want to talk to us?' Maliwan asks, looking sideways at me but lowering the knife just a little bit. 'You know you have blood on your legs?'

I look down. 'I scratched them on some plants, I think.'

'I think they might be able to give us a ride into town,' Dolph says. 'We need to pick up supplies, don't we?'

'No, too dangerous.'

'But Pamela didn't show.'

'She promised,' Maliwan says, with a snarl. 'Where is she?'

Dolph shrugs. 'I don't know. I did say. I did say we shouldn't trust her.'

'Can I ask something?' Steve says then, loudly. No one replies but we all turn to look at him. 'Why are you pointing a knife at us, please? If you're just out here camping, why would you feel the need to do that?'

Maliwan takes a step towards me, lowering the knife to her waist. 'What are the newspapers saying about my boss? Bernie Shuttleworth. I know he's missing.'

'Don't,' Dolph says, raising his arms but not actually making contact with anyone. 'Why would you ask about him? That's nothing to do with us.'

I'm trying to read Maliwan's face but I can't. It's not as easy as I thought it would be, to tell if someone is a criminal just by looking into their eyes and at the shape of their mouth. Back in England, when I had to report on court cases, it was easy to assume that people were guilty when they were framed by glass boxes and had guards standing beside them.

Dolph says to Maliwan: 'They're out here because of the bomb, really. That's the main thing, right? You're not really interested in the other thing.'

'What do you know about that?' I ask, my eyes fixed on the blade. 'The bomb.'

'Nothing, why would I?' Maliwan says. She shifts about on her feet and looks at Dolph as if she doesn't understand the question, but he's scratching at his neck and staring at the sky now.

'And your boss is dead,' I say. 'He's dead.'

'How do you know that?' Maliwan asks in a quiet voice, like a child.

'We saw him,' I tell her.

'Where?'

'On the beach in town. The one by the laundrette.'

Dolph and Maliwan share a look. Maliwan bites her lip and I think I see a tear hang heavy beneath her eye for a moment. Dolph is frowning and shaking his head just slightly.

'You're very calm,' Maliwan says to me. 'It's nice. Dolph keeps talking and shaking, making lots of crazy plans and sweating and trying to light fires. You seem very sensible.'

'Okay,' I say. 'Thank you.'

'Can I talk to you alone?'

# Chapter Twenty-Eight

I think Maliwan is about to murder me. Perhaps she's behind everything and Dolph is the one out here against his will. I dig my fingernails deep into my palms and decide that I'll kill these people if I have to; I've dropped my rock somewhere, but I'll grab a handful of the stones scattered around the doorway to this crooked temple, and I'll smash everyone's heads in. My heart picks up and I get ready to move. But then Maliwan says: 'It's about women's stuff.'

'Oh. Okay.' My voice wavers as the strength drains from me.

We walk to where a lizard is carved into the wall of the temple, and where hornets are flying in and out of a hole in the ground. Maliwan keeps hold of the knife but her arm relaxes. Dolph is watching us from beneath his mess of hair, and peeling bark from a tree; he won't be able to hear anything we say over the noise of the river, which is flowing somewhere behind the temple. Steve tries to follow us but I tell him it's okay, so he waits alone with his arms folded around his chest, his eyes darting from one face to another.

'What is it?' I ask, suddenly unsure of what to do with my hands. Maliwan seems smaller now that we're close to each other. Her arms are skinnier than mine, and she's maybe a foot shorter. Her black hair is wild, with actual leaves stuck in it. I think about pointing this out to her but decide not to; surely that's Dolph's job. Although he has leaves of his own. I keep one eye on him; he's twitching and scratching.

'He wasn't like this before,' Maliwan says. 'He was always a bit nervous. His family are horrible to him. They told him he's stupid so many times that he actually believes it. But he's a scientist. He's very clever. But he is much more nervous now. Much worse.'

'Oh?' I say.

'He's different to the other foreign men I've met. But in a good way. I knew it the very first time we spoke. I love him. Is that man your husband?'

'Steve? Oh no,' I say. 'We work together. He's my friend.'

'Maybe we shouldn't have fallen in love,' Maliwan continues, as if I haven't spoken. 'We're living in the wild now because of it. I'm pregnant,' Maliwan says, her shoulders sagging, like she's been waiting to tell someone this and she expects me to immediately take care of the situation. The way she's staring at me, I wonder if she's even out of her teens yet.

'You haven't told him?' I say, glancing at Dolph. I can't help her with this. I was pregnant for nine weeks. And I killed that baby because of who its father was. I don't know anything.

'I told him. But he doesn't know I'm having pains. They're really bad.'

'Look, I'm really no expert. I think some pain can be normal early on.'

'This doesn't feel normal. Will people be looking for me in town? The police?'

'Maybe.' I peer hard at Maliwan; her dry lips, chipped pink nail varnish, silver birds dangling from her pierced ears. I wish I had better news for this girl.

'Let me come back with you. I need to see a doctor. I can't lose my baby. I love her so much already.'

'If you want a lift, I'll take you,' I say. None of this is what I was expecting. My mouth is dry.

'Thank you.' Maliwan sighs. She puts the knife into her pocket.

'They can come with us,' I say to Steve, walking back towards him with Maliwan by my side. 'I think it's okay.'

'Yeah?' Steve says. He catches me by my elbow and pulls me aside. 'Are you sure? Because I'm really not sure. They both seem crazy.'

'We'll get them back into town, let them go wherever they need to go, and then we'll go straight to the police,' I whisper.

'I think they might try to kill us,' Steve hisses.

'I think the safest thing is to do what they want.'

'What did she say to you?'

I hesitate and then say: 'She's pregnant. She's scared. I feel sorry for her. I want to give her a chance.'

'Where is your car?' Maliwan demands. Dolph has heaved the backpack onto his shoulders and is reaching for his girlfriend's hand.

'Back this way,' Steve points vaguely.

The four of us move off into the trees. We've only gone a few steps when Maliwan lets out a little gasp and doubles over, pressing her fists against her knees. Dolph puts his hand on the small of her back but she jerks him away.

'It's nothing,' she says. 'Keep going.'

'Are you sure? Let me help you.'

'No, not you. Her,' she says pointing at me. 'She is calm. You always panic and make me feel worse.'

'What's going on?' Steve asks.

'I need just one minute,' Maliwan says. 'Feel sick.'

'I need to pee anyway,' Steve says. He looks at me. 'You okay?'

I nod and he steps away through the trees, disappearing almost immediately. I hear sticks snapping beneath his feet but then that sound, too, is absorbed by the forest.

'Are you sure you're just sick?' Dolph says to Maliwan, his face drooping. 'I think I left the water by the tree. I'll go back and get it for you.'

'Okay, okay,' Maliwan says, breathing hard.

'Do you want to sit down?' I ask. She's wrapped her fingers around my wrist now, and I try to think of something to say or do that will make this faith she's placed in me seem justified. I'm a woman older than her, but that doesn't mean I know what I'm doing. She seems to think that it does.

Then we hear a vehicle approaching.

Through the trees I spot a dirt bike slowing down beside the temple, scattering gravel and leaving a train of dust behind it. It stops in the clearing but the engine keeps running so I don't hear what Maliwan says to me. She raises a hand and waves in a way that makes her seem younger still, and gets me thinking about the child I saw at the golf resort. Dolph, who is standing beside the dead tree and swinging a bottle of water, is shouting something at no one in particular. Maliwan makes her way back to the clearing, still bent over slightly, her mouth open. I look around for Steve but can't see him. I follow Maliwan but hang back by the wall of the temple. I watch as the couple greet their visitor.

The engine is cut, and Dolph's voice suddenly seems very loud as he says: 'We were getting worried.'

Stepping down from the bike, the woman removes her helmet and brushes dust from her shirt. I take in the short hair, creased eyes and bony limbs, and realise that we've met before; this is the woman who drove me and Lena back into town last night. Rather than say anything, I press back into the shadows, hoping to remain unnoticed. I'm going to find Steve and get back to the car, because this doesn't feel right.

But the woman, who must be the Pamela that they've been speaking of, nods in my direction, saying: 'Who's that?'

The breeze dies and all of the trees stand still. I meet her gaze. A hornet flies between us, its legs trailing. I can feel Pamela's eyes on me like a weight. She takes a packet of cigarettes from a pocket in her canvas trousers, puts one in her mouth but doesn't light it yet. 'Well?' she says, when no one speaks.

'This is Lucy,' Maliwan says. She was smiling when the bike arrived but seems anxious now, tugging at her top, twisting her feet.

'And who invited Lucy here?'

'No one,' Maliwan says.

'What does she want? Is she bothering you?'

I can't tell if Pamela recognises me or not. She was drunk last night, after all, and seemed, even at the time, to forget that there was someone sliding about on the back seat of her car.

Dolph starts to explain how we bumped into each other, and how I was going to drive him into town to pick up supplies. 'But I guess we don't need her to do that anymore since you're here and, well, do you have anything? Did you bring food and water like you said?'

'What? Oh, here you are.' Frowning, Pamela searches through her pockets and then tosses over a half-eaten chocolate bar in a red wrapper. It lands in the mud near to Maliwan's feet. All the while, Pamela has her eyes on me. 'I find it very strange that a young girl should be out here all alone,' she says. 'In these troubled times.'

Without saying a thing, I decide to return to Steve's car. I don't run because I can't quite believe that I'm in any real danger yet, and the thought of running still feels faintly embarrassing. So, I walk away briskly, as if I have somewhere important to be. In fact, I look at my wrist, although I'm not wearing a watch.

There's a trampling of feet and then Dolph is beside me, his hand on my arm. His grip isn't tight, and he can't look me in the eye, but the feel of him against my skin is enough to make me freeze.

'Just wait a minute,' he says.

'You are the terrorists after all,' I whisper, although it doesn't quite feel true.

'No, no, honestly we're not.' He shakes his head and stares at the ground.

'She doesn't know anything,' Maliwan is saying to Pamela. 'We should let her go.'

'She knows everything. She came out here to trap you. Let her leave, and the police will come for you today. She's a journalist. Didn't she tell you that? Never trust a journalist.'

'What should we do?' Maliwan asks, putting her hands up to her face.

Dolph flinches, like he wants to go to his girlfriend's side, and I take this opportunity to pull away and start to run. I run fast enough to send shockwaves through my knees and up my thighs, making for the trees in shoes that suddenly feel far too big and I know they will make me fall. Who comes out to the jungle in footwear so flimsy? The danger is real now; it's a sharp tingling in my blood.

But I'm headed in the wrong direction. The sound of the river is growing louder and I think the car must be somewhere behind me. I look back and see Dolph in pursuit, his mouth open and his hair bouncing. He's slow, not really trying, and I know that I can outrun him. Perhaps I can loop back towards the car, and surely I'll bump into Steve along the way.

But then I hear the dirt bike start up. This is as fast as I can go; I'm already running like a hunted animal, diving under branches and jumping over thorns and rocks. My only hope is to get into thicker vegetation, but the problem is that by changing course towards the car I've ended up running through just a thin patch of trees.

The bike catches up with me. Pamela looks across and smiles. I feel the burning air around the vehicle, a wind like a predator's breath. And then I catch my feet on something and begin to fall. A dead tree looms up; a big one with holes in it. I have time to think: *Maybe I can climb inside that and hide.* But then I hit the ground, smack my skull against the tree, and the chase is over.

# Chapter Twenty-Nine

I hear a voice. I feel motion. A single moment stretches forever like a dream, and then I become aware that I'm lying inside a moving vehicle, my face pressed against the seat. I'll throw up if I open my eyes.

'Are you awake?' The voice again; a young female voice, Thai accent and an edge of panic.

I try to speak but it comes out in a whisper; the sort of noise someone very elderly would make. I open my eyes, swallow away the nausea, and try again. 'Yes.'

Maliwan looks back from the driving seat. Her eyes are wide, and red at the edges. I remember her in a rush, and I remember the fear. But this is Steve's car; I'm lying on his back seat, so everything must be all right after all. I try to sit up. But I can't move. My wrists are trapped beneath my body. Looking towards my feet, I see blue string wrapped around my ankles. My shoes are gone. Seeing my toes, bleeding and impossibly far away, I feel sick again and shut my eyes tight.

'She wants to kill you,' Maliwan says in a rush. 'So you have to run as soon as we get there, okay? I have my knife, so when we stop I'll cut you free. You need to run fast. You understand? She'll chase you.'

'No, I don't understand! Who is she? What's she doing?'

'She's my boss's wife.'

'She is? What is she doing?' I croak.

'She's helping us.'

'With what? She's not helping me. You bombed Main Street? All of you did it? Why?'

'No, not that. She came in after I hit him. I thought he was hurt. I didn't know he was dead. But she's helping me now. I think she hates him even more than I do. I just wish I hadn't told her about the baby.'

So, this small, pregnant woman killed Bernard Shuttleworth. Steve and I solved that case. It doesn't seem to matter anymore. My tongue feels thick in my mouth.

'Where is Steve?' I manage to say. 'My friend.'

'We never saw him again. But she doesn't know about him, so that is good. She thinks it's just you. We didn't tell her, okay? We both think you seem like nice people. And we're nice people too.'

'But why does she want to kill me? Who does she think I am?'

'You're a witness,' Maliwan says, answering both questions.

'Where is she? Please, can't you just drop me off somewhere? I'm not going to tell anyone you did it. I'm really only interested in the bomber. This is all a mistake.'

'They're right behind us, on that bike. She wanted Dolph with her. I think she's trying to keep us apart. She trusts no one.'

'Okay,' I say, attempting to free my hands by twisting against the rope. 'Where are we going? She won't really kill me, will she? You won't let her?'

'I'm not a murderer! Bernie wasn't meant to die, and I'm not going to kill you. I don't even know you.'

I nod and then I'm nearly sick. I can taste it in my throat. I could use a trip to the toilet too. I might wet myself, actually. This realisation, one that would usually horrify, feels completely unexceptional.

'We're going to the Emerald Lake,' Maliwan is saying. 'You know it? The big hole? She says we can push the car over the edge. Me and Dolph have to do it but it's her idea.'

'Where will I be?' I ask, although I already know.

'You stay in the car.'

I've been to the Emerald Lake before. It's a deep bowl of water in the middle of the forest. Waterfalls drop from it and feed out over the island. It's beautiful. It's going to swallow me. I strain against the ropes.

'We're nearly there,' Maliwan says, 'so get ready, okay?'

I grind my teeth against the seat. I can smell Steve's cigarette smoke in the fabric. I recall a local story about a monster living in the lake; a giant octopus with lots of eyes, who stays coiled in the rocky depths, swallowing any swimmers who dive too deep.

'Help,' I say, too quietly for anyone to hear.

'You must run to the right. There's a cliff in the other direction.'

I can hear the dirt bike. I say, talking too quickly for my words to form: 'Does she have a gun or something? Why are you doing what she tells you?'

'We have to do it this way. We must surprise her. I have to think about my baby.'

'Please don't let her kill me.' I'm remembering my parents, their sweetness, and how they will change if they hear that their daughter is lost after all, after surviving the bomb.

'You have to run,' Maliwan says.

'Can you give me your knife?'

But Maliwan doesn't hear this because the dirt bike has drawn alongside us and the woman, Pamela Shuttleworth, is shouting something. Maliwan slams on the brakes and I roll off the seat so that I'm trapped on the floor, my face against the dirty carpet. I spy a chocolate wrapper under the driver's seat. Steve's favourite kind. I wish he was here.

'Shit,' Maliwan says, scrambling to get out of the car. 'I'm sorry. I didn't mean to stop like that. I never learnt to drive.'

I'm struggling to get up, writhing like a worm. The door beside me opens and Maliwan is there.

'Leave her,' Pamela barks. 'She'll only try talking to you.'

I'm able to see outside by craning my neck, although it causes the blood to pound in my head until it feels like my eyes might burst. The older woman darts forward to grab the car door. Her face is pinched and wet with sweat. I've never seen anger like this; it makes me stay quiet.

'I know you told the police to come for me,' Pamela hisses. 'Did you hatch a plan to trap me while you were stinking up the back of my car? When I was kind enough to drive you home? You understand nothing about this situation. Do you not suppose this island has enough death on its plate, without you feeding it more?'

Pamela slams the door and something falls onto the carpet. Maliwan's knife. Sticking out my tongue, I manage to touch the blade and taste the metal. The others are talking together, but they must have stepped away because their voices are too muffled to be understood. It's mainly Dolph shrieking and Pamela speaking low and hard.

'You're not really going to kill me, are you? I don't know what you mean about the police. I'm looking for the terrorists, that's all.' There's something funny about my voice. I clear my throat but it turns to retching. By the time I've controlled this and spat out a horrible pool of saliva, the car has started to roll forwards and I realise that they really are pushing me towards the cliff. I can hear their feet moving, and the tyres crunching over loose rocks. Nothing else. No talking. I feel like the rest of my life never happened. All there has ever been is this moment, and although it will be over soon and I'll probably be dead, I think this fear will exist forever in some form. This must be how ghosts are made.

'Hey,' I shout in that strange voice. 'Please, don't do this! Please!'

There's arguing outside.

'We can't,' Dolph and Maliwan say.

The car stops.

I sob in a way that I have never heard myself sob before. It scares me back into silence.

'You're choosing a stranger over your own child. I can't say I understand that, but then I've never been a parent, have I?' Pamela Shuttleworth, or someone else, hits the side of the car, hard.

The door opens beside my head and Maliwan gets in, fumbling on the floor for the knife.

'Yes, that's right,' Pamela is saying, 'you may as well cut her free. It doesn't matter now.'

Maliwan lets out a little cry as the door slams shut and hits her elbow. But then she begins sawing at the knots around my wrists.

Someone gets into the front of the car and begins rifling through the glove compartment, which I know is full of Steve's snacks, books and spare batteries. The rope snaps from around my wrists and I spring up, knocking against Maliwan. It's Dolph in the passenger seat, his hands full of junk which he is flinging all over the car as he searches for something, panting hard.

'Thank you,' I whisper, as Maliwan begins cutting my ankles free too. I can barely breathe in this hot, dirty car.

The door beside Dolph swings shut. He looks through the window in surprise, to where Pamela is standing, her hand on the door. She's so small, but looks like she could kill us all with just her fingers.

'Find it,' Pamela says through the half open window, 'otherwise we'll have to rethink the situation.'

'What are you looking for?' I ask, much more loudly than I mean to. I have the knife now, although I don't remember taking it from Maliwan, and I'm hacking at the rope around my ankles.

'Your Dictaphone. Where is it?' Dolph says, peering over the top of the seat. He looks like a gargoyle.

'I don't use one.'

'She says you have one and there's stuff on it can incriminate us all.'

I shake my head, and that's when the car begins to move again. Turning, I see Pamela looking at us, partly blocked by Steve's animal charity stickers in the back window. Her jaw is taut as she pushes, but her eyes are light, moving up to the sky. Dolph and Maliwan go to open their doors but they're too slow, and the car begins to fall with the doors flapping like broken wings. My terror is interrupted by a clear memory of being at the summit of a rollercoaster with my dad when I was about seven years old, his hand on my arm, and my big blue duffel coat rising up around my throat as we began to fall. And now I'm hitting my head against the roof of the car, and the vehicle is diving. The water looks hard like crystal. I'm aware of the air screaming past my head, and of Maliwan screaming too. She has a baby inside her.

'Jump out!' Dolph shouts.

But there isn't time. The water's here.

# Chapter Thirty

When I open my eyes, everything is grey. Thrashing about, I hit metal and what might be someone's flesh. My legs are still strapped together like a mermaid's tail. I kick and kick until something breaks and I'm free. There's a crushing pressure all around me. The car moves, getting sucked down to where the octopus lives. Where are the others? I flip as if an electric current is going through me. I should take off my duffel coat, it's weighing me down. Reaching, I realise that there's nothing around me anymore; no cage of a car. I swim towards where the faintest of lights is rippling.

And then, suddenly, I'm on the rocks, washed up like a piece of rubbish brought in by the tide. I lie on my side for the longest of times, feeling heat from the sun-baked rocks and hearing water drip from my body.

I become aware of someone shouting nearby. At first the sound is neither male nor female. It is nonsense in my ears, but then it takes shape. A man's voice: 'Maliwan, Maliwan!' He screams over and over.

I turn my head slowly, frightened that it will just fall right off my neck. Now I'm able to look out at the water, and can see more than just the grey rocks, and the lines on them like lines on an old man's hand. Dolph breaks from the surface of the lake.

'Maliwan, Maliwan!' he screams, and then he's gone again, back beneath the water.

This scene loops and plays out for a while. I watch him surface, scream, and go under. Each time he disappears I feel certain that he won't come up again, but then he does.

I push with my hands and knees until I can sit awkwardly on the rocks. My mind is clearing and a fresh, uneasy feeling washes over me. I beckon Dolph over, waving my arms, but he goes under once again.

'She's dead,' I whisper, clenching my fists.

Ripples fade and the water is still. I remain motionless while the mosquitoes circle me. I hear them whining but there's a noise in my head too, a hissing like water through a pipe. When Dolph's dark head appears once more, a little closer to shore this time, I struggle to stand, pain shooting through my limbs.

'Come here! Over here!' I shout, and then fall, legs everywhere, back onto the rocks. Fresh pain hits me. Something might be broken somewhere; it's hard to tell where each stab is coming from.

He climbs out of the lake, water dripping from his body and turning the stones black. He doesn't look at me. He puts his hands up to shield his eyes and scan the opposite shore.

'Maliwan!' His voice is a scratchy gasp. Blood trails from gashes on his face and arms and then drips toward the ground. Drops bead on his fingertips. His hair is hanging around his face like tentacles. His skin is a pale shade of blue.

'We need to go,' I say, slowly and carefully forming each word through lips that are suddenly shaking. 'What if she comes back? What if she tries to kill us again?'

I look at the cliffs and at the dense trees all around. Pamela could be anywhere. She could be on her way down to us right now. I feel so weak; she could tip me off these rocks and I would drown slowly in the shallows, looking up at her through the water and the searing sunlight.

'We need to go,' I say again, over the sound of his breathing. I hate looking at the lake.

'No, we can't. She's still out there. We've got to find her.'

'Maliwan? But…' I feel sick, hearing how his words catch in his throat. Doesn't he realise that his girlfriend must be dead? And the baby too.

'Why couldn't you have just given her the Dictaphone?' Dolph still doesn't look at me.

'There is no Dictaphone. She made that up to get you into the car.'

He shakes his head. 'She was trying to help us.'

'I don't think so.'

'No,' Dolph moans. He scrambles back into the lake, the water seeming to reach up for him. 'Maliwan! Maliwan!'

'Don't!' If he goes back in now, he'll never set foot on land again. I'm sure of it. I grab for him but miss completely. And then I slip; my legs go into the water, where pebbles move beneath my feet. Clawing at the rocks, I press my face against them, certain that I'm going to drown after all. All of this happens slowly, like in the cruellest of nightmares.

'I have to keep looking,' Dolph says, his back to me. Either his voice is slurred or my ears are not working properly.

I watch him wade away. Grit is caught in my mouth and eyes. The water is just lapping at my shoulders, but still I feel like it's in my throat, moving towards my lungs. I can't breathe.

'We need to run,' I whisper, the words barely coming out. I look over my shoulder, certain that Pamela Shuttleworth will be here by now, crossing the rocks with a shovel to smash my head, or a knife to pierce my skin.

Dolph stops. He's unsteady, thrashing like he's in a strong current, although there is barely any current at all.

'Hide. We have to hide,' I manage to say, and he comes to me, sinking beneath the surface a couple of heart-stopping times. Together we manage to inch out of the water and back onto the rocks. We keep going, crawling on our hands and knees, and make it to the dusty ground at the edge of the lake, where tourists used to have picnics in happier times.

I know it must be hot here because insects are buzzing and the light makes me half blind, but I'm shivering all the same. Dolph is shaking too. We stare at each other and I watch tears and lake water peel down his face.

'We've got to run,' I say.

'Run.' He nods. 'Now.'

He grabs my hand and we go.

# Chapter Thirty-One

'She was pregnant,' Dolph says, filling the silence that's been hanging between us. He's ahead of me, scrabbling over rocks like he has no feeling in the soles of his feet. His shoes are at the bottom of the lake. His clothes are drying in stiff folds, his hair in spikes. He won't stop moving. He doesn't look at me as he speaks.

'I know.' I struggle to talk, can't catch my breath. I don't trust Dolph, but I feel like we've been bound together, and even if he does turn out to be a murderer or terrorist we will always be the twin survivors of this horrible thing. I need to stay with him for now but I don't want to get too close, so I hang back, feeling like a half tamed animal or neglected child.

'You know? How can you know?' Dolph does look at me now, the question written all over his face; open mouth, wide eyes. If I saw this in a still photograph I'd think that he was screaming.

'She told me. We talked, remember?'

'What else did she tell you?'

'That she killed him.' This is like being drunk; I don't care what I say. Not too much.

'Oh, that.' Dolph stumbles and slides towards the turquoise water. He manages to right himself and continues on, even faster than before. I stay with him. He says: 'I suppose it doesn't matter now, if you know about that.'

'I don't know why she did it though,' I say, but he doesn't reply.

We're following a path around the lake, well-worn by tourists, which dips and rises, sometimes taking us along lips of cliff twenty-feet above the water. We're doing this because Dolph insists Maliwan must be here somewhere. This is our third time circling the lake. I'm hot, heavy and have been stooping to drink from rock-pools. I keep getting this feeling that a third person is with us, and I look over my shoulder expecting to see Maliwan, Steve or, for some reason, my own father. Every time we hear a noise from the bushes we crouch down, put our hands over our mouths and stare at each other, waiting to see if Pamela Shuttleworth is going to reappear and try to hurt us.

Suddenly Dolph stops and squints at the lake, his hands clutching the top of his head, fingers grinding. I wait beside him, breathing hard. This walk has become a sort of hell; eternal and painful. And this is the worst place I have ever been. I feel like the moist trees, the rocks, the water, are hiding a million vicious creatures; fairies with sharp teeth, watching and laughing. It feels worse here than it does at the bomb site. I don't know why. Perhaps it's because this place is nature, and nature is what we are, the blood inside us, and the things that come out of us when we're torn apart.

'She's not here,' I say, because this is it; I can't go on. 'We're not going to find her. And probably not Steve either. I know something horrible's happened to him. It must have done or he'd be here.'

'What? What did you say about Maliwan?'

'You know she's still in the car.'

His eyes twitch and he rubs at his neck, where dirt is caught in creases of skin, and I see that he does know. Tears pool in my eyes; hot enough to burn their lids.

'But what else is there to do?' he says, raising his arms and then dropping them again. 'I don't know what to do, except look for her. She's all I've got. There's nothing else.'

I sit down on a rock, feeling blood rush through my body in a wave, leaving sickness behind it. A bright green bird lands on a branch above my head, and I watch it preen itself, little bits of dust floating from its body towards the ground. Dolph comes to sit beside me. I can smell him; roasted skin, sweat and blood.

'I could be wrong,' I say, although I know I'm not.

Dolph shakes his head and then spits at the ground. 'Sorry,' he says, wiping blood from his lip.

'It's okay.'

'Fuck Pamela,' he says.

'What were you doing out here with her? If Maliwan killed her husband, why were the three of you even together?'

'She said she wanted to help us. But she must have been planning to kill us the whole time. I never wanted to be around her. I knew it was a bad idea but Maliwan trusted her. More than she trusted me. I mean, she trusts me but she thinks I'm an idiot. I wanted to leave the island and never come back. That would have been the right thing to do, wouldn't it?'

'That would probably have worked out better for you,' I agree. 'Did this all happen because he thought you bombed Main Street?'

'No. I never even realised he thought that. It happened because Maliwan was trying to quit her job. Because of the way he was treating her. She told me about it and I persuaded her to leave. We had a whole speech planned. But then he laughed at her and she hit him. I can't talk about it. Oh, God. She can't be dead. She was just here. I can still hear her voice.' He stares hard at the ground.

'I'm sorry.' I mean it, but the words sound like nothing.

'Where do you think she is?' Dolph says after a pause.

'Maliwan? Well, I'm not really sure I believe in heaven, but...'

'No,' Dolph scowls, 'I mean Pamela.'

I'm finding it very difficult to think; my brain wants to shut down. Sleep is on my mind, mainly. And sweet drinks, something with lemon in it, and lots of fizz. Trying to focus, I say: 'Maybe she thinks we're dead. Maybe she's on her way home now.'

'I want to find her. I need to.'

I say: 'If I saw her right now, I think I could kill her.' This is true. Above all the other muddled thoughts and pictures, I see my own hands around that old woman's neck, squeezing and pressing. My vision becomes clear for a moment, and the trees, rocks and water jump out to me, crisp and real.

Dolph says: 'I could definitely kill her. I want to, in fact. That's what I'm going to do. I don't care what happens afterwards.'

The bird flies away and I struggle to breathe for a long moment, willing my throat to open. Dolph doesn't notice. I whisper: 'Shall we try and make it back to town?'

'I guess. I guess it's time. But let's follow the river, okay? Maybe Mal got washed downstream somewhere. I bet that could have happened. We have to keep looking. She would never abandon me. Never ever.'

'Okay.' I'm not sure we'll reach town. I don't know exactly how it'll happen, but I'm going to die soon. I'll help Dolph first though, if I can. And I need to make sure the bomber's caught. The bomber is the most important thing. But if that's really the case, why do I only see Pamela Shuttleworth's face each time I blink?

'Watch out for green. The colour. Remember, Maliwan's top was green?' Dolph says.

'Okay, sure.' I glance around at the greenery we're surrounded by; leaves and tree trunks, lizards and birds. I try to get up but find that I can't. My legs are useless. Accepting this, I prepare to lie down, but Dolph grabs my arm and pulls me to my toes. And then we stumble away, towards where the river falls from the lake in a rush of vapour and miniature rainbows.

# Chapter Thirty-Two

It's as I crack my toes against a rock and swear beneath my breath, that I realise I'm all alone here on the path. I sag against the nearest tree and peer through the gloom, feeling moisture bleed from leaves and onto my skin, making various grazes sting. Moonlight hits patches of river where rocks poke out like teeth. Condensation hangs in the air, insects cry and flit from every corner and my own ragged breath hangs loudly over it all. There's no one else here.

'Dolph?' I call, uncertain of how long it's been since we last spoke. If it turns out that he never existed, was never out here with me at all, like how it happens sometimes at the end of movies, I won't be surprised.

There's no reply. None of the dark shapes move. I'm really on my own.

'Shit,' I whisper, and wrap my arms around the tree, which smells like rot and like something from my childhood. I wish Steve was here. If I make it back to town, I'm going to have to find Kadesadayurat and tell him how stupid I've been, how I've put everyone in danger and now a pregnant woman is dead. And then he'll have to come out here with dogs and helicopters and a good first aid kit, and he'll bring Steve home. I'm trying so hard to believe that's possible.

'Dolph?' I call again, louder, reminding me of how his voice sounded when he was in the lake screaming for his girlfriend. I don't want to think of that; it makes something bubble down there, deep in my throat.

Nothing. Perhaps he fell into the water. Perhaps Pamela has been following us all along, and has snatched him off the path.

Perhaps I ought not to shout, in case she comes for me too. Is she out there? I bet she can see in the dark with those little, lizard eyes.

I'm close to running away, but instead I start back the way I came, moving over the rocks, which are sharp in places, slimy in others. Dolph could easily have fallen. How long is it since I saw him last? It could have been seconds or hours. Time has become meaningless since the moment Steve's car tipped off the cliff.

My feet hit something soft and I trip, palms smacking the ground.

'Huh?' Dolph's voice says. 'Did I fall asleep?'

I can see him now; the glint of his eyes and the darkness of his downturned mouth. I crouch beside him. 'Are you okay?'

'I just sat down for a moment. I was thinking about her and it got too much. I just needed a second and then I guess, I don't know, I just passed out. And then I was dreaming about her.'

From the heaviness of my own body, I say: 'We need to find somewhere to rest, don't we? This is it for today.'

'Here.'

'Not here.'

'Not another temple. We spent three nights there and it's the worst place I've ever been. It was Pamela's idea for us to stay there. She said it would be one night, that's all, and she would make all our problems go away and we could come home. It was so dark and so cold. Bats were hanging upside down off the ceilings. Maliwan didn't even flinch but I was so scared. And we had to try and sleep in a tiny little stone room, thousands of years old and so black, like oil.'

I'm trying to properly make out his face in the darkness, so that he's more than just a broken voice washing into my ears above the roar of the river, but then I hear something else. An engine. Cold ripples pass over my skin. I choke on my own breath. 'What is that?'

'A car. It could be *her*.'

'We must be near the track,' I say.

'Shush.' Dolph grabs hold of my shoulder and holds on tight. I can feel him trembling. It makes me start to shake too.

'This way,' I whisper. 'Let's go see. Come on.'

'I need to find a way to kill her. I would have liked more time to prepare. It's so dark out here.' He tries to close his hands into fists but can't seem to do it.

Together, we rise to our feet and move through tangled plants towards the noise, our feet slipping, insects and webs brushing our faces. Somehow we have ended up holding hands again. This has happened a few times during the walk. The second I realise this I want to let go, but can't because he's gripping so tight. It begins to hurt; I can feel it in my bones. And then there are headlights dancing over the thin trees, and I see Dolph's face like a skull. I freeze, shake his hand out of mine, and watch as he continues towards the road, sidling like a maimed crab through the leaves.

'Stop!' I hiss.

'Why?'

'Danger! It's dangerous. Hide!'

'No, no. It's dangerous for her. *Her!*'

I drag him back down amongst the scratchy bushes. He's still trying to pull away when the vehicle appears; a car slightly larger than Steve's.

'You won't be able to do anything to her right now,' I whisper. 'We're too weak. Look at the state of us. We need to get back into town and sleep and eat and come up with a plan. If we go out there now, she'll really kill us. I know she will.'

The car stops right in front of us. The engine cuts out and the insects become impossibly loud, but not loud enough to cover Dolph's breathing, which is coming out in whistles and whines.

'Shit,' Dolph squeaks, pressing himself into the ground. 'That's a police car.'

'Oh, thank God,' I say, and start to get up. 'Maybe Steve's with them. Steve!'

But then my face is flat upon the dirt, and Dolph's full weight is on my back. I feel his knees sharp against my legs, and his hot, wet breath on my neck. I try to scream but just get a mouth full of mud, grit against my teeth. I struggle to turn my head and he presses a hand to my face, smothering my voice and making it hard to breathe.

I see a door open and a dark figure steps out of the car. A pulse beats hard all through my body, out of time with Dolph's heart which is beating against me, even faster than my own. I can feel the trembling of his body through my clothes.

Something is said in Thai, and then a torch comes on in the man's hand, the light flickering at first but then strong like a pouring liquid, sweeping over the plants and through the trees.

# Chapter Thirty-Three

As insects crawl across the side of my face and mud works its way up my nose, I try to understand what the man with the torch is shouting to other men inside the car. I can't get it; my Thai is less than basic. But there is a tone to their voices which makes Dolph wriggle even deeper into the muck, forcing me down with him.

When the man walks a couple of feet into the undergrowth and kicks at a tree, Dolph's whole body jolts and tightens around me. The man coughs, then he returns to the car and they rumble away.

Dolph springs off me and then sits on the ground in a heap, crushing his hands beneath his knees to keep them still. He can barely speak.

'They're looking for me,' he says. 'Whatever it was that made you and your friend come out here, has made them come out here too. And, just like you, they'll be certain that I've done something terrible. And I haven't. You know that? I haven't done a thing.'

'I could have gone out there alone,' I say in a flat sort of voice. 'You could have let me go.'

'You would have told them I was here. You still think I'm the bomber, don't you? I'll turn myself in for the murder once I've killed Pamela. And I'll take the blame for the bomb too if you want, if that will help anyone. What else is there to do? I'll never go back to work. It would be better just to die.'

The sound of the vehicle fades and we just sit for a while, staring wordlessly towards where the empty road lies invisible in the darkness.

'I hope Steve was in that car,' I say. 'I hope he's safe.'

'He'll be fine. You'll be fine too. You'll see,' Dolph says.

I don't say anything. I rest my chin on my knees and try to calculate the hours until dawn, trying to work out if I can make it. I stare towards Dolph; the energy that I need in order to hate him fizzes and sparks inside me but can't quite catch alight. I think that he is starting to fall asleep, but then he gasps and snaps his head up from where it had wilted towards his chest.

'You were lying to us before, when you said his body was on the beach, weren't you?' he says. 'I'm starting to think maybe I can't trust you. Are you even really a journalist? I know nothing about you.'

'Yes, I am and we really saw it.'

'It can't have been him. It must have been someone else.'

'It was definitely him. Definitely,' I say, close to furious that Dolph can be distrustful of me when he is the one who has been hiding in the jungle for ill-defined reasons.

'I just don't understand that.'

'Why not?' I demand.

'His wife buried it. She buried the body out here somewhere.'

'Did you make her do it? Is that why she was so angry at you?'

'No! She wanted to do it. Honestly, this was all her. She was ordering us about the whole time. And now I keep thinking about how close she was to me; I could see those tiny blue diamonds in her ears, and I could have reached over and pulled them out through the fucking flesh.'

'What do you mean it was all her?' I say, loudly, because he seems to be drifting away into a deep state of muttering and ripping up weeds from the ground.

'Maliwan killed him by mistake. She hit him and then, I don't know, he fell badly, I guess. And then his wife just sort of took over.'

'I don't understand why she would do that,' I say, staring at him. He's just a shape in the darkness; a slightly different shade of black.

'She really didn't mind that he was dead. She was maybe even pleased. How can I explain it? These last few days it's been like going down a tunnel, the tunnel getting tighter, the light growing smaller at the end of it and the tunnel smells like death.'

'You're talking like you have a fever,' I say. 'You should sleep.'

'She wanted to help us. She knew about ... well ... about how her husband was. And once she started helping she wouldn't stop helping. So, it was like it was her thing, not our thing, and we were just along for the ride, doing whatever she told us to.'

'I've heard things about him.'

'I didn't know a thing about it. I had no idea until Mal told me. She got drunk and she told me. I didn't know what he was doing to her. I should have been able to tell. You must think I'm stupid.'

'No. People can hide things.'

'She was eighteen when she started working there. And he was doing *that* with her pretty much from the start. And that's why she hit him. She shouldn't even have been there that morning. She'd quit the day before but had to go back for something. She wanted to ask him something. He fell down and was bleeding everywhere. We didn't even know Pamela was there. She's in the States most of the time. I think, if she hadn't been there, we would have phoned the police ourselves and told them what we'd done. Running just seems stupid. It never works.'

'You're really not a terrorist, are you?'

'No, I told you.'

'Me and Steve have accidentally been chasing the wrong story. We thought we were hot on the heels of a terrorist. We went off in completely the wrong direction. It's all my fault.'

'Well, you can't write about this.'

'I wouldn't know where to start,' I say.

We sit in silence a while longer, the crickets picking up volume around us. He's not a terrorist but he is something.

'I just don't know why he would have ended up on the beach,' Dolph says after a while, his voice muffled like he maybe has his head in his hands.

'Did you actually see her bury him?'

'No. Maliwan wasn't feeling well so we were sitting down for a while. I guess Pamela dragged him off somewhere. I didn't look. I didn't want to see. But she said that she buried him. I saw her holding a shovel at one point.'

'When you find her, you can ask her,' I say.

'Yeah. I guess so. I'm not so bothered about that though. I really just want to hurt her for what she did to Mal. And the baby. Oh, God, the baby. She's taken everything from me.'

'I really am sorry,' I whisper into my knees. I can hear him snuffling.

'I hate her so much. I wish I could go back in time.'

'What were the three of you doing last night?' I ask then. 'We saw her, you know, she gave me and my friend a lift into town. We didn't know who she was.'

'Last night? She wasn't around last night. We didn't see her. She'd just arranged to meet us today with some supplies. We were all alone.'

178

'But she was out here,' I say. 'And you don't know anything about the bike either? You don't know who was shouting?'

'No, no,' Dolph says, rocking backwards and forwards. 'Please, stop with the questions for a bit, will you? I don't want to think about all this. I just need to rest. I need to close my eyes a while.'

I nod slowly. 'Come on, we should find somewhere to shelter. It's not good here.'

We struggle to our feet and step into the road where the car has left deep tracks in the mud. We go the same way, our feet slipping in and out of the grooves.

# Chapter Thirty-Four

I wake up in all kinds of pain. Opening my eyes, I find that ugly flowers have bloomed around us while we slept. I don't try to move yet. Dolph is pressed against me, his arm wrapped around my waist. We were cold last night. It's funny that I don't mind lying this way, when usually I hate to even shake hands. It's like how I can hold a spider in my palms when I'm drunk. Dolph probably thinks he's holding his dead girlfriend.

That thought gets me moving. I sit up, rubbing my arms back to life. They're damp, soft to the touch like playdough, and covered with insect bites. Dolph doesn't stir. What if he's died in his sleep? But his chest is moving as he breathes. His face is like milk and his eyelids are a heavy shade of purple.

We've spent the night beneath a huge tree, nestled between its roots like characters from a fairy tale. We're not far from one of the temples; a big one that tourists like to visit. Last night, I planned on leading us to the temple to sleep but we only made it this far. Dolph had started muttering things I couldn't understand and my legs finally gave out completely, sending me to the ground so that I cut my knees on top of the grazes already there. He dragged me beneath this tree and I slept the darkest sleep I've ever slept.

I need to eat something. It makes me dizzy to lift my hand to my face. I'm afraid to look down at my body because I know it is damaged, and I think that to see the cuts, the ground up toenails, lumps and holes, will only make them hurt more. I decide not to wake Dolph. I'll come back for him after I visit the temple. It can't be far away; we walked into a sign for it last night.

I'm going there because I've remembered that people live around here; some of the poorest islanders, who make a little money selling things to tourists. We forgot about that last night. Perhaps I can find someone and ask for help. We need help at this point; I don't think we can make it on our own. Maybe someone will give us food or water, or give us a lift into town.

Stumbling through a clearing, I see the temple not far away; crooked towers and damaged walls. When I came here before, with Lena, children ran over to ask us for money. Now I'm here alone, limping and trying not to fall.

People live in huts to the side of this main approach. I move that way but it's too quiet, even for this time of the morning. And sure enough, there's nothing here but a row of shacks, all abandoned and partially dismantled. I go inside each one. All I find is a bottle of whiskey, half empty and with greasy fingerprints all over it. The liquid is exactly the right colour to be piss but I unscrew the top, sniff and sip. It is whiskey; just watered down. I drink it in scratchy gulps as I walk back to Dolph. It starts to warm me a little, but it makes me sick too. All of a sudden I need to pee, and I step into the trees to squat there, holding onto rough branches so that I don't fall.

Something rustles to my left. Too large and noisy to be a bird. I stand and straighten my clothes. There's a rustling again. It could be the wind or a monkey, but I run back towards Dolph, twisting my head like an owl to check if I'm being chased, tripping over my own feet and practically sobbing with the fear of it.

Dolph wakes as I approach him. He sits up in a rush and looks around, his fingers clawing the ground. I see his face change as he remembers where he is and what he's doing. He waves at me and then puts his head in his hands.

'I think I heard someone,' I pant, passing him the whiskey. I feel drunk already. I felt drunk before I started drinking.

Dolph puts the bottle to his lips. He doesn't grimace at the taste like I do.

'No one's here,' he says, looking past me at the empty track.

'I think we should get moving. What if she's out here looking for us?'

'Okay,' he says, his voice barely there. 'You all right?'

'I don't know.'

'Well, how do you feel?'

'I feel like I'm really old. My body doesn't work anymore. I want some pancakes and a bath.'

'Is that what old people do in England?' he asks, without any real interest.

'What? No, it's just what I'd like to do.'

'I'd like to drink a gallon of coffee. And bacon. To eat.'

'Bacon would be good.' I nod. Dolph isn't really thinking about food. The expression on his face does not match his words. His eyes flicker. In a clumsy rush, I say: 'I'm so sorry about Maliwan. Really, I am.'

'We should start moving.' He gets slowly to his feet. 'Think you can make it?'

'I hope so,' I say, with a sickly grin. I start walking, moving like a spindly insect. He's just as clumsy beside me. I expect we look quite amusing, struggling down the track like this in our ripped clothes. Amusing or horrifying, I'm not sure which. I start to think about Steve, but shut the thought off before it can grow. I'm glad of all the practice I've had at pushing horrible ideas away. I'll keep them at bay until I get back to Steve's house, but if he's not there, then I will let all the thoughts in, every single awful last one of them.

'You should maybe see a doctor when we get back,' Dolph says then.

'I would think they're all busy,' I say, 'tending to people's burns and blown off limbs.'

'I've got a guy. He's a doctor and a landscape painter. My parents know him, vaguely. I could set you up with him.'

'No, thank you,' I say, something about this suggestion makes my bare toes curl, and I step a little further away from Dolph. 'Why don't you go see him?'

'No, I don't care about me anymore,' he says, and I see his lower lip crack and begin to bleed.

'Okay, well, I'll be fine. Don't worry about me either,' I say. I nearly shut up, but then I add: 'I mean, just yesterday you were on the verge of murdering me. So, I'll not take your concern too seriously.'

'But I didn't murder you, did I? Isn't that what counts? And I've apologised for that, haven't I? Didn't I say sorry to you yesterday?'

'I'm not sure you did, no. Just forget about it.'

'But I am sorry. I am. We were never really going to do it.'

'Okay.' I shrug. He stares at me with wet eyes, so I give him a nod, just to round off the conversation.

Dolph's mouth moves for a moment and then he clears his throat to say: 'You owe me an apology too, you know. Pamela only went really insane after you turned up. I think, perhaps, if you hadn't come out looking for us, Maliwan would still be alive.'

I stare at him for a moment, his face going in and out of focus. 'She was going to kill you both anyway,' I say, but I'm not sure of this at all. My cheeks go cold and my vision fades out for a second, white stars flashing inside my eyeballs. I try to blink the haze away and stumble through a pothole that I can't quite see.

'She didn't have to die like that,' Dolph is saying. 'Maybe if things had happened another way, I would have been able to save her.'

I nod and let him blame me, feeling the blame deep inside.

We walk on, passing the warm bottle between us. I keep my eyes on the horizon and will buildings to appear there. We keep to the edge of the track so that we'll be able to dive quickly into the trees if we hear anyone coming.

'I'm going to find her today,' Dolph says, his words coming out slowly.

'What will you do after that?'

'Kill her, I guess.'

I believe him. 'We should try her hotel. We'll find Steve first, and then we'll all go together.'

'You don't have to help me,' he says.

'I do. You're right about this being my fault. Partly, at least. I'll help you find her.'

# Chapter Thirty-Five

Somehow, we've reached Steve's pale pink house. One of the neighbours have their radio tuned to what sounds like a sports channel, although we can't understand the commentary; the radio, an old fashioned one with crackling speakers, is propped on a window ledge of the building next door. Children are playing further down the street. I can hear them very loudly as I put a hand against the front door to steady myself; it's like they're beating a ball against the inside of my head. My knees shake. We're this close to the house, but I still might not make it. Just behind me, Dolph is biting on his fingers and looking up and down the road.

'You say this is your boyfriend's place?'

'No. My boss. You met him, remember?'

'Oh, shit, yeah. I'm sorry.'

I need Steve to be on the other side of this door. If he's not here, I'm going to be forced to imagine all of the terrible things that could have happened to him, and I'm going to fall apart completely. I don't even have a key for the front door, but usually Steve leaves it unlocked. I try it now. It opens with a click. The radio next door erupts in cheers.

The living room is filled with sunshine. This place is so nice; I don't want to soil it with my grime and hateful thoughts. The patchwork quilt which I've been sleeping under has been left carefully folded on the couch. I stare at it, and will Steve to enter the room, to burst out of his bedroom. He doesn't. Behind me, Dolph slams the door. I want to scream at him to leave, to take his pain elsewhere.

'He's not here,' I say. 'We've left him behind.'

'Anything to eat?' Dolph asks, his face just centimetres from the back of my head; I can feel his breath shifting my hair against my neck.

I slap at my neck as if there's a spider there, and we go to the fridge and lean into it, devouring things from their packets, tearing with our fingers, spilling food down our chins. The cold air makes a pulse beat inside my bruises. We eat like this for minutes, our bodies making little noises, and then our eyes meet and we start to laugh. We laugh hard enough for my stomach to turn, and I shuffle away to stick my head into the sink, staring at the row of cacti there on the window ledge, and the dead flies behind them. Out in the yard, that stray cat is sunning itself. Flies are out there too, hovering over the animal. At least flies won't get to Maliwan's body, I think out of nowhere.

'Are you okay?' Dolph asks, struggling to stop the laughter. His face is wet.

'I don't even know what's funny.'

'Nothing's funny. We're losing our minds.'

The sickness passes and I flop down on the couch.

'I need to go back to the temples and look for Steve,' I say, trying to keep some momentum going. It would be so easy to lie down and stay down for a million years. How will I get out there? I'll have to hire a car or a moped, and I should find a weapon. Someone on this island will be selling guns if I ask around in the right places. I don't know how to use a gun but there'll be a YouTube video for that.

'You don't want to sleep a while?' Dolph says, interrupting my thoughts.

'No, I can't sleep. You can sleep a while if you want. You can have this couch. It's comfy.'

'I'm going to look for Pamela.' Dolph is leaning against the sink, staring at his toes. There's mud on the floor around him. I'm sure we brought it in with us.

I'm trying to think of a way to say goodbye to him when the front door opens, sending a delicate shaft of daylight across the grubby carpet and into my face, dust hanging in the light like glitter, and my face warm like someone's holding a match against it. For a moment, I can't focus on the figures moving through the doorway, but as they stagger towards me they take shape and I see that Steve is here, holding Maliwan upright on her feet.

# Chapter Thirty-Six

'We were so close to getting picked up by the police. They drove right by in that same car we'd seen earlier, do you remember, Lucy? They didn't spot us; it was so dark and we hid at first in case it was Mrs Shuttleworth. When we realised it was the police we jumped out and started waving. At that point, we really didn't care about getting arrested or explaining what the hell we were doing out there. We just wanted to get somewhere safe. They did stop and shine a torch around but we couldn't get to them in time before they drove on. I guess they didn't hear us shouting over the noise of the river. I really thought we were going to die at that point. We just gave up and stayed right where we were at the side of the road. I didn't sleep all night.' Steve looks at Maliwan and says: 'I was watching to make sure you didn't stop breathing.'

Maliwan, who is curled around Dolph on the couch, smiles at Steve. Dolph and I share a look but don't say anything.

'And then we walked all the way back here, certain that the two of you must have died. The longest walk of my life. I need a fucking vacation now, if I didn't already.'

'How did you two find each other?' I ask. I'm sitting on a striped deckchair which Steve has produced from a cupboard. It's covered with a fine layer of sand, my feet don't touch the floor and I'm trying not to fall asleep as I sink into its folds.

'I went back to the temple and he was waiting there.' Maliwan shrugs.

'We didn't see you. I was diving and diving. You can't even swim,' Dolph says. He laces his fingers around hers and holds on tight.

'I just popped out of the car when it hit the water. I was okay. I hurt everywhere but I'm okay.' She looks down at her body like she still can't believe that it's intact. Then she remembers something and pushes a hand into her pocket, pulling out the knife. She holds it flat in her palm so we all can see it. 'I got this back. It fell into my hand as I was coming out of the car. I went straight back up to the cliff so that I could stab Pamela with it. She'd just tried to kill us all. She tried to kill my baby. I thought she had killed both of you. But she was gone already. I didn't know what to do so I went back to the temple.'

'I got lost,' Steve admits. 'I heard a motorbike and shouting so I knew there must be some kind of a problem. But I was too slow getting back. I had trouble even finding the trail. You got knocked out, Lucy?'

'Yeah, but I'm okay. And you made it back here,' I say. 'That's the main thing.'

'Barely. What a fucking witch,' Steve spits. 'Pamela Shuttleworth. What the hell was she doing? Maliwan says she was trying to help in some way but I don't see that at all. You know it's horribly bad for you to be knocked unconscious. We need to get you to a doctor.'

'There's something I should tell you all,' Dolph says. He was resting his cheek on the top of Maliwan's head but he raises his head now, brushing her hair smooth with his hand.

We all look at him and wait for him to speak. He takes a while to manage it, the shape of his mouth changing as he considers which word to use first. Eventually, he says: 'After Lucy blacked out, Pamela told Maliwan to tie her up, and...'

'I didn't want to,' Maliwan cuts in. 'She told me I had to. I tried not to do it tight.'

'While you were doing that,' Dolph continues, 'Pamela was talking to me. She said that if we went to the police and confessed to everything, she'd make sure the baby was always looked after, and she'd give us all the money we ever needed.'

'But you *did* do everything,' I say. 'She didn't kill her husband, Maliwan did. Why would she need to pay you, and why did she even want you to do that after she'd taken the trouble to bring you out to the temples to hide?'

'That's kind of what I said. But she laughed and said that things were more complicated than I realised. And then she said that we were going to have to kill you too, and we'd have to tell the police we'd done that. I said no. She said we didn't have a choice about killing you, but we did have a choice about what happened afterwards.'

'We still might go to prison,' Maliwan says. 'And now we'll have no money for the baby.'

'I have money. My family has more money than the Shuttleworths. I keep telling you that.'

'But I don't want to take your money. I take money from the men I don't like, not from you.'

Dolph stares at her for a moment, grinding his teeth, but then he snaps his gaze back to me, and keeps talking: 'Anyway, I keep thinking about it. When we had his body in the trunk, it sounded like it was moving around. We figured it was just the road. The road was bumpy. And then when we were staying at the temple, we thought that we could hear ghosts wailing.'

'They were ghosts.' Maliwan nods.

'No, what if it was him? And, as well,' he says, looking at me, 'you said you heard shouting and someone stole your bike. And then his body turned up on the beach. That couldn't have happened, could it, if he was buried.'

'He wasn't dead when you took him out there,' I say, suddenly understanding. 'She killed him out there, or let him die. How badly hurt was he?'

'A lot of blood,' Maliwan says. 'I hit him with one of those, what are they called, the horse head.'

'A bookend,' Dolph says. 'A metal one.'

'And when did this happen?' Steve asks.

'Friday. The morning after the bomb went off.'

'I quit the day before,' Maliwan explains. 'But I was very worried about my mum, because I give her most of my money and there was a month I hadn't been paid for yet. I knew he wasn't going to give it to me. And then I heard he was going away for a while because of the explosion, so that really meant I would never get it. I thought if we went back to the resort and if I told him about the baby he would give me the money. But he just laughed at me and said awful things.'

'Like what?' Dolph says.

'It doesn't matter.'

'Weren't you there?' I say. 'I thought you were there.'

'I was waiting outside the room. She thought I'd put her off while she was talking to him. Then she came out and she had blood all over her. I thought he'd hurt her but actually she'd hurt him.'

'And then Pamela was there,' Maliwan says. 'I didn't even know she was on the island. She only comes here once a year and usually none of us even see her. But she wasn't upset at all.'

'She didn't even look surprised,' Dolph agrees. 'She had us wrap him up in all this plastic sheeting. His feet stuck out the end of it with white socks on and blood on the toes. There was blood all over the floor. So much of it. I never thought for a second that he wasn't dead.'

'Jesus,' Steve says.

'And she didn't even introduce herself. I had to try and work out who she was. She had on tons of expensive looking jewellery but her hair was messed up across her forehead, all sweaty. She looked like someone coming out of a party in the early hours, all dishevelled. She reminded me of the people who visit my parents' apartment each weekend. They're always drinking and snarling at each other.'

'So, she suggested burying the body out in the forest?' Steve asks. 'Didn't you think that was strange? Didn't you wonder why she was helping you?'

'Sure,' Dolph says. 'It was really strange. But the whole situation was, and I sort of just did what she said. She had a way of speaking that made us take notice. And we were so scared. We didn't know what to do. It was easy to just follow someone else's instructions, at first anyway.'

'What were you doing at the Imperial Hotel when I saw you?' I ask. 'Was that right before it all happened?'

'No, that was just *after* it all happened. I was supposed to check out that day anyway. I didn't want to just disappear and leave all our stuff there. I still owed a bit on the bill. That would have been suspicious, wouldn't it? So, yeah, we drove straight there afterwards. I've never driven so fast in my whole life. The roads were quiet, so it didn't matter. Oh, but then I hit a monkey. I got out to look and blood was trickling from its ears. It died. Its fingers curled up into fists, like how spiders' legs are when you find them dead in a corner.'

'I hate the monkeys,' Maliwan says. 'People say that *he* brought them here, so who cares?'

'I carried it to the side of the road. It was warm, and the weight of a child.'

'That's horrible. Don't say that,' Maliwan frowns at him.

'You must have driven past me,' I say. 'I was on that road. Wait, was he in the boot of your car when it was parked at the hotel?'

'Yes.' Dolph nods. 'And Maliwan was curled up on the backseat but you probably couldn't see her. When you came out shouting my name I thought perhaps you knew everything, like his arm had come loose and was hanging out the back of the car. I didn't know who you were but you had this look on your face like you were onto us.'

'Oh, I didn't know anything. And I'm still not sure of much now. I'd just finished talking to him. I said goodbye and then you guys arrived, smashed him round the head, packaged him in plastic and got back to the Imperial Hotel before I arrived there. He was waiting there for me.'

'What happened to your car?' Steve asks. 'You dumped it in town.'

'Yeah.' Dolph nods. 'She agreed to let us come into town so we could pick up some supplies. We just went to the little shop by the beach because everything was chaos in the centre, with the bomb going off and all. But once we had our stuff she said we had to leave the car. She drove us back out and left us there.'

'To make it harder for you to escape,' Steve says.

'I guess. And we didn't buy anywhere near enough food. We'd run out by the next day. I tried to catch a bat but it was too fast.'

'She's asleep,' Steve says, nodding towards Maliwan, who has collapsed against Dolph's chest. 'I think I might do the same, just for an hour or so. This is a lot to process and I'm not quite at my best.'

We let Dolph and Maliwan have the couch, and I share Steve's bed, sleeping right along the edge wrapped in a sleeping bag. I'm immediately too hot but don't have the strength to escape from it. I think about how, when we wake up, we're going to have to start investigating the bombing on Main Street all over again. We're right back where we started. I close my eyes tight and picture the road outside my hostel, trying to focus on it hard enough that the flames lick my skin, trying to find a clue somewhere in the scene. I fall asleep and dream of it.

# Chapter Thirty-Seven

Maliwan's had a shower and is wearing some of my clothes, which are slightly too large for her. She keeps grabbing the waist of the shorts to pull them back up. We're crouched together beside the bag which I stuffed full of my belongings when I crept back into the horror of my hostel bedroom. I'm looking for a hairbrush amongst the bundled-up clothes, loose charging cables and dog-eared books.

'I had one. I don't know, maybe I didn't pack it. I actually haven't brushed my hair for a while, now that I think about it.'

'It's okay. I can just tie it back,' Maliwan says.

I sit cross-legged on the floor and watch as she pulls her hair tightly into a ponytail. She looks better now that she's slept and washed, and I can see, beneath the vest top that I've lent to her, the smallest dome of a baby bump.

'How are you feeling?' I ask, looking from the bump to her face.

She knows what I mean straight away. 'I don't have pain anymore.' She shrugs.

'That's good.'

'Is it?' she says. 'I don't feel anything at all now. I just feel empty.'

'You've been through a lot. You'll be okay when things have calmed down,' I suggest, hearing my own lack of conviction clear with each word.

'When will they calm down?' Maliwan laughs, without any mirth.

'I'm going for my shower,' I say. We all woke up from our naps feeling an urgent need to wash, and agreed that Maliwan should go first, followed by myself. Steve and Dolph are waiting out in the courtyard, smoking and not talking to each other.

'I really do feel empty,' Maliwan says, looking hard into my eyes as I stand up. 'I don't think there's a baby in there anymore.'

'Have you had any bleeding?' I ask, having trouble getting the last word out. I think of my own bleeding, last year, and how it had felt like a loss and a gain all at once.

'No.'

'Then it must still be in there.'

'She. Not it,' Maliwan says, gently resting a hand on her stomach.

As I'm gathering fresh clothes and a slightly damp towel from my bag, Steve crumples out his cigarette against the back wall, tosses it towards an overturned watering can and comes inside.

'Twice in one week I've thought you were dead,' he says to me. He pulls me into a hug, my arms already full of things so that I have to just stand there and let him envelop me. I drop a bottle of shampoo onto my foot.

'It's been a bad one,' I manage to say, my face pressed against his shirt which smells of cigarettes and the forest.

'We need to start being a bit more careful,' he says. 'Will you come with me to see Kadesadayurat this afternoon? I've texted him. He's actually in his office for once.'

'We probably should talk to him about everything that's gone on.' I nod. 'But what about them?'

We both look outside to where Maliwan is standing beside Dolph, resting her head on his shoulder and watching as he blows smoke up towards the blue sky and the ragged pigeons on the roof.

'I think we need to find a way of omitting them from the story. Don't you?' Steve says.

'I feel like that too.'

'In the interest of being more careful,' Steve says slowly, 'I'm wondering if maybe we should cease our investigations for a bit. We can hand everything over to Kadesadayurat and let him deal with Mrs Shuttleworth. She shouldn't be too hard to find, an old woman charging around the jungle on a motorbike. And I've completely lost my way when it comes to the bombing. Perhaps we're better off just observing and reporting. Investigative journalism isn't really our thing.'

'But we *are* good at it,' I say. 'Look what we've uncovered. Murder on a luxury resort. We unravelled it all.'

'But we didn't mean to. We stumbled upon that completely by accident.'

'I think we've done really well,' I say, in a quiet voice.

'We have,' Steve agrees. 'But we've made some fairly poor decisions along the way too.'

Steve showers last because he's the only one who doesn't mind if there's no hot water left. He tells Dolph, who has exited the bathroom in Steve's purple dressing gown, that he can borrow some clothes. I watch as Dolph sifts through the contents of a lopsided wardrobe. He fingers the bright material and drags the hangars back and forth across the rail, making a screeching noise against the metal. The sound makes me shiver and I want to push him so that he disappears into the depths of the wardrobe, beyond the shoeboxes and the mounds of ties and belts. Steve's never invited me in here before, but somehow the ordeal that we've all been through together has broken down barriers, and Maliwan is lounging on Steve's bed, painting her toes with some turquoise nail varnish that she found in my bag. Still, I feel like an intruder and I try not to look around, keeping my eyes on the back of Dolph's head, although I would very much like to explore this room just as Steve, I know, would like to ask me questions about why I came to the island.

The shirt Dolph picks out has a setting sun on the back, and the jeans are far too big for him, bunching up strangely. He looks homeless and insane. I'd be wary of him if we passed in the street.

'Do we have a plan?' Maliwan asks, without looking up from her toes.

Dolph finishes buttoning up the shirt and then stares at her, while chewing on his lips. Despite having his girlfriend back by his side, he's still as frightened as he was when we first met him in the forest, I think. More frightened perhaps, because he has something to live for again. I can see fear in the way he tugs at his hair before speaking. He says: 'I think the most important thing is for you to rest. The baby…'

'I can't rest until I know we're safe,' Maliwan interrupts. 'And we won't be safe until we find Pamela. She might try to kill us again. Or she might go to the police and tell them stories about us. They will probably believe her. She's a rich woman and a good liar.'

'We can leave,' Dolph says. 'Come to New York with me.'

Maliwan smiles. 'You're dreaming. I can't leave for a million reasons. What about my mother? And you really want to go back to your family? You are sad every time you talk about them. No. We have to find Pamela. Okay? We have to.'

'Well, I just don't know where to look,' Dolph says, shrugging so that the long sleeves of his shirt flap about.

'She never usually stays at the resort,' Maliwan says. 'I don't think she can stand it there. She just comes for business. She'll sell it now that he's dead, I bet.'

'I think she's staying at the Grand Hotel,' I say, suddenly remembering. But then I remember about our appointment with Kadesadayurat. 'We can look for her there. But Steve and I need to do some work this afternoon for the newspaper. What if we wait and go to the hotel in the morning? It's getting sort of late now, anyway. Dolph's right; you really should rest.'

They look at each other, and then Dolph says: 'Yeah, but the thing is, we don't know how much time we've got. We don't know if maybe she's trying to leave the country. The police might be looking for us already. It's like Maliwan said; Pamela might even have gone to the police herself with a story about us.'

'They would believe her over us.' Maliwan nods.

Dolph looks at her. 'I want you to feel safe. I'm going to make sure we find her, okay? I'll make this right.'

She smiles at him and wriggles her freshly painted toes. I watch something in Dolph's face harden, like he's found a new source of strength as he meets her eyes.

'One night,' I say. 'It'll give us more time to plan. If she's gone to the police then you really ought to stay hidden for now anyway, don't you think?'

Eventually they nod and agree, but I see that they don't like it.

# Chapter Thirty-Eight

'Let's go, then,' I say, my voice catching in my throat.

Steve has been waiting at the open front door while I finish lacing my trainers. The soles of my feet are shredded from the walk back to town; I've put on a thick pair of fluffy, pink socks but now my feet are burning up, which just makes them hurt more.

Standing in the shower gave me some energy back, but the water also made my injuries feel raw. I've discovered grazes and bumps on my skin that I hadn't seen before. Maliwan is curiously unscathed but the same happened to Dolph after his shower; a cut on his cheek has opened up again, bleeding slowly. He rubs at it with the back of his hand, notices blood on his knuckles and licks it off. He's sitting on the couch, reading the latest copy of the *Koh Star*.

'I didn't realise quite how bad it was,' he says, holding up a page of photographs for Maliwan to see. I've already looked at them many times, but still I feel a shiver as I catch a glimpse now.

'We should go there,' Maliwan says. 'It won't feel real until we see it for ourselves. And I need to visit my mother, to tell her I'm okay. She must be very worried.'

I glance at Steve but then I remember that he doesn't know I visited Maliwan's mother's house. No one does. I stay quiet.

'We'll be able to do all that,' Dolph says. 'I think things will get better soon, won't they?'

No one responds to this, and Dolph doesn't look like he really believes it. He stares back down at the newspaper and doesn't turn on from the page showing Main Street and the people suffering there.

'We'll see you guys later,' Steve says to them. 'Help yourselves to whatever. But stay here and stay safe.'

Outside, we stand in the heat, looking up and down the road. Teenagers are sitting on mopeds beside the shop, drinking from bottles. A dog is barking at nothing, spinning in slow circles. It's astonishing to step outside Steve's house and find a certain normality, flowing along as usual.

Of course, we have no car, so we walk to the police station. I develop a way of turning my feet onto their sides so that they don't hurt too badly as I walk on them. Steve manages to roll a cigarette as we move.

'I'm sorry about your car,' I say, as he lights his cigarette with a zippo we found under the couch earlier. 'I'll help you buy a new one.'

'Oh, I don't give a fuck about the car. It's just a thing.'

'It was a nice thing though,' I say.

'Actually, I saw an advert online for a van. I've always quite liked the idea of owning a van.'

'Yeah, think of all the stuff we could put in the back of it,' I say, although I can't think of a single thing and, actually, can barely even keep my thoughts on the van; I look down a side street and think about how I could go that way and be on Main Street in ten minutes. I'll have to go back there soon, before the idea of seeing it becomes too powerfully awful.

'I was online just now, while you were getting ready,' Steve continues, 'and I was scrolling through some photographs on the *New York Times* website. Photos of this island, I mean. The aftermath of the attack. I actually spotted myself in the background of one, speaking to a shell-shocked backpacker in shorts and a bikini top, not far from the bombsite. I remember her. She had a boy's phone number written on her arm in marker pen. She'd no idea what had happened to him, and tried describing him to me, her voice going up and down, her words round and round. I listened, gave her a cigarette and offered to help, but she wandered away while I was still speaking. I'll never know what happened to her. Or the boy.'

'Pamela Shuttleworth couldn't have cared less about the bomb, could she?' I say.

'Oh no, I think she probably considered it a welcome distraction while she got on with her own evil.'

'What are we going to tell Kadesadayurat?'

'Let's find out what he has to say, first of all. And then, I was thinking that you could tell him everything up to the point where Dolph appeared at that temple. So, he can know about Pamela driving you and Lena back that night, and even about the bike going missing and the shouting that you heard.'

'I hope she gets arrested. Even if we've got it wrong and she didn't do anything to her husband, she tried to kill us. Something has to happen to her.'

'She's rich though. She's very rich. I'll bet she's not even on the island anymore, actually.'

'You think she's going to get away with it all?' I say.

Steve shrugs and throws his cigarette into the gutter. 'Let's see what Kadesadayurat says.'

A bird cries mournfully from a roof above our heads. I try to picture what kind it might be, but can only imagine something black and vulture-like, which is not a bird I've ever seen around here; possibly not even a real type of bird at all. 'Okay,' I say. 'Actually, it's going to be a relief to hand this all over to someone.'

The police station, when we reach it, is even busier than the last time we visited. There are journalists waiting in the lobby, talking together in various languages and drinking from plastic cups. People with pale faces and bandages are sitting around the room, backpacks piled beside them. One woman is asleep, leaning against a potted plant. There are two policemen talking on phones behind the reception desk. They recognise us and buzz us through the door which leads to the corridor that Kadesadayurat's office is situated on. Kadesadayurat shares the office with two other officers; it's nearly as small as our own one, and is filled with files, computer monitors, over-flowing waste bins and busy wall charts. It smells, usually, of damp and coffee.

The corridor is packed with people, and we don't make it as far as the office.

'There he is,' Steve says, pointing. Kadesadayurat is standing beside a water cooler.

We wave to him but he doesn't see us, and begins moving towards a door with a neon exit sign above it.

'Kadesadayurat!' Steve shouts, and we run along the corridor, knocking past people and hopping around chairs and filing cabinets. The noise in here is enormous, but Kadesadayurat somehow hears his name being called over the ringing phones, the shouting, and the sounds of faxes coming through on ancient machines. We catch up with him beside a rainbow-striped notice board.

Kadesadayurat nods a greeting to us and crunches on a mint, which I can smell. The police officer is wearing his uniform but missing his hat. Rumpled and sweaty, he looks like he hasn't slept for a while. He's our only real police contact, and has been supplying small pieces of information to the *Koh Star* for a few years now; a mid-ranking officer somewhere in his thirties, he occasionally drinks with Steve and tries unsuccessfully to flirt with me. He always appears to be happy, even when talking about something horrible; a dog drowning in a sewage pipe, his daughter's eczema, a bomb that killed people. He's smiling even now. But he's not happy, of course.

'How are you guys doing?' he says loudly over all the noise, squeezing us each on the shoulder. He doesn't wait for a response. 'Sorry, I've been busy. No time to speak to you. You see Bernard Shuttleworth yesterday? You get my text? I was going to phone you but I was too busy.'

'We saw him.' Steve nods.

'It looks like he was hit by a car. That's what killed him. He'd been beaten first though. Actually, we think he'd been tortured for a couple of days.'

'Oh shit,' Steve says. 'And who do you think did it?'

'His wife. We been out in the jungle, looking for her.'

'You haven't found her?' I say.

'Not yet, but we will.'

'What makes you think that it was her?' Steve asks.

Kadesadayurat stops smiling and takes another mint from his pocket. 'We found some things in her car. We found things *on* her car. Dents and blood. We found things out in the temple that we know came from the golf resort. Tools. Knives from the kitchen there.'

'She tortured him?' I say, remembering what Dolph said about the wailing.

'You blame her? He did not treat his wife with respect,' Kadesadayurat says.

'I guess.' Steve nods, but his face has gone a shade of yellow and I see him swallow, like he's trying not to be sick. I feel that way too; I can suddenly taste the food that I gobbled from the fridge earlier; bad and greasy.

'I hope you find her,' I say.

'We'll find her today.' Kadesadayurat sticks a mint between his teeth, crushes it, and begins to move away down the corridor.

'Wait, wait!' Steve grabs for Kadesadayurat's elbow before he can be absorbed into the mass of arguing, jabbing, rushing people.

'What is it, Steve?'

'Do you have any news about the bomb? Do we still not know who was behind it? We've heard nothing at all.'

'Perhaps, my friend, but I can't tell you,' Kadesadayurat says, smiling again.

'Good news?'

'Perhaps.'

'Really?' Steve says.

'Not yet, but soon.' He winks.

I can hardly bring myself to wonder what he means. I'm afraid that the police know nothing at all, and that the person or people behind the bomb will never be found. Kadesadayurat's mobile phone begins to chirp in his pocket.

'Excuse me,' he says, answering it and turning slightly away from us, talking in Thai at great speed, so that even Steve can't understand him.

I cross my arms and lean against the notice board, getting gently jostled as people pass by. I stare at the stains on the floor and don't bother trying to follow the phone conversation. I think about Bernard Shuttleworth chipping golf balls over the wall at his home, sharing a drink of lemonade with me, and then dying horribly and slowly while I ran around in circles, achieving very little.

'We maybe have good news sooner than I expected,' Kadesadayurat says, spinning around to face us as he puts the phone away in his pocket. He squeezes Steve's arm and then mine, staring into my eyes, our noses almost touching. 'They've made an arrest in Australia.'

'Who?' I ask.

Kadesadayurat laughs, running his hands through his hair and beaming up at the ceiling where a light is flickering. 'I can't tell you that. And don't print anything yet or put anything on that funky website you're always updating. I'm just telling you both because I am your friend, that is all, okay?'

'Okay,' Steve says, smiling but looking bewildered all the same. 'This is good news though, right? Actual good news?'

Several cheers go up around the building, the good news spreading.

'I can't tell you yet. Steve, I must go. We'll talk later.'

'But what about the Shuttleworths?' I say, feeling a spark of panic, my face suddenly hot with sweat. 'People will still look for her, won't they?'

Kadesadayurat doesn't answer. He moves through the crowd, sharing smiles and handshakes. The noise in the building has changed now; an elated roar. Even the ringing of the phones seems less shrill.

We go back outside, where some of the food stalls have returned to the square and there is a smell of smoke and meat. It's as if these people can sense that an arrest has been made, and normality is struggling back to the streets. Steve lights a cigarette and stares up at the sky where there are no clouds and, although it's getting late, the sun is still ferocious.

'Do you think they just arrested the bomber?' I say.

Steve exhales and shrugs his shoulders. 'I have no clue. But God, I hope so.'

# Chapter Thirty-Nine

That evening, Steve cooks up a batch of white, faintly slimy oven chips which we all share from a large blue bowl. The four of us have squeezed onto the sofa. Dolph and Maliwan are curled together beneath the patchwork quilt that I've been sleeping under since the bomb went off. Steve has his laptop propped up on the arm of the sofa. He's scrolling his way through Twitter, shaking his head and occasionally typing with jabbing fingers. I'm squashed between them, resigned to having my leg pressed against Steve's on one side, and Maliwan's feet practically in my lap. I'm trying to watch a black and white Cary Grant film on Steve's small TV while the clicking keyboard and the soft sound of kissing goes on around me.

'This is old. I don't like it,' Maliwan says.

'It's good if you give it a chance,' Dolph says. 'Really funny.'

'Is this the one with the leopard?' Steve asks, looking up from his laptop for a moment.

'Yes, and Katharine Hepburn too. It's honestly very good,' Dolph says. He picked it out for us to watch from a pile of DVDs beside the television. Steve's sister sends DVDs to him occasionally, packaged up with bubble wrap and American comfort food.

'We should go to the rental place, get something new,' Maliwan suggests.

Dolph looks at her. 'You must rest.'

'It's not even nine yet. It's early.'

'Aren't you tired?' he asks her. 'You must be.'

'Very tired. But I don't think I can sleep. My head.'

'Mine too,' I say. My thoughts won't lie still. When I close my eyes, I see flashing lights and unhappy faces. More than anything I want to know what is happening in Australia, but the news is silent and Kadesadayurat hasn't sent us any updates.

We've told Dolph and Maliwan about our conversation with Kadesadayurat. We're cautiously hopeful that the fates of the Shuttleworths will soon be resolved, and that Dolph, Maliwan and their baby will not have to be involved. But we don't know. And not knowing has made all of us restless.

'I want to see the bombsite,' Maliwan says, out of nowhere. She, more than any of us, is struggling with the knowledge that life is carrying on outside while we stay huddled inside this little house, frightened and unsure what to do next.

'Not tonight,' Dolph says. Then he mumbles: 'Maybe not ever.'

'Were you in town when it happened?' I ask them. We haven't spoken about this yet and it feels important to know this part of their story.

'No, we were at our hotel, lying on the bed. I'd been staying there for a couple of weeks so that we could get some privacy. I share a house with four other guys and they're always in and out of my room. And Maliwan doesn't like the bathroom there.'

'Very dirty,' she says.

'Did you hear it?' I ask. 'The bomb?'

'Yeah. Maliwan was looking through photographs on my iPad; an old album from back in college. I was trying to answer her questions about why I used to style my hair that way, who those girls were in my car, and what kind of seal that was exactly. And then we heard the explosion.'

'So loud,' Maliwan says.

'Loud enough to make the windows shake. And then afterwards, when it all went quiet again, everything in the room seemed different somehow. The power didn't go out immediately but then it did and when Maliwan grabbed my hand I could feel her shaking.'

'Did you realise that it was a bomb?' Steve asks.

'We guessed it was. We went down to the dining room and all the guests were gathering down there. No one actually said it but I think we were all scared that there was going to be a follow up; another bomb or men with machine guns. You never know, do you? You hear about that shit all the time now. Everyone thinks the worst.'

'It didn't used to be this bad, did it?' I say.

'The world has always been this way,' Steve says. 'Just it used to happen in places you've never heard of.'

'It feels worse when it happens in a place you know, doesn't it?' Dolph says. 'We stayed in the dining room all night, wrapped in our blankets. The power came on just before dawn and the manager served breakfast. None of the usual waiting staff were there. And it was weird how everything had changed; the air was flat and the piano music, filtered in the same as always, somehow couldn't reach our ears; it sank to the carpet and hung there like a fog. Do you know what I mean?'

'I think so,' I say. Dolph has a weird way of describing things, usually horrible things, but he does it well.

'All we could hear was the muttering about how many people had died, which terrorist group was responsible and then just the screeching of chairs as people got up to leave forever. And a news channel was on, playing on a TV above the bar. There wasn't any sound so we were just staring at pictures of Main Street, destroyed from different camera angles. People were stepping around puddles of blood. I phoned my parents to tell them I was all right. It hadn't occurred to them that I wouldn't be. My mother actually laughed and said they know I don't spend my time in bars.'

'That's horrible,' I say. I can't even remember what I said to my parents when I phoned them that night. I just remember how hollow my voice sounded, like something had fallen out of me as I left the hostel.

'I started crying after breakfast and then I couldn't stop,' Maliwan says. 'I never cry usually.'

'It was hard not to cry. There was such a weird atmosphere,' Dolph tells us. 'These elderly European ladies who were drinking at the bar gave us some tissues. They'd been glaring at us just the night before. There's a look I often get when we're together; like people think I've bought my girlfriend. It's funny, because in fact she's refused all the money I've ever offered. Haven't you?'

'I don't want your money,' she says. 'I've told you this.'

'And then we went to the golf resort, to try and get her pay sorted. The rest you know.'

'I don't like remembering this,' Maliwan says. 'I don't like talking about it. Let's go out.'

'We can't. Not yet,' Dolph says.

'I guess Lucy and I could go to the DVD rental place,' Steve says. 'And we'll pass by the Grand Hotel; just a little look. What do you think, Lucy?'

'Yeah.' I nod, agreeing only because I think Pamela Shuttleworth will be far away from the hotel by this point; if the police can't find her it's unlikely that we will. I don't think I want to see her again. I'm able to replay her voice inside my head, and it makes me shiver, makes my stomach feel tight. I'm terrified of her.

'I like action movies,' Maliwan tells us. She wriggles her toes and I feel them grinding against my thigh. I find myself wishing that they would all just shut up.

'Maybe comedy would be better though, don't you think?' Dolph says, oblivious to the speed of my heart. 'I don't want to see any violence right now, really.'

So, we hand the bowl of chips over to Dolph and Maliwan, who spread themselves out on the sofa, their fingers entwined. Maliwan tries to give me her knife as we're leaving. She tells me to put it up the sleeve of my cardigan.

'In case you see *her*,' she says.

'No, I'm not taking that,' I say.

'Then I'll come with you.'

'No,' Dolph says, a little too loudly. He still has hold of her hand and he pulls her down into the cushions beside him. Maliwan frowns but stays put.

'We won't be long,' Steve says.

The second we step outside I feel like we've made a mistake. The darkness is thick and there's a sour taste in the air. A smell of smoke puts us on edge but we decide that it's the sort of smoke that comes from a bonfire, like people often used to have on the beach.

'That's good, isn't it,' Steve says, 'if they've started doing the bonfires again?'

But nothing feels good as we walk beneath neon signs, no stars in the sky. The bars are quiet but there are some people in them, and the beat of the music gets sucked up through our feet like metal to a magnet, while the hum of anxious conversations floats from the courtyards and from people sat in the darkness at benches, eating hot, sticky food, animals creeping out of the shadows to grab leftovers, large insects clinging to the buildings, lit by streetlights and the headlights of passing vehicles.

'Of course, the video store is near to the bombsite,' Steve says, clearing his throat.

'I know.' I've already thought of this. The store is just off Main Street. It's a little place with a sloping roof; it gets so low that you have to duck at one side of the room where they keep the Kungfu movies. They sell Asian sweets behind the counter and big boxes of beers from sticky refrigerators. I used to like going there after work and then watching films on the flickering TV in the communal room at my hostel, while lizards climbed across the ceiling and a beer grew warm in my hands.

'We won't see her,' I say. 'Will we?'

'No,' Steve says, but he doesn't sound sure. I want to go back to the house but I stay silent. Another part of me needs to see what happens next. I feel my tired heart start to beat harder and faster.

Silently, we walk across town, avoiding eye contact with the people we pass. The video store, where we reach it, is closed and dark.

'Shall we?' Steve says, nodding towards Main Street.

'I guess.'

We come out roughly halfway between the Grand Hotel and the bombsite, and everything seems abruptly quieter and darker. Only a week ago, this place would have been busy with mopeds, tourists and backpackers, laughter and music. We're beside a scuba school office, which is closed, litter piled up by its front door like no one has been in or out for days.

Not far away, the wreckage from the bomb is sitting inside a wreath of flowers. We can faintly see shapes moving, people looking at the hole in the ground, and at the burned tarmac around it. Occasionally we see a camera flash, but the buildings around the crater are all unlit.

'They've put up barriers,' Steve says. 'Makes it looks worse somehow.'

There is a chemical scent in the air, and an underlying odour of soot, quite different to the bonfire smoke that we smelled earlier.

'Let's go to the hotel,' I say. We've come this far.

# Chapter Forty

'Do you think Pamela realises she's wanted by the police?' I ask, as we get closer to the hotel; red awning out the front, spiky plants in pots and a stray dog lying in the gutter, licking itself.

'Yes, that'll be why she was so desperate to have someone else confess for her,' Steve says. 'And I would assume she's aware that they have her car. That'll be why she was riding the little motorbike. It didn't seem to fit with her character.'

'What do you think she'll do if she is here and she spots us?' I say. We're standing across the street from the hotel now, staring at the building and its dark rows of windows.

'She'll try to hurt us,' Steve says with certainty. He presses his forehead with the palm of his hand. I can see him sweating, even through the darkness. My stomach makes a little flip and there's a burning in my throat. I remember how it felt to wake up in the back of Steve's car, certain that I was about to die.

'She won't be here though,' I say. 'She'll be gone by now. She's probably on a flight back to America.'

'Maybe,' he says. 'But I think, maybe not. I believe she's a woman on a mission. I think there are things she wants to do here.'

'She seemed crazy. Maybe she wouldn't have the sense to flee. So, shall we just go inside and ask about her?'

'Why don't we go in there and have a drink,' Steve says. 'They have a really nice bar. They probably wouldn't let us in, usually, dressed like this. But I imagine they're not being too picky at the moment, with most tourists having fled to safer destinations.'

'Okay,' I say, trying to keep my voice from shaking.

We cross the quiet street, the gutter dog raising its head to look at us and then resuming its grooming.

'Don't worry, Mrs Shuttleworth will be long gone from the hotel. She'll be hiding somewhere. Maybe in one of the temples. This is safe for us. Nothing's going to happen. And doesn't it feel a little bit better to be out of the house, doing something?' Steve says, but there is a tremor in his voice too.

'I don't know,' I say. Actually, being near to my hostel and seeing the place where this all began, has got me feeling like we're being chased, and like I need to keep looking over my shoulder. How does Steve know that this is safe? It might not be.

We pass through the revolving glass doors and the air conditioning dries my flushed face. There's a gentle drone of conversation beneath the sound of clinking glasses and jazz music. I can see through to the bar, where a television is playing Sky News, and people are drinking at tables. People bled in here the other night. I wonder if that man, the one sipping a martini beside the tropical fish tank, knows that a girl was shaking right where he's standing. She was missing some of her fingers and staring very quietly at the exact same Japanese Fighting Fish he's looking at.

A man is working behind the reception desk. He has a large, bald head, and is tapping on a keyboard.

'Let's get some drinks,' Steve says.

'I'll catch up with you.'

I watch Steve walk away and then I wander towards reception, my eyes on the man behind it. I'm going to ask him if she's here, just flat-out ask him, because I have to know. But I lose my nerve at the last minute, stopping beside a stand advertising off-shore scuba diving. I pick up a leaflet and stare at it.

And then, all around me, people's phones begin to ring. News crews gather like flocking birds and move towards the door. This must be where they all have been staying. Vans pull up outside. I catch snippets of conversation as people rush by.

'Was at his own address in Melbourne, cocky bastard.'

'I know where we can find the parents.'

The leaflet falls out of my hands and I complete my journey to the reception desk where I try to get the man's attention. He's watching as his guests leave in a flurry of elbows and smart phones.

'What's going on?' I ask, leaning across the desk to meet his eyes.

'I'm not sure,' he says, and then does a double take at my face. I suppose the horrors of the last few days can be seen there, in my pale skin and my unsteady eyes, my dried-up lips and the scrapes and bruises. There's a lump beneath my hair, hard like an elbow, where I fell when Pamela Shuttleworth was chasing me on that bike. The man says: 'Are you okay? Are you staying here?'

'I was actually staying here for a bit after the bomb. Just one night.'

'Oh, I see,' he says in a respectful little whisper.

I look at the people hurrying past. 'Have they caught the bomber? Is that what they're saying?'

'I think so.'

I still can't quite believe that it could be possible. The bomb was such an evil thing that I find it hard to accept a person, a real human person, was behind it. Surely it had to have been a monster of some kind. I whisper, like the crazy person I'm becoming: 'But people *are* monsters.'

Steve is approaching from across the lobby, holding two brightly coloured cocktails.

'What do you know Pamela Shuttleworth? She was staying here,' I ask the man.

'Oh, yes. I checked her in. They think she killed her husband, the old man who owns the golf resort. He turned up dead yesterday and they think she did it. Shocking stuff.'

'Was it only yesterday? Where do you think she could be now?' I have to clamp my fingers around the edge of the desk to keep them from shaking.

'I don't think anyone knows. The police came here to see her. They took her car. She stole a moped or something from one of the porters. No one knows where she went.'

'Try one of these,' Steve is suddenly saying very loudly into my ear. 'They're called Fear Cobras.'

I look sideways at the frothy, purple goo in the glass he's holding towards my face and realise that I need to get outside immediately. Time has snapped like an elastic band, and it's the middle of that night again. I was standing right here, people were bleeding and crying all around me, and I didn't know if another bomb was going to go off. I trip through the doors and out onto the pavement. My lungs feel like they're filled with sand as I suck on the hot air and stare hard at chewing gum stains and discarded cigarettes on the pavement.

A young woman is beside me, dressed in neat khaki shorts and a vest top that somehow manages to look expensive. She's fiddling with a bulky camera and looking up every so often at the vehicles passing by. I can tell she's a journalist before I even notice the ID badge around her neck.

'Have they arrested the bomber?' I say, shuffling to her side and putting one of my grazed hands against her arm. She pulls away and holds her camera tight against her stomach.

217

'Excuse me,' she says in an Australian accent, before stepping towards a van that has stopped beside us, its doors sliding open.

'I'm from the *Koh Star*,' I say, which sounds like a lie. 'I left my phone at home. I've missed all this. Just tell me his name. Please, I need to know.'

'I don't know,' she says, moving away from me. I know that she knows.

'Please.'

'I don't know,' she says, frowning at me. 'But they have got him. You're right about that.'

The woman gets into the van and stares at me as an arm reaches across to slide the door closed. She sees that there is something wrong with me. But I used to be just like you, I think. I had a job just like yours once, before everything changed and I had to become a different sort of writer. A different person.

The van pulls away, and I realise that I can breathe again. That night is over. Some stars are peeping out of the sky, no smoke, no helicopters passing by, and I see a star reflected in the windows of that building over there, the building that people say you can buy opium in if you go up to the lady and say the right combination of words. I stare up there and wonder, as I always do, if the story's true. I might like some opium.

I take a deep breath and go back inside.

# Chapter Forty-One

'There's a chance this is going to turn into a happy ending,' I say to Maliwan the following morning, as we put away a tower of breakfast bowls that we've just finished washing. 'The terrorist has been caught, apparently, and Pamela Shuttleworth is almost certain to be arrested. I bet she won't have a good time in prison *at all*. And you and Dolph can get back to, you know, whatever it is you want to do.'

'She'll be tried for murdering her husband, not for what she did to us.'

'Yeah, but it would get very murky if we tried to get her charged with that. We'd have to mention you hitting him. I think it's better to stay out of it.'

'What sort of journalist are you?' Maliwan says, dropping a handful of spoons noisily into the cutlery drawer. 'Isn't the truth important to you?'

'Sure,' I say, feeling my face flush. 'But I don't think it'll help anyone if you guys go to prison. You didn't mean to kill him. You didn't kill him, in fact. He upset you and you hit him, spur of the moment. She deserves to go to prison for what she did. I don't think it's significant that it started with what you did. She finished it, right? They're saying she tortured him and ran him over with her car. And then she tried to kill the three of us. Four, if you count the baby, which we should, of course.'

'She did kill the baby. The baby's dead,' Maliwan says. She looks at me with a challenge in her eyes.

'You don't know that,' I falter. 'Dolph was talking about taking you to see a doctor, wasn't he? I'm sure the doctor will say everything's fine.'

'I could tell I was pregnant the second it happened. And now I know for certain that I'm not,' she says. 'I don't want to kill Pamela anymore. You're right. They will find her guilty and she will hate prison. That will be worse than death for her. But I wish I could have one chance to talk to her. I want to tell her about the baby. I want to make sure she understands what she did.'

'Maybe you'll still get a chance to do that,' I say.

'No. It's over. Wouldn't you have liked to ask her why? Why she did it? You could have interviewed her for your newspaper.'

'She must really have hated him,' I say, watching as Maliwan spins a copy of the *Koh Star* around on the work surface, her wet fingers soaking the paper and staining it dark.

'I never hated him,' Maliwan says. 'I hated what he did to me but I didn't hate him.'

Steve walks in then, clattering through the front door holding a cardboard box filled with bottles of beer.

'Hello, hello,' he calls.

Maliwan dries her hands on a dirty looking dishcloth and hangs it on a hook at the side of the oven. She goes outside without saying anything and sits beside Dolph, who is petting the stray cat that always seems to be here now.

'How did it go? Any news?' I ask. When I woke up, I found a note on the bed from Steve saying that he had gone to the police station to find out what he could about the bomber. I slept later than usual, having tossed and turned all night; I can't get used to sharing a bed with someone, even if I am cocooned alone in the sleeping bag.

The capturing of the bomber has become official, but we scoured every news outlet we could think of last night and couldn't find any real information other than what we already knew; he has been arrested in Australia.

'Not a thing. They're being very secretive. It's true that they've made an arrest. Everyone seems happy about it, of course. I couldn't corner Kadesadayurat to speak to but I'm sure he'll get in touch with us as soon as he's able.'

'I don't feel like I can relax until I know everything,' I say.

'Things are working out though, aren't they? I mean, obviously, things are still horrible and people have died. But, we're going to get some sort of closure soon...'

'I was starting to think the same thing,' I say, but as I look outside at Dolph and Maliwan, crouched together on a stone step, I'm really not sure closure is a word we ought to be using.

'You know what we should do?' Steve says. 'Go back and interview the owner of the scrapyard. It's a shame not to talk to him, and maybe by the time we get back into town there'll be more information about the bomber.'

I agree. We tell Dolph and Maliwan that we need to work and then we leave them at Steve's place. They're committed to keeping a low profile for now, afraid that Pamela Shuttleworth might still tangle them in the web of her husband's death. We let them keep my phone so that we can get in touch with each other if we need to.

# Chapter Forty-Two

We go to the car hire place at the edge of town. We pick out a black SUV; Steve says that it's the kind of car he's always wanted to own. He drives for once because he's excited about the car, and I'm glad of this because my head hurts and I keep drifting into a state not too far from sleep. Pot holes have the car rattling, and I feel each tremor in my skull. I'm afraid that the adrenaline I've been running on is beginning to dry up; I lean back into the seat and half close my eyes.

And then, rounding a corner, we narrowly miss hitting a van which has stopped crookedly in the middle of the road. I snap fully awake as we brake. It's the kind of van that has an open bed in the back. It's filled with sacks and boxes, some of which have spilled out onto the road.

'What is this now?' Steve says. 'It looks like the opening scene of a zombie movie.'

'There's no one around,' I say, looking into the fields on either side of us.

'I could probably squeeze past and keep going.' Steve twists in his seat, taps his fingers on the wheel and sighs. 'No, we should check it out.'

We climb from the car and immediately hear voices. Circling the vehicle, we come upon an elderly couple standing together by the cab. They're pointing into the trees a little further up the road, where shadows move and everything still looks moist from the recent heavy rain.

Steve asks them, in his slow, careful Thai, what is going on.

They speak quickly, over the top of each other, and Steve does his best to translate for me.

'They nearly hit someone,' he says to me, still looking at the couple as he speaks. The man wrings a hat in his hands, dust coming off it. 'She was lying in the road with something pulled over her. They just managed to swerve in time. She ran away after that.'

The old lady points into the trees again. I strain my eyes but can't see a thing. I feel dizzy from staring too hard and shake my head to clear it.

'They need to leave. I've said we'll help them with their things,' Steve says. Going to the rear of the van, we lift everything back inside while the old couple talk together, too quickly for me to understand anything. The sacks smell of raw meat and petrol. I feel grease on my hands afterwards.

They thank us and continue on their way, apparently happy to hand over all responsibility for the situation to us. I concentrate on the sound of their engine until it disappears, and then it's just the birds and the insects singing from the fields.

'What do you think?' I say to Steve.

'I honestly don't know. I don't see anything, do you?'

'Why would someone be lying in the road? The tarmac would be hot enough to make your skin bubble.'

'People kill themselves that way, sometimes. They wait for a car to crush them. It's definitely not a way I would choose,' Steve says.

Imagining how that would feel, I look into the trees again, and this time, amongst the knotted plants, a figure is standing, hunched over and wrapped in something like a cloak. The shape is grey and fuzzy, and swaying just a little. The harder I stare, the harder it seems to sway. I think they've been there all this time but, like in a magic eye puzzle, I couldn't see them until I looked from this angle, with my eyes tilted this particular way.

Steve sees the person too. 'For fuck's sake,' he says, in a voice that chills me somehow and makes the skin on my arms tighten. And then we start towards the trees, feet sinking through pale mud, huge flies smacking against our faces.

The person is facing away from us and doesn't turn around.

'Hello?' I shout. My own voice makes me uneasy. We get closer and see that it is a woman; her short hair is plastered to her skull, and a piece of dirty rag or carpet hangs from her shoulders. She slowly turns in our direction but stares right through us, to where the car is sitting with its engine ticking, although I'm not sure if she's even focusing on that. And then I recognise her.

'What happened to you?' I say, the words just falling out because I don't have time to think. To Steve, I whisper: 'It's *her*.'

'Shit,' Steve breathes beside me. He stares at Pamela Shuttleworth and reaches slowly for my hand.

I look around for back-up, but the road is empty in either direction for as far as I can see. She's only small. If we can bring ourselves to touch her it should be possible to get her to the car. But then what? We know about the things she's supposed to have done to her husband and I can see the truth of it in her face; the way her cheekbones jut and the way her eyes don't blink.

Steve says to her: 'Did you just get run over, almost?'

She draws the rag tighter around herself. 'It turns out,' she says in a croak, 'that drinking yourself to death is quite difficult. And pills don't seem to work, either. I'm starting to think that I must be invincible.'

'You shouldn't be out here on your own. We can drive you back into town and make sure you're looked after,' Steve says, and I'm amazed by the warmth in his voice. He sounds like someone she can trust, like someone who doesn't think she's going to kill him.

When Pamela Shuttleworth does nothing, just stares, Steve takes a step closer, lifting his arms slowly, the way I would if approaching a timid animal. I move with him but stay slightly back. She's old and small but she tried to kill me yesterday and my body feels heavy in her presence. Up close, she smells awful; dirt and alcohol. I can see her clothes beneath the cloak; they were probably fine and expensive once, but now look grimy and misshapen. Steve takes hold of her arm and he nods at me to take the other. I don't want to, and as I reach out to touch her there's an awful moment where I think I'm going to throw up. I breathe in hard, close my throat and grab onto her. Her arm is surprisingly wiry. I wonder if she can feel my trembling. Steve and I begin steering her towards the road. She lets us do this, and I bite on the insides of my cheeks, trying not to be sick. It takes a while. When we reach the car, she peers at her reflection in one of the windows, her lip curling.

'I've slept outside for one night and aged twenty years,' she says. 'But, then again, perhaps that wasn't what aged me.'

'Let's get you some help,' Steve says.

'Help with what? I'll either go to prison or die. I'd rather die, and I can do that by myself. Probably.'

'Get in the car,' I say in a voice that shakes, opening one of the rear doors. 'Please.'

'I'd like a coffee actually.' She stumbles against the side of the vehicle. She is very drunk, I think. Very, very drunk. Her pupils are huge and black. She looks like a shark or a pointy headed alien. She's all teeth and eyes and bones. She doesn't seem to have recognised me, but I doubt she's able to focus at all.

'I'll buy you a coffee,' I say more brightly. 'We'll go past a stand. But you have to get into the car first.'

Making a noise like a chuckle, Pamela slips towards the ground. Steve catches beneath her armpits and manages to heave her onto the back seat, where she slumps with her head in her lap. As he slams the door I skid around the vehicle, my fingers brushing against the hot metal, and jump into my seat. Steve rushes in beside me and twists the key in the ignition.

'Jesus Christ, let's go, let's go,' he says.

After making a U-turn, he accelerates so hard that the semi-conscious woman slides about noisily. In this confined space, the stench of alcohol is strong enough to make my eyes water.

'Can we lock the doors?' I say, running my fingers along the dashboard and trying to understand the cryptic symbols and dials.

'Maybe this?' Steve says, fumbling with a button. The locks click a few times, and something beeps.

'I'm not sure. But she doesn't look like she's going anywhere anyway, does she?' I whisper.

'I hope not. Where's my phone? We should call ahead to the police.'

'Are we taking her straight to the police?' I hiss. 'What about Dolph and Maliwan?'

'If she tries to implicate them, I'm not sure anyone will believe her. It seems like she's incriminated herself really well. And look at the state of her. What else would you suggest we do?'

'I know. You're right. But I think they wanted a chance to ask her why. She might have killed their baby. I just think it would be nice of us to give them a chance to talk to her.'

'I'm really not sure about that,' Steve says. 'I don't think that's a sensible idea at all.'

'I'm going to send a text to my phone. If they see it then good. If not, at least we tried.'

'I don't know, Lucy,' Steve says, frowning at me. 'How about you just tell them to wait at the police station. They can talk to her as we get her from the car to the building.'

'Okay,' I agree. Steve passes me his phone and I concentrate on keeping my hands from shaking as I text. I hope that they see the message. Maliwan's certainty that she has lost her baby has left me feeling a grimy sort of guilt; I know that if I think about it too hard I'll be able to blame myself for everything bad that has happened lately. I'd like to be able to help her in at least this one small way.

'Are you awake? Are you okay back there?' Steve asks over his shoulder, but there's no reply.

'It's better if she's unconscious,' I say. 'I keep expecting to feel her hands closing around my neck.'

'Me too.'

'You know who I am. You know what I've done. Don't you?' she says then, her voice a growl. I sneak a look and see that her head is tilted back, revealing the roof of her open mouth, and I can see up her little, dark nostrils. Steve jumps and swerves across the road, but there are no other cars so it's okay. Still, my heart flutters.

'Yeah, I've heard bits,' Steve says, after a pause. 'I'm a journalist, so...'

'Do you know he has twelve children, and not a single one with me?'

'Oh?' Steve squeezes the steering wheel hard. I'm holding my breath and can't seem to stop.

'The thirteenth was on its way. But the mother's dead. The baby too, of course. So, it'll never be born. Unlucky for some, like they say.'

'What happened to them?' Steve asks, although of course he knows that Maliwan is safe inside his home right now. Pamela Shuttleworth doesn't answer.

The air in the car is too cold and I'm beginning to shiver; I slap at the vents on the dashboard, desperate to shut them off. Steve is driving faster than I have ever known him to drive and part of me hopes that he'll swerve off the road and kill our passenger, who has no seatbelt on and would probably smash through the windscreen. I'm afraid to look at her. Every time I do she seems larger, closer. But, still, I keep looking. I can't help myself.

'I know you,' she says, the next time I look around. 'I know your face.'

I shudder and turn away towards the windscreen, digging my fingertips hard into my knees. I hear her beginning to laugh behind us; Steve and I glance at each other, our eyes wide.

'So, what do you want?' Pamela says then, exasperated all of a sudden, like we're wasting her time.

'We're just getting you back into town, we're just...' Steve says.

I interrupt him; a rush of energy has all the hairs on my arms standing on end: 'Why did you do it? Maliwan was pregnant. You knew that. How could you?' I stare at her over the back of my seat, trying to meet her unfocused eyes, and then trying not to look away from them in fear.

'They made their own choices.'

'But they were having a baby,' I say. I can smell the alcohol all around her. It's hurting my throat.

She laughs. 'Oh, *they* weren't having a baby, you silly girl.'

'What?'

'It was *his*! Of course it was! That's what this is all about. Don't you see? He offered her an abortion and she hit him. She was hoping for money.'

'His?' I say, not following her for a moment. But then I think of Bernard Shuttleworth, the way he crunched on his ice cubes and leered at me.

'But they're all dead now, so what does it matter,' she says with certainty. Neither of us correct her. She sighs, like she's satisfied with her plan and the way it all worked out. It doesn't seem to bother her that I'm here, seemingly okay.

'And your husband's dead too,' Steve says quietly, holding onto the steering wheel with two tight fists.

'Gosh, he took a long time about it,' she says with another of her dry laughs. 'I thought he was going to die fifteen years ago when he had his first heart attack, but he just kept hanging on and having a wonderful time. I'm not sure he was even dead when I threw him into the river. I had so much more planned for him.'

'What happened?' Steve asks, staring at the road ahead.

'I just wanted a child.'

'So, you...'

'He tried to escape. I had to run him down and then it all just felt a bit flat after that. It was time to get rid of him.'

Steve and I look at each other. I think I'm about to be sick and begin bunching up my top so that I can catch the vomit in it and not stain the rented car. But, instead, I pant and wheeze and nothing comes out of me, while that lady continues to chuckle right behind us.

'Look, kids,' she says suddenly. 'Hand yourselves in and I'll help you. I have a lot of money. I mean *a lot*. I'll make it worth your while. Go to prison for me. It's even better this way, without a baby involved. You tell them you killed him. You killed them all.'

'We'll certainly think about it,' Steve says loudly. 'But let's go get those coffees first.'

Pamela doesn't reply, but when I peek back at her I see that she's smiling, showing all of her pointy little teeth. She stays that way until the expression is no longer a smile. It's not an expression I can read at all. Her eyes are the colour of metal, looking at nothing.

'Go faster,' I whisper.

# Chapter Forty-Three

Only one more block to travel before we reach the police station. Dolph and Maliwan haven't replied to the text message I sent, and I suppose I'm relieved in a way. Once we've handed Pamela Shuttleworth over to the police it will be the end for her, and we can continue on without her. If we stop to talk outside the police station it just increases the chances of something going wrong.

The roads are busy in town today. Steve has to brake when a little car pulls away from the kerb, and then a group of women on mopeds swarm around us. We crawl along behind them and then get stuck at a set of temporary traffic lights. Some of the mopeds edge around the lights and keep going, but we're stuck as the oncoming traffic flows in a noisy, polluted wave either side of us.

'Come on, come on,' Steve says, whistling under his breath and tapping at the steering wheel with his chewed-up nails.

Some military vehicles and refuse trucks rumble across the crossroad, dust and little scraps of debris tumbling from the backs of them.

'I suppose that's why the traffic's so bad all of a sudden,' I say. 'Maybe they're clearing out the bomb site.'

Steve's about to speak, but he freezes as a door opens in the back of our car and Pamela Shuttleworth flings herself out, landing on her feet like a mangy cat. She runs through the traffic, seemingly unaware of the mopeds, cars and people shouting from bicycles. A scarf trails from her neck and falls to the ground, where it's ripped up by tyres.

The light turns green and our lane of traffic begins to move, but Steve remains frozen, his mouth half open and his eyes following her erratic route along the street.

'Go after her!' I cry.

He accelerates hard, overtakes some mopeds, and we turn right at the crossroads. There are lumps of concrete in the road, fallen from the passing trucks, and we bounce over them so that I hit my shoulder against the door.

'She's there, she's there!' I say, hopping about in my seat. She's just passing a group of backpackers who are eating street food as they walk, and then she disappears behind a row of street vendors who are selling noodles, meat on sticks, umbrellas, porcelain dragons, all twinkling and glistening beneath the sun.

Steve bumps the car onto the kerb and brakes so hard that the wheels skid and we hit a dustbin. I'm still sitting there, listening to the noise of metal on metal, when one of the backpackers appears at my window and mouths a question at me. Her eyes are wide and she straightens her glasses as she stares at me.

'We're fine, we're fine. Sorry,' I say, opening my door and tumbling out of it, the air so furiously hot that I can feel it sitting heavy in my lungs as I struggle to take a breath.

'You crashed?' the girl says in a French accent.

Steve appears beside me, sweat pouring down his face. 'Everything's okay, don't worry,' he says to the girl. He puts a hot hand against my shoulder and pushes me along the pavement, away from the car and past the stalls. The people working there watch us pass. A couple of them are laughing at us, but the others have hard, closed looks upon their faces. I want to tell them that we're not bringing more trouble to their town; we're trying to stop it.

'I don't see her anywhere,' I gasp.

'We can't lose her now.'

I look along the road to where the police station is sitting, hazy through the heat. We were so close, but there is a sea of people between us and it; the road is busy with people piled on top of mopeds and push bikes, trucks bump past leaving dust in the air which I can smell over the frying of the food. People are wandering past the stalls and talking together beside metal tables which glitter in the sunshine. Brightly-coloured baskets are filled with produce, and one lonely bird with a hat on its head sits tethered to a perch. Westerners, still faintly dazed from the events of the week, move through the throng, some stopping to buy things or to gently finger the bags and clothes hanging from rails, to point at the ornaments, to eat the food. Empty crates are stacked about into crooked towers, and litter has piled up along the edge of the road. Steve and I stare thorough this ocean of movement and noise and shifting, anxious faces. Pamela Shuttleworth is nowhere to be seen.

We walk along the street until we're level with the police station. Then we cross over, dodging the mopeds, and walk back until we're standing opposite our abandoned hire car. An elderly Thai man is standing beside the vehicle, shaking his head at the way we've left it.

'We lost her,' Steve says. 'She's gone.'

'She wanted to die,' I say.

'You think that's what she's gone to do?'

I shrug. My body feels heavy and I want to sit down, but I stay standing. I check Steve's phone, which is in my pocket. Dolph and Maliwan haven't replied to the message I sent from the car. I don't want them to know how badly we've messed up.

'Let's look a while longer,' Steve says. 'She's old and drunk. How far could she possibly have gone?'

So, we walk up and down, peering into any open shops and cafés, checking the alleys that run between buildings and asking the taxi drivers if they've seen her. Steve tries to describe her in Thai, gesturing wildly and scrunching up his face, then nodding hopefully as people shake their heads. She's gone.

By the time we return to the car, some of the stalls are being packed up and the number of people passing by has thinned. Men are loading crates onto the back of a van, shouting at each other as they do so, and scaring the pigeons away.

'Look,' Steve says, touching my arm.

Where the crates have been shifted away from the wall, an opening to an alleyway has appeared. There are torn posters pasted to the bricks and slimy vegetables on the ground, where someone must have tipped them out after closing up their food stand. Dark shadows are cast by the walls and the passage is only narrow, but we head over there and squeeze around the remaining crates, the men ignoring us and continuing their yelled conversation.

'This would be a fine hiding place,' Steve says.

I agree, and follow him into the shadows.

# Chapter Forty-Four

Pamela is folded on the ground like a dead bird.

She is at the very end of the passageway, which turns at a right angle and runs behind the buildings before stopping at a dead end. There a several padlocked doors along the way, and a coil of barbed wire along the top of the back wall, partially fallen from position so that it hangs towards us like a snake.

Steve drops to his knees beside her and reaches out with his hands. But he can't quite bring himself to make contact; his palms hover just above the curve of her back, which reminds me of the way a roast chicken looks once it's had all the meat hacked away.

'Oh shit,' I say. 'What do we do? Shall I go for help?'

Her cheek is flat against the concrete. I can't seem to pull my eyes away from her twisted face, the sticky pink mucus that has run from her mouth to the ground, and the way her fingers look, all grey and twisted up beneath her. But her eyes, half open, still have a knowing glint in them. I can tell that she's dead. Her body is no different to the rotten vegetables that are strewn on the ground here, slimy grey leaves turning to nothing.

Steve, still on his knees, looks up at me. I've been hanging back by the wall, but as his eyes meet mine I shuffle forwards, my feet knocking against a pile of damp cardboard boxes and scaring a family of cockroaches out from beneath it.

'We should check for a pulse,' he mutters, reaching slowly towards her neck.

'Be careful,' I whisper, like she still might rise up and grab him, dig her claws into his arm.

He touches her for just a second and then pulls his hand away like it's been burned.

'Jesus Christ,' he says, biting his lip. 'She's definitely dead. I can feel it.'

I force myself to go closer and help him to his feet.

'What the hell do we do now?' he says, covering his face with his hands. I can see his whole body shaking.

'I think we should leave. Let's just go. Okay?'

'Okay.' He nods, his face still hidden behind his hands.

And so we leave.

# Chapter Forty-Five

I spot what I think is a bloody handprint on the frame of Steve's front door, but he says that it's charcoal from a barbeque he made a mess of last summer.

'I should clean it off but it's fairly ingrained into the wood now,' he says. He doesn't sound sure though, and we both look at it for a while, reluctant to go inside.

When we do step through the door, Dolph and Maliwan are not here. If it wasn't for the menthol cigarettes stubbed out in the giant shell by the back door, or the cotton wool pads in the bathroom bin, smeared with pink nail varnish, it would be easy to believe that they were never here at all.

My phone is on the coffee table. I pick it up and read the message that I sent to it earlier, trying to imagine how Dolph and Maliwan would have felt when they read it and what they might have done next.

'Do you think they're coming back?' Steve asks as he opens the fridge and peers inside. He just stands there, not taking anything out. The light from inside of it stains his body a washed-out shade of yellow.

'I don't think we'll ever see them again.'

I come through to the kitchen and notice the bubbles in the sink, mounds of them, and the way that the tiles around the sink have been scrubbed clean, whiter than they have ever been.

'Steve?' I say. 'How do you think she died?'

'She *did* want to kill herself. You said that.' He's still staring into the fridge.

'Yes. But do you think that's what happened?'

'I don't know.' Finally, he pulls a bottle of champagne out from the door of the fridge, closing it with his elbow. Then he rummages through the cupboards, only discovering one champagne flute. He grabs a cylindrical vase from the window ledge, tipping spare change and a couple of crusty paint brushes from it, and uses this as a second glass.

'Don't you want to save that for when you have something to celebrate?' I suggest, looking at the bottle of expensive champagne. I sit on the couch and try to imagine Dolph and Maliwan sleeping here. I can't quite picture them. They're already slipping away. No one except Steve and I know that they were ever in our lives, now that Pamela Shuttleworth is dead. We can pretend none of it happened, if we want.

'It's been sitting in here for months,' Steve says. 'She was a terrible person. Did you notice how she moved like a praying mantis? But I would still prefer not to have seen her like that. Don't you feel the same?'

'It was horrible.' I nod, but that word isn't big enough to explain how revolted I am, or the way that the memory of what we found in that alley is turning into something dark and stirring, which will always be waiting for me when I try to sleep, try to think, try to move on and be a good person.

'I wonder how long it will be until someone finds her,' Steve says. He carefully twists the cork in the champagne bottle until it opens with a sigh into his fist. He pours us each a generous helping. I don't much want any alcohol, I already feel sick, but I accept the glass and take a sip, feeling the bubbles pop against my nose.

'We should have told someone,' I say, surprising myself as I down the champagne with ease. It tastes like fresh air. I don't object as Steve fills my glass back up. 'We still could.'

'Yes,' Steve says, but neither of us make any effort to pick up a phone.

'Whose baby do you think it was?' I ask. The idea that the baby might not be Dolph's has left me feeling strange in my stomach; there's a gnawing in the hollow where I once held a man's baby.

'I have a horrible feeling that it *was* his. Bernard Shuttleworth's.'

'Me too.'

Steve pours us some more champagne and then the bottle is empty. He goes into the kitchen to see what else he can find. There's a nearly-full bottle of red wine beside the bin. He pulls out the stopper and gives it a sniff. 'I used this to cook with the night the bomb went off. I was going to throw it out but I think it's still good. Have some?'

'Sure,' I say, because the champagne has lit a gentle warmth inside me, which is slowly melting away the cold horror of everything that has come before it.

We continue to drink as the light outside the window turns orange and then is extinguished. We finish everything alcoholic in the house; miniature bottles of whiskey, a can of beer with fluff stuck to it which had rolled beneath Steve's bed, a lemony liquor in a bottle shaped like a parrot. Eventually we remember that Steve had purchased beers for the four of us to enjoy tonight, and he finds them in the fridge.

'It's funny how plans change,' he says.

There are several times during the evening when we think that we hear people outside the door. Twice we open it to find no one there. Once there is a cat eating a frog, and the final time we open it just as some teenagers are passing by, glaring at us and then laughing.

'They're definitely not coming back,' Steve says. 'Perhaps they've left the island by now.'

'I expect you're right,' I say, and I'm not sure how I feel about it. 'We should have all said goodbye to each other. We'd sort of become partners.'

'Partners in what exactly? I'm not good with goodbyes at the best of times. I wouldn't even know where to begin with that one. This is probably for the best. We weren't really partners. We were thrown together and then we were thrown apart again. Make sense?'

'I think so,' I say.

'*We're* partners though, you and I.'

Steve puts a romantic comedy on the television but I find it hard to follow; people are hiding in closets and running after buses. Neither of us laugh. I'm no longer enjoying my drink very much; the bubbles are rising at the back of my throat, and the lights are starting to spin as my eyes roll from side to side. I slump into the cushions and slide towards Steve, who is still drinking at speed and is checking the news on his phone.

'We need to find Kadesadayurat tomorrow and convince him to tell us something about the bomber,' Steve says. 'I need to know. It's driving me mad.'

'Me too. Without a name or anything, I can't quite believe that it's real.'

'And then I think perhaps we should leave for a while.'

'Leave where?' I ask, my brain slow.

'The island. There's been so much damage done over this last week and we've been part of it somehow. We should go away. I want to go someplace I've never been to before. Somewhere that hasn't been ruined yet.'

'I thought you wanted to visit your daughter.'

'I do. I'll go there. I've never been there before. It's called Cork.'

'Will you come back?' I ask, feeling a pressure at the back of my throat, and tears heavy in my eyes. I want to ask him not to leave me, and perhaps I will, because the alcohol is beginning to loosen words that I wouldn't usually speak.

'Of course. This is my home. But, Lucy, I honestly think you should go somewhere too.' He pauses for a moment, and then adds: 'You're better than this newspaper, you know? You're not washed-up like me.'

I laugh, throw some more lager down my throat and try to think of something to say.

'I mean it though,' Steve says. 'What are you doing here?'

'Are you really going to ask me about that right now? I just like it here, okay?' I attempt to take another swig of my drink but knock the bottle hard against my teeth. I laugh at myself and slide further into the cushions, where I can feel dust and stale crisps collected in the folds.

'Oh, you're drunk,' Steve says, his face suddenly right beside mine, and in that moment, I think I know how to fix things. I know how to show him how important he is to me, how close we've become not just as colleagues but as people. I know how to birth a little good thing into the night when everything that has come before it has been ugly and bad. And, most of all, I know how to fix the emptiness that has been screaming inside me ever since that day when I became pregnant and forgot how to be near men.

I turn my face to kiss Steve, feeling his moustache against my lips and the beer in his mouth mix with the beer in mine. I realise instantly that I've made a horrible mistake because the shape of his mouth feels wrong, he is pulling away from me, holding up his hands and shaking his head.

'What are you doing, you drunken idiot?' he says to me. He laughs and then looks almost frightened.

'I have no idea. I'm so sorry.'

'I could be your dad,' he says. 'And besides that, you realise I'm gay, right? I thought you knew that.'

'No,' I say, unable to keep myself from sobbing, which makes me feel even more stupid. I've held onto my tears for days and now I'm crying over this. 'I guess I never thought about it.'

'I figured you knew because I know and we always seem to get each other. We clicked the moment we met. You remember, at the dock? I knew we were going to be best friends. Best friends. Not this. You know that. You're just drunk. Don't worry about it.' Steve puts an arm around my shoulder and pulls me close to him.

And then he tells me about his wife, Henrietta, and how he expected her to be relieved when he told her that he was gay.

'She'd said, once before, that she'd rather die than be without me. I thought that was just something people say. I'd known things weren't as they ought to be for a long time, and assumed she must have felt it too. But I was wrong and, despite everything, she did not want a divorce.'

'What did you do?'

'I went ahead with it anyway. It was much easier and less expensive than I'd imagined. The lawyer's office was next door to a juice bar, and I would bring back a special, brightly-coloured juice for Jenna after each visit. They had a way of layering it, so the juice was in stripes.'

'So, Jenna stayed with Henrietta, after the divorce?' I ask, trying to piece together the fragments of information that he's given me in the past.

'No. We never got as far as discussing that,' Steve says. 'We were still doing things together as a family during that time, while I was arranging everything, legally. I thought it was unhealthy but Henrietta said she didn't want to disrupt Jenna's life any sooner than we had to. So, we were waiting for a train to take us to a museum. We were going to visit an exhibition about Vikings. Something like that. She tried to jump in front of a train.'

'What? Who? Your wife?'

'She was at the other end of the platform. Said she was going to pick us up some coffee and a juice box for Jenna. She looked back at us to make sure I was watching, and then she jumped. But she fucked up the timing. A man pulled her back onto the platform before the train was anywhere near her. But she was screaming and hitting him and someone called the police. Then she was screaming and hitting me, saying all sorts of insane things. It was so ugly, Lucy.'

'How old was Jenna?'

'Very little. But old enough that she still remembers snippets about that day. She remembers the snow. It started coming down as we walked to the station. She had on a bright pink coat, with rabbit ears on the hood. As a policewoman carried her away, Jenna put her hood up and snuggled into the stranger's shoulder. That's what I see when I remember that day. My bunny in someone else's arms.'

'You got her back though, right?'

'Henrietta was in hospital for a while. She told everyone that it was my fault, that I'd been lying to her for years and cheating on her with men. I didn't. I didn't do that. But it seemed best for Jenna to have a fresh start with her grandparents after all that. I regret that decision now. More than anything. She grew up on a farm with them, and they were kind and they tried not to speak ill of us in front of her. Henrietta's family actually blamed me for what happened, and so did some members of my own family. They're all religious. I think perhaps Jenna blames me too, in some small way, but luckily for me she's an independent thinker. Anyway, it never mattered what they thought or what they said snidely over coffee, because I already blamed myself. I always will.'

'It's not your fault. You were just trying to be honest, right?'

I realise that Steve is looking at me as if he's expecting something in return for his story, like we'd made some sort of deal. But we hadn't. Steve has been desperate to share the tale of his dramatically failed marriage since I moved here. We went out for cocktails during my first weekend on the island and he told me it was his wedding anniversary, then his face clouded and he'd been on the brink of saying more, until one of his friends interrupted us, a DJ who has since moved on to Hong Kong. Steve's come close to telling me the full story many times since then, and has sprinkled hints all over the place.

I focus now on his nose, trying to ignore the shadows which are flickering from the corners of the dim room behind him. I could be sick. I take a long drink from the bottle which has grown warm in my hands.

'I don't know,' I say. 'Something bad happened to me and I quit my job. It's in the past. I'm forgetting it a bit more every day. Especially now, when so many other horrible things have happened.'

'That's not how it works though,' Steve says. 'Big horrible things don't dilute the smaller horrible things. They just all morph together.'

'I expect you're right.'

'You don't have to tell me anything,' he says. 'It's okay. But I'm always happy to listen, if you ever decide that you want me to.'

I sit silently for a moment, breathing slowly and watching as the lights from a passing car rise over the wall in the back yard.

'My parents' neighbour raped me,' I say, looking down, as if the words have fallen into my lap. The strangeness of saying them out loud makes me want to giggle.

I'd taken a week off work to dog-sit while my mum and dad went to Majorca. They have a Dalmatian and a terrier, both rescue dogs and terrified of kennels. I walked the dogs, slept in a bed more comfortable than my own, and watched movies on a huge TV. I lit my mum's scented candles every evening so that no one would know I'd been smoking in the kitchen. I used to smoke a lot back then.

Arthur often smiled at me from his kitchen window. He seemed like a completely normal man. He had a wife and children, a ceramic hedgehog by the front door, a sunflower that grew right up to the first floor windows. But he worked unusual hours and was often home alone during the day. When he knocked on the door I let him in, because there didn't seem any reason not to.

After he left, I straightened the clothes he'd tugged at, and I sat on the stairs with a dog either side of me. I stroked them until my fingers hurt. Libby, the terrier, licked my grazed knees. I sat there for about an hour, because I had no idea what to do next. In the end, I decided to do nothing. I decided to pretend like it never happened. I never told anyone, and I never cried except for during that evening, into the dogs' necks. I never saw him again.

It's strange to think that if he hadn't raped me I wouldn't have been here when the bomb went off. I would have seen it on the news like everyone else. I might even have wished that I could be out here, to cover a story that really meant something. That would have been a stupid thing to wish for, but we all wish for stupid things sometimes.

I know I should have gone to the police about what he did to me. Not for my own sake, but for the sake of all the women he might rape in the future. But I didn't go to the police and I don't think I ever will now; I'm a coward. My mum has mentioned that she has new next-door neighbours. After a noisy marriage break-up, the wife and children went away and then he sold up and moved on too. He could be anywhere.

I'm usually very good at switching off any thoughts I have of him. Thoughts of the pregnancy too. I have to breathe in a certain way, and I picture my brain like a slab of ice, so that everything just has to slide off it. But the bad thoughts creep in anyway, through the ice, when I'm feeling miserable for one reason or another. I've let them in a few times since moving here, and I've had to scream into my pillow, scratch at my arms. Sometimes I think I see him on the other side of a crowded bar, or bobbing about in the sea. I hope that one day I'll be able to forget about him entirely, but I don't think that's likely. Perhaps if he hadn't got me pregnant.

'Shit,' Steve says, when I've spat out a garbled version of the story that I relive during every night that I can't sleep. I watch his face change and I wish that I hadn't told him.

'You think less of me now,' I say, realising that this has been my biggest fear all along.

'Not at all. I think a little more of you every day. That will never change. I hate *him* though.'

He opens a final bottle of beer which we pass between us, and we stare at the television while we drink, although we don't have it switched on. There's an orange candle flickering on top of the TV, like a Halloween pumpkin. Steve falls asleep before I do, and I grab the bottle out of his hands as it begins to tip. I lean back into the cushions, which smell of cheap deodorant. Steve stirs and smiles in his sleep. It'll be good to sleep, so long as I don't dream. Am I safe now? Are any of us safe? I close my eyes and find they're wet with tears. As the sobs come I try to stifle them so I won't wake Steve, pulling my cardigan up over my face like a shroud.

# Chapter Forty-Six

We wake early, too hungover to sleep. Steve fries eggs and some pink meat in a blackened skillet. My slice of the meat has hairs growing from it, but I eat it all anyway, mopping up the grease and pale-yellow yolk with a piece of stale bread.

'You might be hoping that I don't remember much about last night; that I was too drunk. But I remember it all, I'm afraid.'

'Oh,' I say, looking at Steve with my hand stopped halfway to my mouth, a chunk of bread between my twitching fingers.

'And I just want to say, in the cold light of day, with no alcohol involved; I think you're wonderful, Lucy, and you don't need to feel ashamed about any of it. Not about a single thing, okay?'

'Okay,' I say, and I manage to smile, just a little bit.

After we've eaten and have started on our second mugs of strong coffee, we switch on the laptop and Steve books himself a flight to visit his daughter in Ireland. He fills out his credit card details incorrectly, and has to restart the checkout process, swearing and spilling tobacco over the keyboard as he rolls a cigarette. Once he's done, he goes outside to smoke with a smile on his face, and I take his place at the keyboard. My fingers twitch. I half close my eyes and try to picture myself somewhere new.

When Steve comes back inside he has a bunch of purple and yellow flowers in his fist, mud dropping from their tangled roots onto the floor.

'Let's take these to the bombsite,' he says. 'I feel like it's time. We need to leave some flowers before they start clearing them all away.'

'Okay,' I say, staring at the confirmation email I've just opened. I'm not sure how I feel. As soon as I settle on one emotion, another comes along and chases it away. I pull my hands into fists to stop them shaking.

'Did you do it?' he asks.

I nod.

'And?'

'Australia,' I say. 'I'm going to spend six weeks there. Is that okay? Is that too long?'

'Sounds perfect to me.' He smiles. 'You're not going there to work though, are you? You know that's where they're supposed to have caught the bomber?'

'Maybe that's part of it,' I admit.

'Of course it is. You can't let go of a thing, can you?' But he's smiling as he says this, so maybe it's okay.

We go to the bombsite. Neither of us suggests going back to the place near to the police station where we found Pamela Shuttleworth yesterday. We haven't discussed it, but I think we have both decided to write ourselves out of that story. Perhaps I'll regret that one day, but it feels like the right thing to do at the moment.

There is still a grey sort of light in the morning sky, like the night is clinging to the rooftops. The streets are quiet. As soon as we leave the house, we stop speaking. When we get to Main Street, pass the Grand Hotel and then approach the crater, Steve loops his arm around mine and I'm glad, because my legs feel hollow and there's a hissing in my ears.

A lot of the debris has been cleared away, but there is still this dark hole in the ground, which looks somehow organic, like a cancer has ripped through it. There are still strips of metal and wood, fallen from the buildings and scattered about the place. I can't tell what any of them used to be. And there are dark stains which I know were once fresh blood. The buildings look like they're filled with ghosts, and I think it will be a good idea to tear them all down.

'You can feel it, can't you?' Steve says.

I nod. I know what he means. The air feels different here. Thing looks slightly better; attempts have been made to fix the damage and take the shock away, but the victims are still dead and maimed. And, just as I knew there would be, horrible vibrations run up and down the street. I can sense them heading out through the jungle, beneath the temples and to the deserted golf resort. I think the feeling here will be worse at night, when most people have gone to bed, and the birds and stray dogs have settled. This hum of energy will rise up in the air like a siren, and it'll feel as if the bomb has only just gone off, and the people are still screaming.

We add our flowers to the piles already here. There are many sealed cards, soft toys, and some pint glasses filled with rainwater and sodden, ruined notes. Some of the flowers have started to die, but most are still in bloom. Still, there's a dusty smell of rotting petals in the air.

Shielding my eyes from the rising sun, I look up at my hostel, fairly certain that this will be the last time I ever see it. It looks unreal, like a stage set. Two green birds are sitting together on the ledge of my bedroom window, feathers puffed up, eyes closed into slits.

'Let's go,' Steve says. 'It makes me too sad to stay here long.'

It's as we turn to walk away, that our attention is drawn across the road by the sound of metal scraping along the ground. A woman dressed all in black is dragging a stack of chairs along the pavement in front of the ice cream parlour, moving towards a little white van parked beyond the place where the road is cordoned off. The glass has been shattered from the shop front, but the door is intact, and she has opened it. The interior is charred, tables and chairs upturned, ruined. We walk closer and see that the counter is still standing at the back of the room, and brightly coloured sprinkles are scattered across the blackened floor. She is halfway through clearing them. Jelly beans, pink shrimps and little, bright things are in a mound beside a dustpan and brush. Sauces have been spilled and dried in pink and brown puddles. Melted plastic containers lie on the tiles in distorted shapes.

'Hello?' I say, looking away from all this and back to the woman.

She places the chairs down carefully and turns to see us. I recognise her straight away. She is small and slim, her hair tied neatly back. But her face, usually crinkled into a smile, is strained. There are shadows beneath her eyes. She nods at me, a flicker of recognition crossing her face, and then she wipes her hands on an apron around her waist. Her hands are black with soot.

'Hi,' I say. 'You're the owner.'

'Yes, yes,' she says, and tries to force a smile.

'Sorry about your café,' I say. Steve, beside me, is still staring at the remains of this place, where we have spent afternoons watching the world go by.

'Yes, very sad for us.' She nods.

'We heard that the bomb may have been in one of your plant pots,' Steve says, glancing at the lip of the crater where the pots used to stand.

She runs a hand through her hair, catching a strand on her ring and pulling it loose from the ponytail. She looks at her feet as she speaks. 'The police said we could come back in today. They finished looking. I thought if I come here early, I could clear up before reporters came. You're fast. You are the first people here.'

Steve and I look at each other, trying to overcome our hangovers and understand what she means.

'You've been away, right? When did you get back?' I ask.

'Few days ago. We didn't know anything. We just saw on the TV same as everyone else and we were so worried. We didn't know.'

'Who was looking after the place while you were away?' Steve asks, using a tone of voice to imply that he knows the answer but has momentarily forgotten.

She stares at us, wiping her hands on the apron again, as if it's a reflex. 'I give one interview to you,' she says. 'And then I'll speak to no one else. My husband says we should stay quiet, but I think it's important that people know we had nothing to do with it. No idea. We would never want this.' She points at the destroyed road, the place where people died.

'I understand,' I say.

'The police keep his name secret so far, but they will tell today. Everything will change.'

I nod. People are starting to move around now, further up the street. We can hear mopeds passing somewhere nearby, dogs are barking and there is a smell of breakfast food frying, which makes my stomach bubble. A black van turns onto the street and begins rolling towards us.

'No time,' she says. She pulls a loop of keys from a pocket in her apron and locks the front door, out of habit I suppose, and she looks at us with an embarrassed smile when she realises what she's done. She pulls a gummy sweet off the edge of her shoe and throws it inside, onto the pile that she had been sweeping. It starts a little landslide.

We walk together to our office, where we pour her an iced tea which she takes tiny sips from. And then she tells us about her son, who she loved very much when he was a small child.

'I know I shouldn't love him anymore,' she says.

She describes how he would volunteer to test all of the ice cream flavours, as if he was doing an important job for his parents. He would sing songs of nonsense from a chair behind the counter, and he kissed her face, befriended the chickens which they kept out the back. But then he went to a boarding school on the mainland, and he began to view life in a new, serious way. He no longer spoke very often, but he gave thoughtful presents and hugged his mother when she met him at the port.

'I wanted to keep him here, and he could work in the café with us, but my husband wanted better for him. He went to a very good school. Very good. We don't just have this place, we have café all over Thailand. This was first one though. We were all born here.'

And then she tells us how, after he finished school, their son wanted to stay on the island for a while, to serve ice cream and do very little else, but they discouraged him, and helped him get a place at university in Australia. And that was when he really began to drift away, not speaking to them for months, then speaking to them on the phone and saying strange things, words that did not sound like his own.

'He was lonely,' his mother says. 'He met the wrong people. These ideas, they were not his ideas.'

She smiles as she remembers how pleased she was when he offered to watch the café for them while they went to visit her sister on the mainland.

'My sister has breast cancer,' she says. 'We've wanted to visit her for a long time but been too busy with work.'

'When did you find out that he was the bomber?' I ask, forcing myself to meet her eyes. I have my fingers clamped around a pen, pressing down hard on a pad of paper.

'He saw the police were coming for him. He phoned me. He said sorry, not for what he did, but for how it's going to affect his father and me. We cannot stay here now. Everyone will hate us. But he wasn't sorry about the people he hurt. He was glad the tourists died. They used to be so kind to him. When he was here and he helped me in the café, they would give him foreign coins for his collection and he practiced his English with them. His English very good. Such a clever boy.'

'He made the bomb?'

'He made it in the café, out the back where we keep all the boxes. I don't know who taught him that, but he was always good at making things. He fix the bug zapper. The electric thing on the wall.'

'And then he left before the bomb went off?'

She nods. 'I think so. I think he set a timer and then he went back to university. But we did not have much time to speak on the phone. He could see the police coming. He hung up when they were outside the house. Until he called, we thought that he had been killed. But then he phoned and say the police coming and he's sorry, he knew we wouldn't like what he did, but it was important and someone had to do it.'

'Where is he now?' I ask.

'They bringing him back to Thailand. I might be able to visit him, but I don't know if I want to. I don't know if I should.'

'Thank you for talking to us,' I say. 'I can see how hard it is for you.'

'I always liked you both. Iced coffees your favourite.' She smiles.

'You did the best iced coffees in town,' Steve tells her.

'They will execute him,' she says then, the smile sitting like a ghost upon her face.

After that, she doesn't want to talk to us. We say goodbye and watch from the top of the steps as she walks away, her head bowed.

'Will they?' I say to Steve, as she turns a corner and is gone.

'What?'

'Execute him.'

'Probably.'

We go back inside, the door swinging shut behind us. I look at the notebook I've left on the table, pages filled with urgent shorthand.

'Well, there's a story for you,' Steve says.

# A NOTE TO THE READER

Dear Reader

I wanted to take a minute to thank you for reading *Running in Circles*. When I started writing this story, I couldn't be sure if anyone except for my friends and family would ever read it, so it feels amazing to know that there are people out there purchasing and (hopefully) enjoying my work. It's taken me several years and numerous re-drafts to get to this point!

Lucy and Steve feel like old friends to me now, and it's exciting to be able to share their adventures with the world. I've put some elements of my own life into their stories; I trained as a journalist and travelled in Asia. Thankfully I've never lived through anything as dramatic as the events depicted in *Running in Circles*, but it still feels like a very personal tale to me.

Reviews are really important to new writers like myself, so if you get the chance to leave a review on either **Amazon** or **Goodreads**, I would really appreciate it. I'd love to hear your thoughts. You can also follow me on **Twitter/ClaireEsnail** or **Instagram/ClaireGrayIsHere**

I'm working on a follow up to *Running in Circles* at the moment. Lucy is no longer in Thailand but she's still getting herself mixed up with some questionable people while struggling to uncover sinister goings on. I'm very grateful to Sapere Books for picking up *Running in Circles* and for giving me the opportunity to further explore the world its characters inhabit.

Thanks again for taking the time to read my work!

Claire Gray

**clairegrayauthor.com**

**Sapere Books** is an exciting new publisher of brilliant fiction and popular history.

To find out more about our latest releases and our monthly bargain books visit our website: **saperebooks.com**

34930139R00153

Printed in Poland
by Amazon Fulfillment
Poland Sp. z o.o., Wrocław